Praise for
DONNA GRANT

5! Top Pick! "An absolutely must read! From beginning to end, it's an incredible ride."
—*Night Owl Romance*

5 Hearts! "I definitely recommend *Dangerous Highlander*, even to skeptics of paranormal romance – you just may fall in love with the MacLeods."
—*The Romance Reader*

5 Angels! Recommended Read! "*Forbidden Highlander* blew me away."
—*Fallen Angel Reviews*

5 Tombstones! "Another fantastic series that melds the paranormal with the historical life of the Scottish highlander in this arousing and exciting adventure. The men of MacLeod castle are a delicious combination of devoted brother, loyal highlander Lord and demonic God that ooze sex appeal and inspire some very erotic daydreams as they face their faults and accept their fate."
—*Bitten By Books*

4 Stars! "Grant creates a vivid picture of Britain centuries after the Celts and Druids tried to expel the Romans, deftly merging magic and history. The result is a wonderfully dark, delightfully well-written tale. Readers will eagerly await the next Dark Sword book."
—*Romantic Times BOOKreviews*

Don't miss these other spellbinding novels by
DONNA GRANT

DARK KING SERIES
Dark Heat
Darkest Flame
Fire Rising
Burning Desire
Hot Blooded

DARK WARRIOR SERIES
Midnight's Master
Midnight's Lover
Midnight's Seduction
Midnight's Warrior
Midnight's Kiss
Midnight's Captive
Midnight's Temptation
Midnight's Promise
Midnight's Surrender

DARK SWORD SERIES
Dangerous Highlander
Forbidden Highlander
Wicked Highlander
Untamed Highlander
Shadow Highlander
Darkest Highlander

SHIELD SERIES
A Dark Guardian
A Kind of Magic
A Dark Seduction
A Forbidden Temptation
A Warrior's Heart

DRUIDS GLEN SERIES
Highland Mist
Highland Nights
Highland Dawn
Highland Fires
Highland Magic
Dragonfyre

SISTERS OF MAGIC TRILOGY
Shadow Magic
Echoes of Magic
Dangerous Magic

Royal Chronicles Novella Series
Prince of Desire
Prince of Seduction
Prince of Love
Prince of Passion

Wicked Treasures Novella Series
Seized by Passion
Enticed by Ecstasy
Captured by Desire

**And look for more anticipated novels
from Donna Grant**

The Craving (Rogues of Scotland)
Darkest Flame (Dark Kings)
Wild Dream – (Chiasson)
Fire Rising – (Dark Kings)

coming soon!

A WARRIOR'S HEART

THE SHIELDS

DONNA GRANT

A WARRIOR'S HEART

Cover design © 2012 by Croco Designs

ISBN 13: 978-0988208476 (ebook)
ISBN 13: 978-0988208483 (print)

www.DonnaGrant.com

Available in ebook and print editions

CHAPTER ONE

England, 1123
Stone Crest Castle

If Jayna had known what she would become, she would have plunged the dagger into Gabriel's heart when she'd had the chance. That decision had cost her her soul.

And she paid for it every day.

She didn't like what she had become, but her mother had told her that in order to survive, one had to adjust. Jayna had certainly adjusted.

As she stared at the imposing mass of rocks that was Stone Crest Castle, she thought about the people within its thick walls. A shiver raced over her skin, but it wasn't due to the icy night air.

She had finally found Gabriel.

And it was time he paid for his crimes.

Jayna smiled with anticipation, her heart pounding with excitement. She'd waited so long for this moment that she almost couldn't believe it had arrived. Yet it had, and she was going to carry out all the ways she'd thought of to make Gabriel pay.

She pulled the hood of her cloak up to cover her head and face. Getting into the castle wasn't going to be easy, but she was certainly up to the challenge. After all, she had waited nearly an eternity to see the look on Gabriel's face when she confronted him.

"Gloating already?"

Jayna stiffened when the familiar wash of air moved around her. He might not have a form, but he was the most powerful being in any of the realms.

"I know I shouldn't," she answered as she kept her eyes on the castle.

A tsking sound came from behind her then a warmth enveloped her. "My dear, Jayna, did I teach you nothing?"

She smiled a true smile and breathed deeply. "You taught me to survive, and for that I owe you everything."

"Do you think I kept you alive just so you could mete out your revenge against Gabriel?"

For the first time in centuries, Jayna felt a gnawing sense of worry. "I assumed so, aye."

"That was part of it, my dear," he whispered in her ear. "Once I regain my form, I'm going to need a queen. Someone who knows how to rule with beauty, grace, and the iron fist of vengeance. In other words, Jayna, I need you."

Jayna didn't know what to say. For too many years all she had cared about was finding Gabriel and killing him. Never had she thought about a husband or family. It had always been about Gabriel.

As if reading her mind, he asked, "Just what had you planned on doing once you killed Gabriel?"

"I don't know. I've never thought about it."

"I think the time has come for you to think about many things. My mission is nearly complete. For the first time since time began, evil will dominate the realms. No longer will good triumph and evil be punished. It will be our time. Think about it."

And just as suddenly as he had appeared, he vanished. Jayna pushed aside his words. She needed to focus on Gabriel, on finding him and sinking her blade deep into his heart as he had done to her so very, very long ago.

CHAPTER TWO

Gabriel splayed his hands against the cold stones of the battlements and looked over the valley, missing Laird bitterly. He hadn't wanted to care for the wolfhound as he did, and it was because the dog meant so much that Gabriel had begged Aimery to take Laird to the Realm of the Fae.

Until the Great Evil was gone.

The merriment inside the great hall reached Gabriel even outside, and though he hadn't wanted to hurt Hugh or Mina's feelings, he hadn't been able to celebrate.

Too much had happened in Scotland. In the back of his mind, he always knew he didn't wish to discover his memories. He had feared they would be as tarnished as the nightmares that plagued him, nightmares he had never told anyone about.

Nightmares that showed him unspeakable horrors and deeds.

When the Fae had found him, Gabriel had been all but dead. Yet, with their healing abilities, the Fae had restored him but they hadn't been able to help him with his memory. For a long time he craved knowledge of his past, who he was, if he had a family or a wife. He wanted to know details.

Yet always there was this underlying fear that someone was coming after him. The Fae assured him it was only due to his extensive injuries, and for a while, Gabriel had believed them.

Until recently.

Discovering he was immortal should have been a joyous occasion. Instead, it had only made him realize his past was deep and dark. A place he wanted no part of. He would like nothing better than to say he was the man he had become, but only fools discounted their pasts.

He had sinned.

He knew it in the marrow of his bones.

How he had sinned was the question, but he had a sneaking suspicion he would find out very soon.

"There you are," Cole said as he sauntered up, a big smile on his face and a mug of ale in his hand. "Mina demanded I find you and give you your ale."

Gabriel tried to smile as he accepted the mug. "I wouldn't wish to upset the lady of the castle. But I imagine it was more likely Hugh that sent you to find me."

"All right," Cole said with a loud sigh as he leaned his back against the stones and looked at Gabriel. The smile was gone and worry showed in his dark eyes. "We all know something is bothering you. What we don't know, is why you aren't coming to us for help. We are your family, your brothers."

"I'm fine," he lied. "I'm just worried that the Great Evil isn't done with us. Now that all four of the Chosen have been found, he can be defeated."

Cole raised his brows at Gabriel's words. "We're all worried about the Great Evil, and if you expect me to believe the words you just spoke, you don't know me as well as you should."

Gabriel raked a hand through his hair. "Cole, sometimes things are better left alone."

"Like your past."

"By the gods," Gabriel bellowed and pushed away from the wall and faced his friend. "Leave it alone. I beg you."

"Nay."

"Please."

"As I said earlier, we are your family, and family look out for one another."

Gabriel shook his head as he realized the futility of arguing with Cole.

"Have you remembered your past?"

Gabriel cringed and turned his back to Cole. "Nay."

"The only thing you know is that you're immortal. That shouldn't be something for you to fear."

"What I fear is my past," Gabriel said softly.

Cole moved until he stood in front of him. "Your past is exactly that, my brother. It doesn't matter what you did or who you were. We know who you are now, and that's what counts."

Gabriel felt something touch his hand and looked down at the mug of ale. He took it and looked up to see Cole smile before he walked off.

The ale was just what Gabriel needed. He leaned his head back and took a long drink. He glanced out over the land again and could have sworn he saw something move near the forest. With a step closer to the wall, he stared at the spot and waited but nothing stirred.

Gabriel took a deep breath and decided he had done enough worrying for the night. The four Chosen had been found, and the end of the Great Evil was coming. It was time to celebrate. With his family, his brothers.

When Gabriel reached the great hall, he stopped at the

balcony that overlooked the massive room and gazed down. The people of Stone Crest dined on roasted pheasant and potatoes.

His eyes traveled to the dais where the Shields sat. Hugh, their leader, and his wife Mina sat at the center of the table. Hugh had not only found his mate upon coming to Stone Crest, but he had found a home, as well.

To the right of Hugh was Roderick. Roderick was an immortal prince from the realm of Thales. To Roderick's right was his wife, Elle. Next to Elle sat Nicole, who Gabriel and Val had battled a griffin to free, and then Val, a Roman general.

On the left of Mina sat Shannon and Cole. The empty chair beside Cole was Gabriel's spot. Gabriel wanted to join them, needed to join them, but he found it more than difficult. Each of the Shields had found their mates while battling the Great Evil, and though Gabriel would never admit it, he longed to find a woman for himself, as well.

The yearning he felt deep inside his chest when he watched his friends with their wives left him feeling desolate and as though he would never be whole. It was almost as if he had lost his mate.

With a deep sigh, he made his feet move and descended the stairs that led into the great hall. Cheers rose from the Shields as he approached. Gabriel smiled and raised his mug of ale as he walked the length of the long table to his seat.

"I'm glad you joined us," Cole said as he leaned toward him. "We were becoming concerned."

Gabriel sank into his chair and looked at the trencher laden with food. He shrugged and began eating. Cole knew him well enough to know that he didn't wish to talk. Though from the corner of his eye, Gabriel could see Hugh and the others glancing at him from time to time.

What began as a very tasty meal soon lost all flavor as he pretended to act as though all was fine. When he finished, he pushed back his trencher, drained his mug of ale and forced a smile as he looked to Mina.

"The meal was excellent, my lady."

Mina smiled, her blue-green eyes reflecting worry. "I'll be sure to tell the cook."

He rose and started around the table when Hugh stopped him. "Where are you going?"

"You all celebrate. I'll keep the first watch," he threw over his shoulder.

Hugh sighed loudly as he leaned back in his chair. "I worry about him. He hasn't been the same since he and Val returned from Scotland."

"Nay," Val said softly. "It was like discovering his immortality made things worse."

Nicole, Val's mate, tsked as she threaded her fingers within his. "Give him time, love," she said, her Scottish accent thick.

"We don't have a lot of time," Roderick stated.

Hugh looked to his wife and held out his hand for her as he stood. "Are you ready for bed, my love?"

Mina smiled as she accepted Hugh's hand. "Always."

Hugh tucked Mina's arm in his and looked at his men. "The Fae are guarding Stone Crest. However, I think it would be vigilant of us to keep a lookout ourselves. The Great Evil hasn't been foolish before. I doubt he'll start now."

~ ~ ~

Gabriel leaned his head back and sniffed the wind. It was faint, very discernible, but he was able to smell it. Evil.

He shifted his shoulders as his hand gripped the

smooth wood of his bow. The need to kill the Great Evil was overwhelming, and for only an instant, Gabriel almost left Stone Crest to do that.

"Your thoughts are troubled," a smooth, deep voice said from beside him.

Calm instantly surrounded Gabriel. He didn't need to look to his left to know it was Aimery. The Fae Commander had always managed to quiet the thoughts in his mind.

"The evil is nearly here."

"Nay, Gabriel. It already is here."

Gabriel turned to Aimery. He needed to see the truth in the Fae's shimmering blue eyes to believe him. But Aimery wouldn't look at him. The Fae's gaze was directed over the land, to the forest Gabriel had stared at most of the evening before he joined the others in the great hall.

"The smell of evil is faint."

"I know," Aimery said softly. "It's not the Great Evil, nor anything as great as the griffon. This evil is something different."

Gabriel understood now. "It's something we won't expect."

"Exactly." Aimery faced him then. "Why were you thinking of finding the evil by yourself?"

He shrugged, unsure now of anything. "I had a powerful urge to seek it out and kill it myself."

"That would be folly, my friend."

Gabriel saw the doubt in the Fae's mystical eyes. "I'm not part of the evil."

For long moments, Aimery stared at him. "Nothing we have ever done has opened your past, Gabriel. We don't know who you were, your family, or even where you were from."

"I know." Aimery wasn't telling him anything he didn't

already know.

Aimery crossed his arms over his chest causing his long flaxen hair to shift in the breeze. "Though immortality isn't an obscure occurrence, there are few races throughout the realms which are immortal."

Gabriel's stomach clenched and the blood in his veins ran like ice. "What are you saying?"

"I've sent out runners to the realms which are immortal."

He turned away, unable to hold the Fae's gaze any longer. Aimery had always been someone Gabriel looked up to. He had been the one to find Gabriel, and even helped to nurse him back to health. He owed Aimery greatly, but there was one thing he feared above all, and that was letting Aimery and the Shields down.

"I don't want to know," Gabriel finally said. He braced his hands against the stones once more and let his head drop.

"What do you fear?"

Gabriel lifted his head slightly and glanced at Aimery. The Fae stood regal in his tunic of silver with blue threads that matched the blue in his shimmering eyes perfectly.

"You know of what I fear by reading my thoughts. Why do you want me to speak them?"

"Because I think you need to hear them aloud."

Gabriel shook his head. "Nay. I have a duty, Aimery. I gave my word, my vow, to the Shields. My word is all that I own in this world. I refuse to lose it now."

"No one doubts you, Gabriel. The Shields all know that you are one with them. They simply worry about you."

A wry chuckle escaped Gabriel as he let his head drop between his arms again. "And you, Aimery? Do you know that I am one with the Shields?"

"Aye."

But Gabriel knew the truth by hearing the hesitation in Aimery's voice. He didn't prod the Fae more. There was no need. Gabriel had the answers he sought.

CHAPTER THREE

Jayna couldn't stop her hands from shaking. All night she had remained in the woods watching the castle as a lone man walked the battlements while she waited for the rising sun.

Snow began to fall, thick and heavy just a few hours before dawn, but Jayna hadn't minded. She stayed huddled under the pine trees. But now the time had come. It was time to venture into the castle and find Gabriel. Find him and kill him.

She took a deep breath to calm her racing heart. After she adjusted her cloak and ensured the hood hid her face, she began her walk to the road that would take her to the castle gates.

At this time of the morning, not many people ventured from their homes, and Jayna knew it was going to be decidedly difficult to get into the castle by herself. She was going to need help.

She stopped as she reached the long, winding road. To her left was the imposing castle. She was anxious to get inside the castle walls and find Gabriel, but too many years of searching had taught her some measure of patience.

Her options were few. She was just about to step back into the forest and wait until later in the day when she heard something down the road. She peered to her right and strained to hear just what was making all the racket so early in the morn.

The rickety old wagon being pulled by an equally old horse turned the corner in the road, and Jayna couldn't help but smile. She now had her way into the castle.

"Damme, ol' Ruth," the old man cursed as he tried to get the horse to move faster. "I know 'tis cold. Believe me, me old bones feel it just as yours do, but yer load isn't that heavy."

Jayna stood waiting in the middle of the road, but it appeared the old man hadn't seen her and the horse wasn't going to stop.

"Do you need some help, sir?" she said. When he didn't answer, she spoke louder and hid her smile when he jumped.

He stood just a few strides from her as he came to a halt and looked at her as if she had just sprung up from the earth. He looked to be a kindly old man with tufts of white hair poking out of his head and his face a mass of lines and wrinkles against skin so pale she could see his veins.

"A lass? Helping me? Nay, girl. I should be the one helpin' ye."

Jayna walked to the mare and patted Ruth's neck as she looked at the wagon.

"I'd offer ye a ride, lass, but I'm afraid ol' Ruth just cannot bear it."

She waved away his words. "I'm hale and hearty, sir. Let me lend you a hand to get out of this cold. Where are you going?"

"To the castle. I've got some food for me

granddaughter that I need to get to her and her young-uns."

Jayna picked up one of the bags of food. It wasn't as heavy as she first perceived, so she grabbed another one. With a bag in each arm, she walked until she stood beside the old man.

"That should help Ruth a bit, aye?"

He smiled, showing several missing teeth. "They call me Jobbins."

"Good morn, Jobbins. I'm Jayna."

"You speak like a lady, Jayna. Are you sure you should be out here alone?" he asked looking around.

Jayna laughed. "Come, Jobbins. 'Tis cold and your granddaughter needs her food."

Behind her, she heard Jobbins coaxing Ol' Ruth to get moving again. Surprisingly, the mare did move a bit faster. Jayna didn't like how she worried about the mare or Jobbins. It had been a long time since she had interacted with people, and she hadn't expected to feel the ache for her family after so long.

She wasn't given long to dwell on her thoughts as they reached the massive wooden gates of Stone Crest castle. Jayna slowed her steps until Jobbins was even with her. She hoped the old man would vouch for her when the menacing looking guards stopped them.

Yet, the guards called to Jobbins by his name, as they asked about his family and even how Ol' Ruth was holding up in the weather. Never once did they ask about her, though one of the guards did watch her suspiciously.

Jayna walked with Jobbins through the gate and into the bailey. She let her eyes roam around the large enclosure as she continued to follow him. Her heart raced with anticipation. Gabriel was in the castle. He was so close she could almost feel him.

At long last she would have her revenge.

"Jayna, lass, Ol' Ruth and I sure do appreciate yer help this cold morn'," Jobbins said as he stopped the cart. Jayna opened her mouth to tell him it was no problem when several children ran up.

She watched Jobbins with his great-grandchildren, the love he held for them shining brightly in his eyes. Jayna felt her eyes begin to sting and she hastily blinked and turned to find a young woman standing beside her.

"Good morn," the woman said.

Jayna glanced at the woman to find her black hair pulled back in a neat plait and her figure slightly plump from childbirth. "Good morn."

"Did Grandda talk you into helping him?" she asked with a friendly smile.

Jayna returned the smile. "Nay, I insisted since Ruth was having a hard time. My name is Jayna."

"Thank you for your help. I'm Lizzie," she said as she took one of the bags out of Jayna's hand. "Every winter I expect it to be Ruth's last, yet every season she lives on. I'm not sure what we'll do when that mare finally does leave us."

With the children helping Jobbins and Lizzie, the small cart was emptied of food within no time at all. Jayna stood by Ol' Ruth and petted the tall mare as Jobbins argued with Lizzie about leaving. Lizzie finally got her way and convinced Jobbins to stay for a while.

"I need to see ta Ol' Ruth," Jobbins said.

"All right, but make sure you come straight back. There's no reason for you to be staying by yourself in those hills when there's room for you here."

Jobbins tsked, but Jayna could see he liked his granddaughter's attention. "Thank ye again for all yer help, Jayna. If ye ever need anything ye can find me here or in my cottage in the hills. Ye cannot miss it. Just follow the road and then take the left fork."

Jayna waved as Jobbins walked Ol' Ruth to the stables. With a deep breath, she turned toward the castle and stopped dead in her tracks. Coming toward her was none other than Gabriel.

She had wondered if she would be able to recognize him after so long a time, but he hadn't changed at all. His tall frame still bulged with muscles and his gait was that of a man with a purpose. His face no longer held the boyish charm it once did, and instead, was closed and unforgiving.

With one hand on the hilt of his sword and the other arm swinging beside him, he made his way toward her. Even from a distance she could see his molten silver eyes, eyes that had once held warmth and promise now were as cold and hard as a lake in winter.

Jayna made herself walk toward him. It wasn't time for her to attack. First, she needed to study him, to get close to him.

He was nearly upon her when she raised her gaze to his face. She knew he couldn't see within the hood of her cloak, which was the only reason she allowed herself a glance at his face. It was leaner, harder. And his hair was longer, well past his shoulders now.

As she drew alongside him, she could still make out the red strands mixed with the varying shades of brown. A smile pulled at her lips as she moved past him.

He was within her reach. Just a little more time and then Gabriel would die.

~ ~ ~

Gabriel stopped in mid-stride. He turned and looked at the woman that had just passed him. There had been something familiar about her, something that nagged just out of memory. Which was distinctly odd since he had seen nothing of her face.

He watched as she disappeared amid the people of the bailey, and though a part of him wanted to follow her to discover who she was, he knew it would be folly. The Shields needed him more than he needed to satisfy his curiosity.

"Well?" Cole asked impatiently as Gabriel walked up.

Cole had been found by the Fae as well, though the reason he couldn't remember his realm is that he had been but a small child and the realm had been destroyed by the Great Evil.

"Val and Hugh haven't returned from their look to the east. I searched the forest and found where someone had stood all night."

"Did you smell any evil?" Roderick asked.

Gabriel leaned against the thick curtain wall that surrounded the castle. "A faint whiff, nothing definite."

Roderick growled and raked a hand down his face. "Cole and I searched the south woods and found nothing."

"Did you venture to the monastery?" Gabriel asked.

Both men shook their head. "I think we should all search there."

"Maybe so," Cole said as he leaned against the stones with his hand. "I don't like that place, and I don't think Mina nor Elle wish to return anytime soon."

"They don't need to," Gabriel answered. "I think it better if the four Chosen stay inside the walls of the castle." As he looked at his two friends he realized something else, as well. "You both should stay and protect your mates."

Roderick shook his head. "I'm not going to leave you, Hugh, and Val to fight this evil alone."

Gabriel pushed away from the wall and looked at the four women as they walked from the castle laughing and talking like old friends. He wondered what it was like to find a connection to the past, something or someone that would help to heal the void within him. The four Chosen had found that in each other and they were as close as if they were sisters.

"Nay, that's not what I mean, Roderick," he said. "All of you need to defend your mates."

Cole's dark eyes narrowed on him. "We are brothers in his, Gabriel. You cannot fight this alone, nor will I let you."

How could Gabriel tell them that he knew he had to fight this alone, that his four friends must protect their women in order for the evil to be vanquished?

"We haven't even found the evil yet," he said in answer to Cole. "Until we do, it's all a moot point."

"Speaking of the creature," Roderick said. "Don't either of you find it strange that it hasn't shown itself yet?"

Gabriel nodded. "I've been thinking on that. Before, the creatures have always been large and powerful, beasts that no ordinary man could defeat."

"True," Cole said. "First the gargoyle, the harpies, a minotaur, and then the griffon, a beast so pure it was thought never to turn evil."

"Yet it did," Gabriel said. "Each creature has been more powerful than the last."

"What are you getting at?" Roderick asked.

"Just as Aimery told me last night. We need to look for the unexpected. This is the Great Evil's last chance to end this and gain power."

Cole smiled as understanding filled his dark eyes. "The Great Evil isn't going to send us a mythological beast to battle."

"He's going to send us something we'd never suspect," Gabriel finished.

Roderick whistled. "By the gods, what are we going to do?"

"Keep the women safe," Gabriel said.

"Easier said than done," Cole muttered. "All I hear from Shannon is that she wants to help us hunt the evil."

Gabriel glanced around the bailey hoping to see the cloaked woman again, but many wore black nondescript cloaks, making his search in vain.

He turned back to his friends. "Have the women stumbled across anything that would show them what they need to do to kill the Great Evil once and for all?"

"Nay," Roderick answered. "They try not to show it, but I know they're frustrated. All of them assumed that once the fourth was found, they would have the answers."

Cole inhaled deeply. "You've the right of it. Shannon said they've tried nearly everything they can think of, but nothing seems to work. She's afraid there will come a time when they must band together, and none of them know what to do, which will mean the Great Evil will win."

"I wish he had a name," Gabriel mumbled. "I want to see his face, to know what he is."

Cole grinned. "You always were more prepared once you got a look at the creatures."

"I'm not sure seeing the Great Evil will aid us," Roderick said.

"Meaning?" Cole asked.

Roderick turned away from watching his wife to look at his fellow Shields. "Meaning, Gabriel is right. No matter what, we won't be prepared for whatever is sent to us, even if it's the Great Evil himself."

"True," Gabriel admitted. "However, I think it's the not knowing that is eating away at everyone."

"The not knowing what, or when," Cole corrected.

Roderick nodded. "You've the right of it, Cole."

"Well, I need more," Gabriel said. "I'm heading out to the monastery."

"I'll come with you," Cole said.

Roderick crossed his arms over his chest. "You think there's something there?"

Gabriel shrugged. "I have no idea, but because two battles with the creatures were at the monastery, there might be something there."

"Good luck then," Roderick said. "I'll stay behind with the women. I don't like leaving them alone."

"Keep them together," Cole said over his shoulder as he followed Gabriel to the stables.

As the two men hurried into the stables, the stable boys moved out of the way since they all knew the Shields liked to saddle their own mounts.

Gabriel had just finished fastening his saddle and mounting when Cole walked his horse up.

"Ready?"

Gabriel nodded. "Ready."

They clicked their horses into a trot and rode out of the dimly lit stables into the bright morning sun. The horses snorted, creating clouds out of their breath. Gabriel's eyes roamed the bailey, though he wasn't sure what he looked for.

They approached the castle gate and Cole called out a greeting to the guards who hastily opened the massive structure enough so that they could pass through.

Once they left the bailey and heard the gate close behind them, Gabriel nudged his mount into a gallop. Winter had England firmly in her grasp as was evident by the blanket of white on the ground and the ice covering the lakes.

It wasn't until they reached the line of trees at the edge of the forest that Gabriel felt it. He pulled back on the reins and brought his gelding to a stop.

"What is it?" Cole asked as he drew alongside him.

Gabriel's gaze roamed over the castle. "Someone is watching us."

Cole chuckled. "It is probably nothing more than a servant or one of Stone Crest's people seeing what we are about. I've never seen you so edgy before," Cole said as he moved his horse into the forest.

Gabriel hesitated a moment. He wasn't uneasy by nature, but he couldn't stop the niggling in his mind that something was going to happen. To him.

And it wasn't going to be good.

CHAPTER FOUR

Jayna stood atop the battlement and stared after Gabriel and the other man as they rode to the forest. When Gabriel stopped his mount and turned to watch the castle, she knew he had felt her gaze.

And she was glad of it.

She was curious to know if he could feel his impending doom. Just the thought that he might be a bit frightened brought a smile to her lips.

It was hard for her to admit, even to herself, that seeing Gabriel for the first time since...well, since he ruined her life had upset her more than she had thought. She hadn't known exactly what she would feel, but the excitement of finally capturing her prize had outweighed the fear of seeing him again.

Laughter from the bailey below reached her. Jayna drew her thin cloak tighter around her and looked over the side to see four women huddled together laughing and talking.

At one time she'd had friends, people she could laugh with and spend time with. But that was before Gabriel.

Now, as she stared at the four beautiful women, she felt a pull within her, a longing for her old life she hadn't felt in many years.

Suddenly, one of the women looked up at Jayna. She had eyes the color of a clear blue sky, and long auburn hair pulled away from her face in a thick braid.

"Hello," the woman said.

Jayna jerked and realized she was staring. She gave a nod to the woman and turned away. When she glanced back at the forest, Gabriel and the other man had ridden into the thick trees.

For so long Jayna had been on her own, keeping to herself at all times. She realized that might not have been the wisest choice since she would have to mingle with the people of Stone Crest in order to get close enough to Gabriel to kill him. And then get out before anyone realized she had been the one to kill him.

"Excuse me," a soft, feminine voice said from beside Jayna.

She turned her head and saw the woman from below standing beside her.

"Forgive me," the woman said, her accent different than any Jayna had ever heard. "I don't mean to intrude, but you look so lonely up here. Would you like to join me and my friends?"

Jayna found that she was afraid to speak. The woman was so poised and elegant that Jayna knew she would look crude and inept in front of this woman. At one time, Jayna had been the most graceful of women, but time had a way of changing people.

She finally shook her head and began to turn away when a hand touched her arm.

"It's cold," the woman said again. "Come inside and warm yourself by the fire for a bit."

Jayna hadn't realized she was shivering until that moment. She had been concentrating on Gabriel so hard that everything else ceased to exist. Just then her stomach rumbled.

The woman's smile never faltered as she stared at Jayna. "My name is Elle, and as I'm sure you have guessed, I'm not from here."

Jayna licked her lips. This woman was obviously a lady and would be able to get her close to Gabriel, therefore, completing her mission early. "Thank you," she finally said. "I'm Jayna."

Elle's smiled widened. "What a pretty name. It's so feminine and strong at the same time. Come, Jayna," she said and held out her hand. "The others are anxious to meet you."

Jayna wasn't sure what she had gotten herself into. She knew how catty women could be at times, but Elle seemed genuinely friendly, and, God help her, but Jayna needed a friend.

She took Elle's hand and together they walked down the stairs to the bailey and then into the great hall where the other women were already seated at one of the tables.

"Elle, you did it," said a woman with hair so black it nearly shown blue and a thick Scottish accent.

Another woman with strawberry blonde hair only nodded as she smiled. "I knew she would. She's very tenacious."

Elle laughed and came to stand at the head of the table. "Allow me to introduce to you Jayna."

Jayna felt four pairs of eyes on her and began to grow nervous. One slip with these women and she would be kicked out of Stone Crest and her one chance to kill Gabriel would be gone.

"Good morn," she said.

"I know you won't remember their names, but I'll introduce you," Elle said. "To my right is Nicole, who is from Scotland. Beside her is Shannon."

"Hello," Shannon said.

An accent different from Nicole's, but similar to Elle's, Jayna noted. She made a mental note to remind herself that Shannon had the wavy brunette hair and soft brown eyes.

"I'm Mina," said the woman with strawberry blonde hair and the most unusual blue-green eyes. "I'm mistress of Stone Crest, and I would like to welcome you to my home."

Jayna swallowed and pushed back the hood of her cloak so that everyone could see her. "Thank you for your hospitality."

Elle pulled her to the table and Jayna found herself sitting between Mina and Elle. Trenchers of food were brought and placed in front of them. The smell of the warm food made Jayna's mouth water and her stomach grumble loudly.

"Was that your stomach again, Shannon?" Nicole asked.

Shannon laughed. "I can't help it that I like to eat, but as a matter of fact, it wasn't."

"I think we might be frightening our guest," Mina said and slid a glance at Jayna.

"Not at all," Jayna assured them. "I do apologize, but it was my stomach you heard."

Shannon grinned at Jayna before she threw Nicole an 'I told you so' look. "They're used to me eating a lot, Jayna, so don't hold back."

"You have such an unusual accent," Jayna said after she had swallowed her first delicious bite. "Where are you from?"

She didn't miss Shannon trading a look with Elle. Both

women became very focused on their meal, letting Jayna know they were hiding a secret.

"It's very far away across the seas," Shannon finally answered.

But Jayna wasn't fooled. She knew they were keeping something from her, but it wasn't like she didn't have secrets of her own. She almost laughed aloud when she imagined their faces if she told them she wasn't even from their time.

She focused on her meal as the women began to talk again. The conversation turned to their men and what they were hunting. Jayna kept quiet as she savored her hot meal, the warmth of the nearby fire, and the friendly conversation. But she didn't intrude on the talk. Instead, she listened and learned much more than she ever anticipated.

It seemed Gabriel was part of a group of warriors, but warriors of what, Jayna didn't know. When she was finally finished, she leaned back in her chair as the conversation quieted.

"Feel better now?" Mina asked.

Jayna nodded, feeling a little out of place next to such a gracious, beautiful lady of the castle. Mina had an aura around her that spoke of steely resolve and a gentle heart. In other words, she was the kind of woman Jayna knew would defend her loved ones to the death.

"The meal was delicious, aye," she said. "I appreciate your hospitality and your kindness. I will leave now, my lady," Jayna and started to rise.

Mina put a hand on her arm to halt her. "Please sit," she said softly. "I haven't seen you around Stone Crest before. From where do you hail?"

Jayna had known this question would come, and she was prepared for it. "Nowhere and everywhere. I travel, taking what work I can in exchange for a warm meal and a dry place to sleep."

"An odd thing to hear a woman doing," Nicole said, her Scottish accent thickening a bit. "You must be able to defend yourself if you're still alive."

Jayna smiled as she pulled a dagger from the sleeve of her gown. The women smiled and laughed as they watch Jayna replace the weapon. "I learned very early on that the world was a cruel place, and if I wanted a place in it I must be able to defend myself."

"Who taught you?" Elle asked.

"My parents died when I was very little which left me in the care of my drunken uncle who cared more about his sword than he did anything else. When I was about sixteen summers he went into a rage and beat me. I waited until he passed out, grabbed one of his daggers and some food and left. I've been on my own ever since."

Jayna hated lying to them, but she didn't have a choice. She had to sound sympathetic to them or they wouldn't believe her.

"How awful," Mina said sadly.

Shannon did a very unladylike snort. "I would have killed him."

"I can't imagine what you've been through," Elle said and placed her hand atop Jayna's.

Nicole sat forward to get Mina's attention. "Mina, isn't there some place she can stay for a while? It's terribly cold out, and Jayna has no place to go."

Jayna watched as Mina chewed her lower lip.

"I must speak with Hugh first," Mina said. "You know what is going on, and I don't want to do anything until he arrives."

"Very true," Elle agreed with a nod. "I can't believe I forgot."

Jayna hurriedly rose to her feet. "Thank you, my ladies, for everything. However, I wouldn't want you to put yourselves in any kind of trouble with your husbands. I'll be on my way."

"Nay," Mina said and as she stood with Jayna. "I cannot let you leave, not in this weather. There'll be more snow soon."

Jayna looked down to hide her smile. She swallowed and slowly raised her gaze to meet Mina's. "I would not wish for you to argue with your husband."

"Let me talk to him first," Mina begged. "He'll wish to speak with you before allowing you to stay, but I'm sure he'll welcome you."

"Are you at war?" Jayna asked.

The women exchanged glances before Shannon answered. "In a manner. Precautions must be taken, though I'm sure you understand."

"Of course." Jayna found herself curious at just what was going on. She had no doubt she would know the answer before the end of the night.

Mina stepped around her chair and smiled to Jayna. "Come with me."

Since she didn't have much of an option, Jayna followed Lady Mina as her gaze swept the great hall from side to side. It was an impressive castle. Its sheer size would intimidate the most virile of men.

As Mina left the great hall and began to ascend the stairs, Jayna glanced over her shoulder to see the other ladies talking quietly with their heads together as if their lives depended upon some secret.

Jayna nearly laughed aloud at that prospect. She had once been a grand lady in charge of a great house, and she remembered quite vividly how frivolous her life had been.

"I know you don't wish to tell us who you really are,"

Mina said softly as she turned to the left and walked down a long hallway. "My husband, Hugh, will ask, and you can rest assured that he would never tell your secret."

Jayna clasped her hands in front of her as she followed Mina. "Not even to you?"

There was no mistaking the slight tightening of Mina's smile. "If you ask him not to, nay, he will not. Hugh is a man of his word."

"Why are you telling me this?"

"Because I think you are more than what you say. By your speech and bearing, I'd say you are a lady."

Jayna sighed and stopped walking. Had she been so ready for friendship that she had let down her guard? She watched as Mina turned to stare at her. "Anyone can act like a well-bred lady."

"Not anyone," Mina said with a soft smile. "Keep your secrets for now, but follow me so that you can rest."

Rest. Jayna hadn't truly rested in...too long to remember. Ever since that awful day that had changed her life forever. She had refused to relax until Gabriel was dead.

Then she could think about her future.

Jayna was so lost in thought she didn't pay attention to where Mina led her. As she chided herself, Jayna scanned the deserted hallway and glanced over her shoulder.

"If you keep to this hallway, you'll find the stairway leading to the great hall," Mina said.

Jayna narrowed her eyes. How had Mina known what she was thinking? Jayna didn't respond to her comment. Instead, she touched the dagger hidden up her sleeve.

Suddenly, Mina stopped at a doorway and gestured inside. "I hope this is suitable."

Jayna walked into the room and gazed at the hearth and a fire that was being stoked by a servant. Above the hearth was a large tapestry depicting a knight leaving his wife for battle. On the other side of the room stood a bed with thick blood red fabric that she could pull around the bed to ward off the chill. There were a small table with two chairs, a chest near the bed, and a few pegs on the walls.

"This will do perfectly," Jayna said as she walked to the roaring fire. "I appreciate your hospitality." And she meant it.

"Would you care for a bath?"

Jayna blinked and moved her gaze to Mina. "It wouldn't be too much trouble?"

Mina laughed. "We have a bathing chamber that I can take you to whenever you would like."

"Why are you being so nice? You don't know me."

She folded her hands together and regarded Jayna solemnly. "I'm nice because you are in need. However, I can honestly say that if you hurt anyone at Stone Crest, I'll kill you."

And Jayna knew she would. She had never met a woman like Mina, a woman who was not only graceful and kind, but had steel running through her. She hated to admit it, but she genuinely liked Mina.

"Should I worry about you?" Mina asked.

Jayna turned and walked to the table as she contemplated the tapestry. "I didn't come to Stone Crest to harm you."

"What do you fear, Jayna? There is great sadness in your hazel eyes. Sadness and fear. Burdens that a lady such as yourself should never know."

Jayna took a step away from Mina. "Fate has a way of forcing herself upon us. I was dealt my Fate."

Mina sighed and briefly closed her eyes. "Revenge won't heal the pain within you."

Shaken, Jayna put a chair between her and Mina. How did Mina know just what to say to prick the sturdy stone walls she had built around herself? How did Mina know about her pain and fear? About her revenge?

Jayna knew she hid those emotions well. To the world she appeared a woman on her own, ready for whatever life threw at her. No one had ever known the deep despair that sometimes overwhelmed her, or the longing she had for her family and her people. No one.

Until now.

"I'm sorry," Mina said suddenly. "I'm not sure what came over me just now. It was as though I could feel your pain. Or someone's pain." Her gaze studied Jayna as if she were trying to decipher if what she had felt was real or not.

"No apologies," Jayna said. "I think I'd like to rest for a while."

"Of course. I'll return in a couple of hours to check on you."

Jayna waited until the door closed behind Mina before she closed her eyes and sighed heavily. Killing Gabriel might not be as easy as she first thought. Not as long as Mina was around.

CHAPTER FIVE

Gabriel stopped his horse in front of the ancient monastery and stared at the crumbling stones.

"It was never much to look at," Cole said quietly.

"Nay. Strange that a holy place would call to the creatures."

Cole dismounted and dropped his horse's reins. "I thought that myself. Once holy, always holy."

"Right," Gabriel answered as he too dismounted and went to stand beside Cole. "Evil such as these creatures shouldn't be able to touch a place such as a monastery."

"Hmmm," Cole said as he scratched his chin. "A question in need of answering. Shall we look inside?"

Gabriel grinned as Cole cocked an eyebrow before walking through the arched stone gateway of the monastery. Gabriel's eyes scanned the top of the monastery as he recalled when he, Hugh and Cole had knocked the stone gargoyle off the roof.

Just as before, remnants of the monks could be seen in the statues of gargoyles at the top of the monastery used to ward off evil. Holy or not, the monks were also superstitious, not that Gabriel could blame them after everything he had seen while a Shield.

"I wonder," Cole said, "if the Fae hadn't given Hugh the clue that the gargoyle could be killed while it slept, would we have won that day?"

Gabriel turned to his friend and shrugged. "I like to think everything happens for a reason."

"I agree. I just can't help thinking Earth would've been destroyed ages ago if the Fae hadn't been here to help. Without us, the evil would win."

Gabriel knew that Cole was bothered that the Chosen hadn't figured out how to destroy the Great Evil yet. "Shannon and the others are strong and intelligent. They'll figure it all out."

Cole nodded absently and walked into the monastery. Gabriel followed. Instantly, the musty smell of disuse assaulted Gabriel. The entry was large with ceilings that soared high above them. Balconies looking down into the entry could be seen from every floor above them.

Bookshelves that had already been knocked over were now crushed, the books nothing more than dust after the two battles that raged within the holy walls.

"I don't smell evil," Cole said as he picked his way through the debris.

"Me, neither."

Just as Gabriel was about to turn and leave, he spotted something oozing off a fallen bookcase. "Cole," he called out as he squatted down to get a better look at the nearly clear, thick substance.

"What did you find?" Cole asked as he knelt beside Gabriel. "Well. That's interesting. What do you suppose it is?"

"I don't have any idea." Gabriel reached out and touched it, then rubbed it between his finger and thumb.

"Its almost sticky, and easily pliable." He leaned down to sniff his fingers. "There's no smell to it."

Cole stood and looked around the chamber. "Whatever it is, it has left its mark on the place."

Gabriel rose and followed Cole's gaze to see other spots throughout the chamber. "It's clear, so we might have overlooked it. I wonder how many other spots this substance can be found throughout this place."

"Let's find out," Cole said with a smile as he unhooked his double-headed war axe and started toward the doorway that would lead him to the chambers below.

Gabriel turned and made for the stairs leading to the floors above. He had gone about twenty steps when he encountered another puddle of the clear liquid. He decided to take a chance and venture onto the roof to see if any of the substance was up there, as well.

When he stepped out onto the roof he unsheathed his sword, preferring it to his bow for the time being. His eyes scanned the surroundings. The tree limbs were laden with snow, and the forest was unusually quiet.

Out of the corner of his eye, Gabriel saw movement. He spun around with his sword raised only to encounter...nothing. He could have sworn he had seen something.

He slowly lowered the sword and walked around the roof with slow, measured steps. The hair on the back of his neck stood on end. Someone, or something, watched him.

Suddenly, a loud whoosh sounded behind him. Gabriel spun around and blinked.

"It cannot be," he whispered.

The evil laughter echoed around the silence of the forest. "Oh, but it is," the gargoyle said as it hovered above him. "You didn't honestly think you'd be rid of me with just a little shove, did you?"

"Gabriel," Cole shouted as he ran out onto the roof, then skidded to a halt. "By the gods."

"Be warned, Shields," the gargoyle said as he flew higher. "Your time is at an end."

Gabriel leaned against the side of the roof and let out a breath. "You did see it, aye?"

"Aye," Cole said, his mouth twisted with anger. "At least we know what we're fighting."

"And how to kill it," Gabriel reminded him.

Cole laughed. "If this is all the Great Evil thinks will stop us, he's wrong."

Gabriel straightened and sheathed his sword. "What did you find below?"

"More of the substance. You?"

"The same. I followed it up here and that's when I encountered the gargoyle."

"Let's return and tell Hugh. He and the others should've returned to Stone Crest by now."

Gabriel nodded and followed Cole back into the monastery and down the stairs. Again he felt as though someone watched him, but no matter how hard he looked, he didn't find anyone.

He ran outside and hurriedly mounted. With one last look to the skies, Gabriel whistled to his horse and set out at a run to Stone Crest.

By the time he and Cole pulled their mounts to a halt inside the bailey, Hugh, Val and Roderick were making their way towards them.

"We know what we're fighting," Cole said as he jumped to the ground.

Hugh nodded. "As do we."

"I can't believe it didn't die the first time," Cole continued as he walked around his horse to the other

Shields.

Gabriel dismounted and patted his horse on the neck as the stable boys came to get the horses.

Val ran a hand down his face. "I never thought to see it again. We've never had to fight the same creature twice."

"At least the gargoyle is easy to kill," Cole stated.

"Gargoyle?" Hugh repeated.

Gabriel narrowed his gaze as he looked to his leader. There was something in Hugh's tone that didn't bode well. "Aye. The gargoyle."

"You must be mistaken," Val said. "It's the harpy that's returned."

"Nay," Cole said. "I saw the gargoyle with my own eyes and heard it speak. It said that our time was running out."

Hugh raised his hand for quiet. When they were all looking at him, he lowered his voice and said, "I know what I saw, and it was a harpy."

"Be that as it may, it was the gargoyle that we saw," Gabriel said.

Hugh nodded. "All right. Let's compare. What I saw was a creature with wings that clanked so loudly as they beat that you could hardly hear yourself think."

"Nay," Cole said. "Ours had wide, thin wings."

"The creature we saw had the face and upper body of a beautiful woman with long, flaming red hair."

Gabriel shook his head. "Our creature had a hideously shaped face with a long snout and red, beady eyes."

Hugh cursed as he paced before them. "You describe the gargoyle, yet I know we saw the harpy."

"By the gods," Val muttered. "We're not fighting one creature, but two."

The men looked to each other, then as one turned toward the castle. They must talk privately, not in the middle of the bailey were anyone could overhear them.

Yet, they didn't get farther than the great hall before Mina stopped Hugh.

"I must speak with you," she called out to him.

"Can it wait?"

She hesitated a moment, then nodded. "Aye."

Hugh gave her a small smile before he hurried up the stairs to one of the tower chambers that they used when needing to discuss something privately. It was well away from the rest of the castle, and situated so that they could hear someone coming up the stairs.

"What are we going to do?" Roderick asked once they were in the tower chamber.

Hugh sank onto one of the chairs, his head in his hands. "Aimery will have to be notified immediately. We've battled both creatures, and we know how to kill them."

"I hate to say it," Gabriel said, "but I highly doubt that both creatures have come back the same as before."

Val sighed. "Meaning they won't be as easy to kill."

"That's my thought," Gabriel said with a shrug. "It makes sense if you think that every creature we've battled has gotten stronger and more deadly with each one we've killed."

"Gabriel's right," Cole said.

Hugh raised his head and steepled his hands in front of his face. "All right. We need to come up with a plan of action. Both creatures fly, which makes their attack on the castle most likely at night so we can't see them. The harpy we can hear coming by the clacking of her wings."

Roderick moved to the door. "I'll have the guards doubled and tell them to keep their eyes on the skies."

"They'll need to rotate shifts since we'll need the battlements fully guarded at night as well," Val said as he stood and followed Roderick from the tower.

Hugh sighed and leaned back against the stone wall. "We've battled these creatures. We know their weaknesses."

"Aye," Gabriel said, sensing his leader's worry. "The gargoyle can only attack at night, so during the day we find it and kill it as before."

Cole nodded. "If they're smart, which they've shown in the past, one will attack at night while the other attacks during the day."

"Which would leave us being attacked constantly," Hugh murmured.

Gabriel lowered himself on one of the chairs. "It's a good strategy for them. It'll leave us locked in the castle for fear of leaving."

"And we can't chance leaving with the Chosen," Cole said. "Our women are the key to the demise of the Great Evil. He'll be coming for them."

Hugh nodded slowly. "I thought I'd finally found my future when I found Mina, but now that's threatened." His gaze moved to Cole then to Gabriel. "I cannot lose Mina."

"You won't," Gabriel promised as he rose. "Go to her. I'll make sure everything is prepared for an attack tonight."

Hugh walked past him and out of the tower. Gabriel watched his leader for several moments before Cole moved beside him.

"I know how Hugh feels. Shannon is my life. Without her I'm nothing."

Gabriel looked to his friend and saw the concern in Cole's brown eyes. "We're all together now. We'll get through this as we have everything else before."

Cole tried to smile but failed before he moved past him and down the stairs. For long moments, Gabriel stayed in the tower by himself. Before, the Shields had been invincible because they had cared for no one but themselves. Gabriel couldn't help but wonder just how different things would be now that his brothers were more concerned with the lives of their wives than the deaths of the creatures.

He turned and walked to the window, which was nothing more than an arrow slit in the stones. His eyes scanned the frozen ground of Stone Crest, hoping against hope that he would see something or find some way to save the men that were his family.

Yet, there was nothing.

Just as with his memory – blank.

CHAPTER SIX

Mina twiddled her thumbs as she sat before the great hearth and contemplated her new guest. She still wasn't sure what had happened in the chamber with Jayna, but Mina was sure of one thing: she *had* felt the despair, loneliness, and revenge.

A shadow moved near her and then a figure leaned over her to kiss her cheek. She turned her head and smiled up at her husband. That's when she saw the despondency in his beautiful brown eyes. "Hugh?"

He sighed as he took his chair beside her. "We know what we're fighting."

"That's good, though."

"Maybe." He dropped his head back and reached for her hand. His warm fingers closed over hers, and Mina felt a chill go through her.

"Hugh, please."

"The gargoyle is back, and so is the harpy."

She sucked in a breath and gaped at him. "Nay."

He slowly nodded as he closed his eyes. "Aye, my love. Val and I saw the harpy while Cole and Gabriel saw the gargoyle."

"Do the others know?" She knew she must tell the other Chosen soon so everyone could prepare.

Hugh nodded. "I'm sure my men are telling them."

Though he had said nothing, Mina knew her husband worried for their people. They had lost so many when the harpy and gargoyle had last attacked them.

She squeezed his hand. "We've prepared our people. Everything will be fine."

He opened his eyes and turned his head toward her. A small smile played on his lips. "You sound so sure."

"You aren't the leader of the Shields for nothing, my lord," she said with a smile. "You've kept your men alive all these years, and together we'll save our people."

He lifted her hand and kissed it as he rubbed his thumb over her skin. "Enough of this for now. Tell me what you needed me for earlier."

Mina took a deep breath. "We've a guest."

"A guest?" Hugh repeated and sat forward. "Who?"

"A woman. She says she's a traveler."

"But," he prompted.

Mina shrugged and rose to pace before the hearth. "When I walked her to her chamber, I caught a glimpse of something." She wrung her hands as she searched for the right word. "It was as if I felt her emotions so clearly."

"And what were they?"

"Despair. Seclusion. Revenge." She turned to face her husband and watched as he rose and came towards her.

"Do you think she's here to hurt someone?"

She shrugged. "I'm not sure. She seems nice, and the others really enjoyed her company. She just...seems so lonely."

"What was her story? Why is she traveling alone?"

"She told us that her parents died when she was young,

and she was raised by an uncle that beat her. She ran away as soon as she could and has been on her own ever since."

"And you believe her?"

Mina chuckled. "Shannon and Elle did because they come from a time where that is possible. However, Nicole and I knew better. The possibility of a young woman such as Jayna surviving on her own all these years without something happening to her is near impossible."

"Exactly. So, what is she hiding?" Hugh asked as he pulled her into his arms.

"She also claims she's a peasant, but all you have to do is look at her and hear her speak to know she's nobility."

"Very peculiar, don't you think?"

Mina rested her head on Hugh's muscular chest. "Is it coincidence that she arrives here now when the Shields are getting ready to fight the creatures and the Chosen are trying to figure out how to destroy the evil?" She leaned her head back and looked into Hugh's eyes. "I've always trusted your instincts. Will you talk with her yourself?"

"If it'll put your mind at ease, aye. Besides, we cannot take any chances."

Mina hugged him then rose up on her tiptoes to kiss him. "She's in the east wing."

~ ~ ~

Hugh stepped from the stairs and turned down the hallway that would lead to Jayna's chamber. He was curious to see this woman, not because he wondered what she looked like, but because Mina had literally felt her emotions. He had never heard such a thing, but he wasn't surprised by it.

He lifted his hand and knocked on the door. "It's Lord Hugh. I'd have a word with you, please."

A soft shuffle from within and then the door opened. Hugh found himself staring at a slender woman with a wrinkled, out-of-fashion gown. Her blonde hair was pulled away from her face in a long plait down her back, and her hazel eyes stared into his, patiently waiting.

"You're Jayna?"

She gave a stiff nod. "I am, my lord." She stepped aside and allowed him to enter.

Hugh cast a glance around the chamber and only found a black cloak that had seen too many days hanging on one of the pegs. No other items of clothing could be seen.

He stopped before the hearth and clasped his hands behind his back as he regarded her. "My wife tells me that you're a traveler."

She nodded. "I find it suits me."

"How is it that you have survived as long as you have?"

"I'm quick-witted, which has gotten me out of several situations that could've proven ill-fated," she replied in a tone one would use if they were talking down to a servant.

Mina was right, Hugh thought. Jayna is no commoner. "Mina says you ran away from your uncle. He could be looking for you."

Jayna laughed softly. "He was always too drunk to even know I was around, my lord. I was probably gone for months before he realized I wasn't there."

"Any other family?"

"Nay."

Hugh scratched his chin as he contemplated the situation. "Tell me, Jayna, what brought you to Stone Crest?"

She shrugged. "My feet, I suppose, my lord. I was on the road this morning when I encountered an elderly man with a horse that was more dead than alive. He was headed here and I offered my aid to him."

It was a good story, and one Hugh could check for himself since he knew she spoke of Jobbins and his mare Ol' Ruth.

"May I ask you a question, my lord?" Jayna asked.

"Of course."

"Are you at war with someone?"

A frisson of fear snaked down Hugh's spine. "Why do you ask?"

"The guards have doubled since I've been here, and it is highly unlikely that they are for me."

Hugh smiled despite himself. Jayna had spunk. Whatever she had endured in her years traveling, if she did indeed travel, it had only made her stronger.

"We are at war. In fact, it might be prudent for you to leave soon, though with the storm about to blow in, you might be here for a few days."

"I've no wish to be caught in a war between two lords," she said as she stood as still as stone. "Though Lady Mina worries I might freeze to death, I've been in worse and will survive. If it is all right with you, I'll be on my way."

Hugh clenched his jaw as he debated on whether to let her leave or not. "I cannot, in good conscience, allow you to leave in such vile weather."

If they were lucky, the storm would hold off the creatures long enough for Jayna to leave before he had one more innocent to think about.

"Please, Jayna. Mina will never forgive me if you leave now."

"If you're sure," she said hesitantly.

Hugh nodded, all the while wondering if he'd made the greatest mistake of his life. He walked out of the chamber and into the hallway, but still he couldn't get his instincts to tell him if he had done wrong or right.

He found Mina still before the hearth in the great hall,

her expression one of contemplation. She hurried to him as soon as she saw him.

"Well?"

He shrugged. "I couldn't tell one way or another, my love. There's a storm brewing to the west, a nasty one at that. I couldn't let her leave and be out in it."

"And if she's part of the evil?"

"I'll have Gabriel keep watch over her. If she's an innocent, well...we'll have to make sure we get her out in time."

~ ~ ~

Jayna smiled as Hugh left her chamber. She had expected him to ask more questions, but the longer he stayed, the more she realized he was the type of man where actions spoke louder than words. She would have to be careful because she knew he would be watching her.

She yawned and decided it was a good time to test the bathing chambers Mina had spoken of. Jayna walked out of her room and turned toward the stairs. Just before she reached the stairs she encountered one of the servants.

"Can you take me to the bathing chamber?" she asked.

The girl, several years younger than her, smiled and bobbed her dark head. "This way, milady."

Jayna knew she should correct her, but it felt good to be noticed for what she really was – a lady. She followed the young girl down several flights of stairs and hallways until she found herself standing outside a large open chamber with curtains blocking anyone from seeing inside.

"There are cloths to wash with as well as to dry off," the girl explained. "No one is inside, milady, and the water is hot."

Jayna nodded her thanks as she pushed open the

material and stepped through them. Her eyes grew round as she looked at the sheer size of the wooden tub. Two, possibly three, grown men could easily fit inside it.

The water beckoned her, and God help her, Jayna couldn't wait to climb inside. She couldn't remember the last time she had taken a hot bath. Usually, she only had enough water to wash her face, though there had been times she had bathed in any streams or ponds she had come across.

Once her old gown and underclothes were off, she dipped her toe into the water. A sigh escaped her as chills raced across her skin and the steam from the water molded her hair to her face.

She slipped into the water, surprised to find how deep the tub was. She leaned back against the sides as the heat flowed over her, enveloping her in a cocoon of warmth and relaxation.

How long she sat in the water she had no idea. She must have dozed because when she opened her eyes she felt disoriented for a moment. The water had begun to chill, so she hurriedly washed her hair and body and then hopped out of the tub to dry off and put her clothes back on.

It was one of the many times she wished she had another gown, but it was easier to move around without lugging a bag of clothes around. At least that's what she kept telling herself.

She leaned forward and flipped her hair over to wring out the water as best she could. Then, she wrapped the cloth around her as she reached for her gown. Except it wasn't there.

"I hope you don't mind," Mina said as she walked into the chamber. "I had your gown taken to be washed. Elle is more your size, so she loaned you one of her gowns until yours is clean."

Jayna swallowed. "Thank you. That is too kind."

Mina waved away her words. "Nonsense. Let me know if you need anything else."

She could only stare at the gown in her hand. It was exquisite. Not quite blue, but not quite green. It wasn't just the gown that Mina had given her, but undergarments, as well.

With her hair still hanging wet and tangled about her, Jayna hurried to put on the clean clothes. She smoothed her hand over the soft material of the gown. The wide, trailing sleeves and deep hem held a floral pattern that matched the color of the gown. And once she wrapped the braided belt twice around her waist, then let its length land nearly to her feet, she felt like a queen.

How long had it been since she had dressed as a lady? How long had it been since she had acted like a person of her station should? The years had passed by in a blur because she had been focused on one thing...Gabriel.

Just for a moment, one instant in time, she wanted to forget the past and the revenge that ruled her world. She wanted to forget the Great Evil. She just wanted to be Lady Jayna, a woman who searched for her future.

She sighed and slowly walked from the chamber. It was her own chamber that she sought, for there she could sit before the fire and comb out her hair as she tried to forget the past.

CHAPTER SEVEN

Gabriel barely had time to wash up and change before supper. The food was more than delicious at Stone Crest, but sitting at the long table with the men he called brothers and their wives was becoming harder and harder. It just drove home how alone he was in the world.

As he hurriedly descended the steps he recalled that Hugh had asked to speak to him before the evening meal. Time had gotten away from Gabriel as he checked the armory. Whatever it was, he knew Hugh would speak to him later.

It wasn't until he started toward the dais that he noticed a woman in the chair beside his. For an instant, he was sure he recognized the woman. He slowed his steps and studied her face. It was the face of an angel, one so beautiful and graceful that it couldn't possibly be real.

Her golden blonde hair was parted down the middle and hung over her breasts in two thick plaits. As he made his way toward the dais, he saw the welcoming smile she bestowed upon anyone that passed near her. Her lips were full and her mouth wide, erotic lips that he suddenly yearned to feel on his skin.

Gabriel stopped and tried to swallow. He couldn't get closer to her yet, not when he hadn't had his fill of looking at her. He needed to see more of her creamy skin, unmarked by a blemish. He needed to see her gently arching brows lift gracefully at something Val said. He needed to see her striking hazel eyes crinkle at the corners as she laughed.

He *knew* her.

"Gabriel?"

He jerked and turned his head to find Hugh at his elbow.

"Is everything all right?"

Gabriel nodded, unable to find his voice, and angry with Hugh for breaking into his examination of the woman.

"She is quite beautiful isn't she?" Hugh asked softly.

Gabriel made himself turn his back to the dais as he looked to Hugh. "Who is she?"

"First, tell me why you were staring at her as if you know her?"

"Because I think I do."

"What?" Hugh asked, bewilderment widening his eyes. "How?"

Gabriel sighed and ran a hand down his face. "I don't know. It's just when I first saw her...I felt as if I knew her."

"Could she have been someone you bedded?"

Gabriel flattened his lips as he shook his head. "I may bed my fair share of women, but I do remember their faces. She's not one of them."

"You haven't been at Stone Crest long enough to have forgotten her, and if I take her at her word, she just arrived here today."

"Maybe she simply looks like someone from my past," Gabriel finally admitted.

Hugh clamped a hand on his shoulder. "Has any more come to you?"

He shook his head, unwilling and unable to speak more of a past he feared more than death itself. "Mina waits for you. Come, we must eat."

"Her name is Jayna," Hugh said before he could walk away. "Mina welcomed her, but with everything going on, wanted to make sure that Jayna wasn't part of the evil."

"I'm sure you spoke with her. What did you discern?"

"Nothing." Hugh sighed. "She claims to be a commoner, but I don't think she is."

Gabriel glanced over his shoulder at her. "Just look at the way she sits and you can tell she isn't. Nay, she's no more common than I am royalty."

"She also claims to be a traveler. She ran away from a drunk, abusive uncle some years ago and has been on her own ever since."

"What do you think of that?"

"I think she's partly telling the truth, but I think there's more to it."

"You want me to keep a close eye on her?"

"Aye," Hugh said with a half smile. "We all are, but if I ask one of the others to keep close to her, there just might be some jealous wives."

Gabriel chuckled. "Nay, I'll do it."

"You're a good man," Hugh said as he walked to the dais.

Gabriel found it quite easy to make his way to a table that he wanted to avoid most days. It was odd to find that he was looking forward to a bit of a mystery to solve. There was definitely something about Jayna that sparked his interest.

If it was somehow related to his thinking he knew her, or the fact her story had huge flaws in it, he didn't know.

But he most certainly was going to find out.

~ ~ ~

Jayna struggled to keep the smile on her face as Gabriel walked toward her. It had been an unexpected surprise to find that she would be seated next to him. She fingered the dagger up her sleeve, the one she would use to end it all.

She waited for him to recognize her, to call her a fraud and make her attack. She slid the dagger out so the pommel fit into her hand. Her legs were poised to jump up and strike as soon as he opened his mouth.

"You must be Jayna," Gabriel said with a polite nod as he took his seat beside her.

Jayna could only stare. She couldn't believe he didn't recognize her. Or maybe he did and he was biding his time, much like she was doing.

Being this close to him made her remember the Gabriel she'd once known, the Gabriel that she had given her heart to. The Gabriel that had smiled and charmed and wooed her like no other.

"Are Mina and the others taking good care of you?"

She blinked at his conversational tone. His deep voice had always made her heart skip a beat, and to her horror, it was doing so again. How could someone she hates so much still affect her in such a manner? It didn't seem fair.

"Aye," she finally answered. "Lady Mina has been an exceptional host."

"Mina is one of the finest ladies around. So are Elle, Shannon, and Nicole. Hugh tells me that you might be staying for a few days due to the storm."

She nodded and glanced at him before turning her attention to putting the dagger back up her sleeve without him noticing. "Lord Hugh assures me that the storm will be fierce, and that neither he, nor Lady Mina, could, in good conscience, let me leave."

"I agree with them," he said and turned so that he half faced her. "Tell me, how have you survived on your own? I find it extremely difficult to comprehend."

Jayna inwardly grimaced. She had to say just the right thing without revealing herself, all the while trying to determine if Gabriel was playing her. "Fate has been kind to me, in a way. Women aren't safe to travel alone, which is why I learned to use a bow and arrow, as well as a dagger, very effectively."

"Impressive. Where are your weapons now?"

She turned toward him and let her eyes roam over his handsome face. "My dagger is never far. However, I've also learned from past experience that whenever I come across a village or castle, they don't like seeing a woman with a bow and arrow."

He grinned, his eyes crinkling at the corners. "Ah, you hide it before entering a castle or village."

"Precisely."

"And you aren't afraid of someone stealing it?"

"If they find it, let them keep it since they've earned it. Yet, I doubt anyone will find them."

"That good, are you?" he asked with a quirk of his lips.

"Aye."

He chuckled then. "You've spirit, Jayna. I'm surprised that fire within you hasn't found you a husband."

"Who says I want a husband, my lord?"

He waved away her words. "No 'my lords' for me. My name is Gabriel."

She nodded her head as she studied his eyes. Gabriel always spoke through his eyes, his expressions there for all the world to see. If someone was looking.

And she was.

"How long have you lived at Stone Crest?"

He shrugged and drank from his goblet. "Not long. Only a week or so. The time before that I was here for a few weeks."

"I thought you lived here?"

"Nay. I also travel."

She smiled and found his eyes drawn to her lips. Suddenly a thought took root. If he really didn't remember her, she could become close to him by seducing him. Women had done it down through the ages. It was the oldest trick in the book, and a proven one at that.

"Ah, someone who understands my need to see new things," she said softly.

"Hmm. The difference is, I don't go because I want to, I go because I must."

"So you don't get to choose where you venture to next?"

He shook his head. "I go where I am told."

It was difficult to comprehend that Gabriel would take orders from anyone, let alone a lowly lord such as Hugh. "How did you come to be in Hugh's service?"

He looked at her with his molten silver eyes as if weighing her to see if she was trustworthy. "Hugh is not my liege lord, he is my leader."

"Of what?" Jayna found herself interested. There had been hints of being at war, yet no one had said with who.

"We are called the Shields. Hugh leads me, Val, Roderick, and Cole. We battle mythological creatures sent here by an evil bent on destroying this realm."

The room suddenly spun around Jayna as his words sunk in. She tried to grab hold of the table but found only air instead. Large, warm hands gripped her arms to steady her.

"Jayna? Are you all right?"

She waited until the room stopped spinning before she opened her eyes to see his worried gaze on her. She knew then he didn't know who she was or why she was here. She could kill him tonight, but it wouldn't be the same unless he really knew who she was.

"Val," Gabriel said over her head.

Jayna felt rather than saw Val turn towards them. "Is something amiss?" Val asked.

"It's Jayna. I think she's sick."

She shook her head and pulled her gaze away from Gabriel's. "I'm fine. It must be the wine I drank on an empty stomach."

For a moment, she didn't think the men would believe her, then Val turned back to his wife and Gabriel released her.

"You don't believe me, do you?" he asked as he turned to face the table.

She couldn't very well tell him she did when she hadn't seen anything at Stone Crest. He really would be suspicious then. "It's rather difficult to believe something like that without seeing it for yourself."

"Unfortunately, you just might get the chance."

"That's why you're defending the castle as if some lord were about to invade?"

"Aye," he said as their food arrived. He looked at her as she eyed the food and said, "It's the best food I've ever eaten."

Jayna barely tasted the food as she tried to formulate a new plan of attack for Gabriel. She needed to know why he didn't recognize her. For her revenge to be complete, he needed to remember her.

They ate in silence while down the table was full of laughter and much talk. By the time the meal ended, Jayna decided more questions were the way to go.

"I apologize if I offended you," she said softly and shyly looked at him. Her act paid off as he turned toward her.

"You didn't."

"I'm relieved. Would you then tell me more about the...Shields did you call them?"

"Aye, the Shields. It's the name the Fae gave us."

"Fae?" She shouldn't be surprised to know they were involved. After all, if all the Great Evil had told her about the Fae were true, they were very protective of Earth.

"They really do exist, Jayna. I know all this is hard to believe, but I speak the truth."

She nodded woodenly, her heart thumping wildly. "There are many myths and legends that roam these lands, and like most people, I love to hear grand tales but they are hard to believe unless I see them for myself."

"Pray you don't, because if you do, you'll have found yourself in the middle of this war," he said solemnly.

She sat back and clasped her hands in her lap. "You asked me about my family, but don't you have family that needs you? A wife and children?"

He chuckled again, the sound rich and full. "Nay, no wife and children. There isn't time."

"Your brethren seem to have found the time," she pointed out.

He looked down the table, and she was amazed to see a hint of sadness in his silver depths. "Aye, they have, but those women aren't just any women. They're special, and will help us end the Great Evil once and for all."

"Great Evil?" she asked, hoping he didn't detect a hint of fear in her voice.

"Aye," he said and drank deeply from his goblet. "He has already destroyed Cole's realm. Roderick's realm has been fighting the evil for a while, and we're all hoping we can end it before Thales is destroyed."

Jayna swallowed hard. She didn't like what she heard. Surely Gabriel was mistaken. She knew what she had aligned herself with was evil, and she even knew he fought the Fae on several occasions. But the rest...the rest she knew nothing about.

She focused on Gabriel, on luring more information out of him because the end was near for her and she couldn't wait to see him lying dead on the ground.

CHAPTER EIGHT

Gabriel thought he detected a moment of panic in Jayna's beautiful hazel eyes as he spoke of the evil and realms being destroyed.

"That's what we're here for," he reassured her.

"What?"

"To fight the creatures the Great Evil sends to destroy villages. That's how it starts. He lures someone with the promise of power, and he gives them an unusual blue stone about the size of a child's fist and smooth as silk."

"What do they do with it?" she asked, edging closer to him.

He shrugged and glanced around the hall before returning his attention to her. "They call up the creatures with the stones. Whoever has the stones controls the beasts."

She scrunched up her face, her large eyes filled with doubt. "A small blue stone controls creatures released to annihilate the world?"

He grinned. Not many commoners would know such words, yet he said nothing regarding her speech. Instead he said, "Aye. Outlandish isn't it? We learned early on that if we destroy the stone, it kills the creatures. However, sometimes it's harder to find the stone than it is to discover who controls it."

"Hmm," she said softly and ran her finger around the top of her goblet. "Why lure someone with the stone? If this Great Evil is so powerful, why can't he release the creatures himself?"

"Good question. That is one we haven't been able to answer, though we do know he likes to pull people to him, to bind them so that they'll never be free. Men are weak creatures when it comes to power. Most want it so badly they would do unspeakable crimes to attain it."

Jayna nodded. "I've known some women like that as well."

"Aye. I've never understood why the thought of power held such sway over a person."

"It doesn't you?"

He shook his head, wondering if the piercing way she looked at him held more meaning than just her words. "There are some men who are natural born leaders, such as Hugh. Men sense that he can be trusted, that he can, and will, lead them out of any fight. Men willingly die for leaders like Hugh. But natural leaders most often don't seek the power that could be theirs."

He glanced down the table and saw Hugh give him a penetrating look, one meant to let Gabriel know he needed to delve deeper into Jayna's past to see what he could discover. Unfortunately, that meant spending a lot of time with her.

Gabriel both looked forward to it and worried over it. There was something about Jayna that told him he knew her. It was the how of it that went unanswered. Yet she didn't appear to know him, so maybe he was wrong.

But his instincts had never been wrong before.

"Did you have a chance to explore the castle today?" he asked.

She smiled shyly and shook her head. "I admit I was intimidated and stayed in my chamber."

"Would you like a small tour now so you can get your bearings?"

"Aye, that would be nice. Thank you."

Gabriel stood and held out his hand to help her rise. It was another test. If she didn't take it, she could very well be a commoner who was a great actress that had picked up a good vocabulary. But if she did take it, she was a born and bred lady.

His grin widened as she placed her hand in his and allowed him to help her rise. Her skin was cool and soft in his. Her long fingers were slim, and her nails cut short.

He admired her curves in the form-fitting bodice of her gown. She stood nearly to the top of his chin as she held herself regally, waiting for him to lead her.

"This way," he said as he led her around the dais and toward the solar.

Her steps were graceful, smooth and unhurried. Gabriel found himself admiring her until he remembered that she could very well be a spy from the Great Evil.

"Tell me something of yourself. Something of a time before you joined the Shields," she suddenly requested.

Gabriel guided her to the right. "That is the solar. It's Mina's favorite chamber, and it's also where she set up Hugh's chessboard. It's one of his favorite pastimes, so if you cannot find him anywhere else, look here."

She nodded and glanced at him before turning her attention forward as they walked. "You aren't going to answer me, are you?"

He shrugged and walked farther down the hall. It

wasn't until they had left the laughter and conversations of the great hall that he spoke. "I don't have any memory of anything before the Shields."

"What?"

Gabriel was confused at the surprise and hint of anger that shown in her hazel eyes.

"You recall nothing?"

He shook his head and moved forward. "The Fae found me by one of their doorways. I was wounded and near dead, but through their magic and healing abilities they were able to save me."

"In return you felt obligated to join the Shields?"

"Nay. I wanted to do something, something worthwhile, as I tried to regain my memories."

She was silent for a moment before she asked, "And how long has that been?"

"Too long," he answered and steered her into the armory.

He felt her stiffen beside him.

"Why did you bring me here?"

Gabriel turned and looked at her. "All that I told you tonight is the truth. We Shields have fought and died to keep the Great Evil from destroying Earth. Too many have perished, and too much has been sacrificed for us to lose now."

"What are you trying to say?" she said as she took a step back. Her face was devoid of expression, but her gaze held his.

"I'm saying that if you're here to spy for him, or if you're here to prevent us from succeeding, you have two options. You can leave now, and no harm will come to you. Or. You can stay. But once we discover you're in league with the Great Evil, your death will be swift."

If he frightened her, she was good at hiding it. Gabriel

watched her carefully for any signs that she had come to Stone Crest other than the reason she had given.

"Since I'm having a rather difficult time coming to grips with the fact of all you've said regarding this...Great Evil...I can assure you, I'm not here to prevent the Shields from their mission."

For some reason, he believed her. Maybe it was the conviction shining in her hazel eyes, or maybe it was because he wanted her to be innocent. Whatever the reason, he simply nodded and held out his arm for her as they walked from the chamber.

"Why the armory though?" she asked as he closed the door behind them.

"I wanted you to see the extensive weapons Hugh has gathered at Stone Crest. There's a weapon for nearly every person."

She said no more as he moved down the hall to the stairs. He let her walk ahead of him, his gaze straying to the gentle sway of her hips as she glided up the steep stairs.

"To the right," he said as she neared a landing. He motioned down the hall once he stepped beside her. The hall was lit with the occasional torch while the shadows grew as the sun sank lower into the sky.

"The castle is easy to navigate once you learn the layout. Down this hall you will find Hugh and Mina's chamber, should you need her. The rest of the Shields are placed throughout the upper floors."

"Where is your chamber?"

He turned his head to look at her, but her face was hidden in shadow. "On the floor above us."

"Mine is in the east tower."

He swallowed and tried to remember that she wasn't telling him this because she wanted him to visit her tonight. But then, why did she tell him?

He glanced at her again as they slowly walked down the hall. A torch cast her face in amber light and he saw her watching him. Her mouth was slightly parted and her eyes...inviting.

Gabriel took a deep breath and forced his gaze forward. He was seeing things that weren't there. It might have been awhile since he'd relieved the ache of his cock, but it had never caused him to act like this before.

To want like this before.

And he didn't even know her.

"You said you were wounded?" Her voice was soft, almost a whisper.

He knew she spoke of when the Fae found him. "Aye."

"Did someone attack you?"

"I wish I knew," he said after a moment. "I've been told my mind has blocked the past because something painful must have happened."

"Such as?"

He shrugged and clasped his hands behind his back. "Could be anything. Losing my family, seeing someone I loved killed, or a betrayal."

"I could see how those events would traumatize someone," she said with a small nod. "I've never encountered anyone who lost their memory before. Forgive me if I pry too much."

He waved away her words. "I've lived with it a long time now. I've been lucky enough to have men as close to me as brothers who have gone out of their way to try and help me remember. Even the Fae tried many things. Yet, no memories return. I think maybe it's better this way."

"You could have a wife or children," she said. "They could be waiting for you."

Gabriel shook his head. "I don't think so." He stopped and leaned back against the cool stones. "I'd like to think that if I did have a wife or a family that I would feel some sort of...connection...to them."

"Possibly. Do you know where you're from?"

This was one answer he knew. One answer out of many. "I do know that I'm not from this realm."

"How do you know that?" she asked, her head cocked slightly to the side.

Gabriel shrugged, not yet ready to tell her of his immortality. "Just something I figured out."

Suddenly Jayna smiled. "I think you're not speaking the entire truth."

"We all have our secrets, you included," he said as he pushed off from the wall.

"Ah, secrets. It is a part of who we are, I think. If everyone knew everything about everyone else, what mystery would life hold?"

Gabriel chuckled as he continued down the hall. "A philosopher, aye? Secrets or no, you are a mystery for sure."

"Do you like mysteries, Gabriel?"

Maybe it was in the way she said his name, like a whisper of seduction, of knowing his very soul. Or maybe it was because she was a mystery, but whatever it was, he felt a jolt run through him.

"Why do you ask?"

She lifted a dainty shoulder and glanced at him through her lashes. "One never knows what a man will like. Some men like innocence, some seductresses, some mysterious, and other men like to be dominated. Which one are you?"

Gabriel's heart raced at her words. His blood felt like it was on fire as he tried in vain to forget there was a stunningly beautiful woman walking beside him.

He finally found his voice to answer, "I like my women honest."

She chuckled. "Honesty. How...odd when most men

are anything but."

Gabriel watched Jayna as she walked a little ahead of him. What was her game? What was she doing at Stone Crest now of all times? And why the hell did he want her so badly?

CHAPTER NINE

Soon. Soon it would be his time again to rule Earth. It had been so long since he'd had a form, human or no. He yearned to be able to look at himself in the mirror again, to taste food, to feel a woman's body beneath his.

The small snatches of time he'd been able to gather enough power to appear human were few and far between, and they never lasted for longer than half an hour.

He laughed then.

They might have taken away his form, banished him to the ends of time, but they never expected him to become so powerful that he was able to destroy realms.

And they didn't even know who he was.

He couldn't wait for them to see just how he doled out revenge upon the Realm of Nations.

But until then, he needed to concentrate on Earth. He had assumed it would be easy to destroy, but the Fae had meddled more than they should have and prevented its collapse.

Yet, he had one surprise the Fae and their special army of Shields weren't expecting. A surprise that would deal the final blow that would bring down the realm of Earth and the Fae realm with it.

How he wished he could rub his hands together in anticipation. Instead, he simply existed.

"My lord?"

He waited for the creature to come closer. "I'm here. How goes it today?"

"They think both the harpy and the gargoyle have returned," it said, breathing heavily.

"Good, good. Ready everything for tomorrow on my command."

"Aye, my lord."

He waited until the creature had departed before he turned his gaze to Stone Crest castle. They thought him gone, hidden away from view, but he was here, waiting. And here he would stay until his plan was carried out.

Tomorrow would start it all.

~ ~ ~

"Well?" Hugh asked as Gabriel walked into the solar.

Gabriel shrugged. Most of the people and servants had either returned to their homes or bedded down for the night in the great hall. "I didn't learn anything new. Yet. Give me a few days."

"We may not have a few days."

Mina tapped her finger on her chin. "I think she likes you."

Gabriel was taken aback. "Likes me?"

"Aye. She flirted with you when she didn't flirt with any other."

He shrugged and glanced at Hugh. "The rest of the men were taken, Mina, though I thank you for the flattery."

"She may have something," Hugh said as he sat back in

his chair. "You'll be close to her in the next few days, and we know that women tend to share their secrets once a man has bedded them."

"Hugh," Mina said in exasperation.

He shrugged. "It's the truth, love." He turned back to Gabriel. "What do you think?"

Gabriel didn't want to tell them he thought it was a splendid idea because he wasn't quite ready to face the fact that he was attracted to Jayna, and only after one meeting.

"I suppose you might be right," he answered. "I'll take whatever opportunities present themselves." He finally looked around the solar. "Where is everyone else?"

"To their chambers," Mina answered.

Gabriel had seen the many looks over supper. Everyone was worried and frightened, and they were spending as much time together as they could. He looked to Mina and Hugh. "What are you two still doing down here?"

"We wanted to hear from you," Hugh said. "But now that I have, I'm going to take my wife to bed."

Gabriel grinned as Hugh and Mina smiled at each other as they walked from the solar. Once they were gone, Gabriel sank into the chair Hugh had vacated and looked at the chessboard.

The wind howled outside. The storm Hugh spoke of would be here in a day or so. Tomorrow would be a good time to take another look in the woods.

He released a breath as he thought of Jayna. He would bring her and have her show him her bow and just how well she had hidden it. If she even had a bow.

The smile vanished as he thought of his brethren. The Shields were all he had, his only family. He could not – and would not – let anything happen to them. As much as his body might be attracted to Jayna, he still couldn't help but think she might somehow be connected to the Great Evil.

But how?

What harm could she do? Before, the Great Evil had sent creatures bent on killing, but no matter how Gabriel looked at it, he didn't see how Jayna could harm them.

There was always poison, but in order for her to tamper with any of their food she would have to get into the kitchens. And he knew that would never happen. It was a testament to Hugh's leadership that his people were loyal to him. They would gladly die for him rather than see him come to harm.

Other than killing each of the Shields off, Jayna couldn't touch them. Just in case she was aligned with the evil, Gabriel would make sure she wasn't privy to any information that could harm them.

He sighed and ran his hand down his face. Jayna had asked many questions about his past and his memory loss. Questions that no one else had dared to ask.

"Aimery," he called out softly. "Aimery, please."

In a blink, Aimery stood before him in his silver tunic, and pants threaded with the same unusual blue that matched his swirling eyes. His long flaxen hair hung straight down the middle of his back, and as usual, he had several rows of tiny braids near his temple. "What is it?"

"I need to know what happened the night I was found."

Aimery sighed and took the chair opposite Gabriel. "I've told you this many times."

"I know, but I'm looking for anything that might trigger some memories. I haven't asked about that night in a very long time."

"Aye," Aimery nodded. "I wasn't there when they originally found you, but I was called in soon after. You were almost too gone for us to save, but we combined our magic and brought you back from the brink of death."

Gabriel nodded, remembering this from previous tellings. "My wounds. What kind did I have?"

"Too many to count. You were covered in blood. Besides the many cuts along your arms, chest, and face, you had a broken leg and the burn on your palm that you keep hidden from everyone."

Gabriel swallowed and fisted the hand Aimery spoke of. There had always been something about the burn that bothered him, almost as though it would speak of an evil past.

"The cuts must not have been very deep since I have no scars."

Aimery studied him a moment. "Some weren't, but others were."

"If I'm immortal, then how was it I was near the brink of death?"

"Do you forget so easily that though Roderick is immortal, he can be killed? The Fae can also die. Now, tell me, what do you remember?"

"Nothing," he answered automatically. Then his mind flashed a scene in his head of several Fae leaning over him. "I...I told you what herbs to use."

Aimery sat back and smiled ruefully. "You did. You had a fever and were delirious, and we almost didn't listen to you. Is this the first time you remember that?"

"Aye. Why didn't you tell me before?"

"I thought you knew."

Gabriel leaned forward and rested his elbows on his knees with his head in his hands. "I need details, Aimery."

"Why all of a sudden?"

He shook his head. "I don't know."

"You were in and out of consciousness, Gabriel. The fever that riddled your body left you ranting and mumbling when you weren't telling us what herbs we needed to use to save you."

Gabriel raised his head to look at Aimery. "Did I know what realm I was in?"

"I don't think so."

"What did I say during my ramblings?"

"Nothing that made a lot of sense," Aimery replied. "Most of the time you kept repeating that you were sorry, but for what we never figured out."

Gabriel had hoped questioning Aimery would give him some answers when all it did was give him more questions. "Did I say anyone's name?"

"If you did, I never heard it. You think you left someone behind? A wife?"

"I don't know. Jayna asked –"

"Jayna? Who is Jayna," Aimery asked.

Gabriel straightened in his chair. "She came to the castle early this morning. Mina and the other women took her in and offered her a place to stay for awhile."

"Did anyone question her?"

"Aye, both Hugh and I have. Hugh has asked that I stay near her for the next couple of days while she's here to see if I can discover why she's really here."

Aimery shut his eyes, and for a long moment he was quiet. When he opened his eyes there was doubt shining there. "She's here for revenge. It beats strong within her, it's what drives her."

"Mina said the same thing. Revenge for what, none of us know as of yet, but I'll find out what it is."

"She's not a commoner as she claims."

Gabriel laughed. "Aye, we all know that for a lie as well."

"She's cloaked her mind, Gabriel. Be careful."

"We will."

Aimery crossed his arms over his chest. "Now tell me what it is that Jayna said to you."

"She asked if I had left a wife or family behind. I said I hadn't because I didn't feel them. But that made me start to question myself. Did I leave someone behind?"

"I wish I could help you with that answer, but your mind hasn't shut just you out, it's shut even the Fae from prying into it. Whatever you have locked away, you never wanted to remember."

"And that scares the hell out of me. What could it have been?"

Aimery shrugged. "Any number of things. What makes one man sick with worry, another won't think twice about."

"Have you heard word from any realms with immortals? Have you perhaps found where I'm from?"

The sadness in Aimery's unusual swirling blue eyes spoke louder than any words. "Nay, Gabriel. I'm sorry."

Gabriel rose to his feet and blew out a breath as he began to slowly walk around the solar. "I've gone this long without answers, I'll survive longer."

"You might survive, my friend, but I know how much you want the truth."

"I used to want to know everything. Now I'm not so sure. Like you said, my mind has blocked my past for a reason."

He heard a sigh behind him and then the creak of the chair as Aimery rose. Gabriel turned to face the Fae commander.

"I planned to visit tomorrow," Aimery said as he moved away from the chess table. "However, I've learned what I needed to tonight."

"Jayna?"

"Nay, though I'm glad to know that, as well. I know of the harpy and the gargoyle. I must report to the king and queen. My army is still standing guard around the castle and Hugh's lands. They've detected evil."

Gabriel nodded. "The creatures?"

"I suspect it's more than just the creatures. It's time to finish this once and for all. Be vigilant, Gabriel."

"I'll let Hugh know."

"If I'm able, I'll return on the morrow."

And with that he was gone.

Gabriel slowly walked from the solar and up the stairs to his quiet, lonely chamber.

It wasn't until he undressed and crawled into bed that he found himself thinking of a certain golden-haired beauty with tempting hazel eyes.

CHAPTER TEN

Jayna yawned as she stretched beneath the warmth of her covers. The coolness of the chamber moved over her skin as she raised her arms over her head. She slipped out of the covers and rose from the bed. Her feet met the icy stones on the floor as she pulled a blanket around her shoulders and padded to the hearth to stroke the fire to life.

Once that was done and heat once again began to fill her chamber, she turned to dress and found another gown hanging beside the one she wore the previous night. Someone must have come into her chamber during the night or early that morning.

She glanced out the window to see light already brightening the sky. She never slept past dawn, and she never allowed anyone to sneak up on her. Yet both had occurred. Whoever had come into her chamber hadn't wanted to hurt her, but what if they had? She'd be dead now instead of eyeing a new gown.

What was wrong with her? Was she letting the supposed safeness of the castle, the warm, soft bed and the companionship of a few women yank down defenses that had pulled her through a catastrophe that would have killed most women?

Jayna vowed not let herself get dragged into complacency while she was here because it would end as soon as Gabriel was dead.

She still couldn't believe he didn't have any memory of the past. He spoke of injuries, but the last time she had seen him, there were no injuries.

Just thinking of that awful day left her sick to her stomach. She had pushed aside those hideous images long ago, yet she drudged them up now.

Jayna didn't like the direction of her thoughts. She quickly dressed in the dark blue gown left for her. Once she was clothed, she pulled the comb through her long tresses as she sat before the fire.

She hadn't wanted to face the truth last night, but she had learned a hard lesson during her life – it was better to face the truth at the beginning than at the end when mistakes were made.

So, she admitted to herself that she had enjoyed Gabriel's company yesterday. She hadn't known what to expect when he had sat beside her, and she most certainly expected him to recognize who she was. But once he hadn't, she let herself go, let herself be something she hadn't been in so very long.

She flirted and talked, but it had been so she could seduce him to make him remember just what he had done.

But...as they had walked among the dimly lit corridors of the castle she might have forgotten, just for a moment, who she was and why she was there.

Her longing for her old life, the joy and happiness she had felt before Gabriel destroyed everything, was stronger than she ever knew. If she were a weaker woman, it might frighten her, but she had seen horrors people only dreamed about. And that made her stronger than most. It also allowed her to face her fears and her wants head on.

"Don't go, Jayna. If you seek your revenge on Gabriel you'll only succeed in becoming what he is. Let it go. Live your life," her mother said.

"I cannot. He must pay for what he's done."

"Oh, child. If you leave, you're sentencing yourself to death."

Her mother had been right, but even now, she wouldn't change things. In killing Gabriel, she would sentence herself to death, but she was ready for it, welcomed it actually.

Hurt, long buried, rose up to choke her. Jayna blinked away the moisture that gathered in her eyes, making the fire swim before her. She concentrated on combing out the tangles in her hair to keep from thinking of her mother and the life she had left behind.

Try as she might to ignore the memories, she could still recall her mother's warm brown eyes and they way they would light up when she laughed.

Jayna finished plaiting her hair and sighed. She had come this far, she couldn't fail now. Not when she was so close to finishing.

A soft knock on her door brought her out of her reverie. "Enter," she called out, not wanting to leave the warmth of the fire.

"Did you sleep well?" a deep, smooth voice asked.

She turned her head to see Gabriel leaning against the door, a fur-lined cloak of black around his shoulder and something dark draped over his arm.

"I did, thank you," she replied as she climbed to her feet. "I was just about to go down to the great hall."

She felt his gaze as she walked toward him, but she couldn't quite meet his eyes this morning. At one time, she had thought he was the man of her heart, a man who she could trust and who would be by her side forever. She had thought she was prepared to face him, prepared to feel any memories that crept up on her.

She had been wrong.

"Jayna?"

She took a deep breath and walked out of her chamber as Gabriel shut the door behind her.

"Are you well this morning?" he asked, concern making his voice soft.

"Aye," she answered and forced a smile. She certainly couldn't tell him that at one time she would have walked barefoot over hot coals for him, or that she used to daydream about what their children would look like.

A chill raced through her and she brought her arms up to wrap around her waist.

Lightning fast, he pulled her to a halt as his hand touched her forehead. "There is no fever."

"I'm fine," she said as she stepped back.

She knew by the set of his chin he didn't believe her. Gabriel had always known when she lied.

"I was going to suggest going for a ride this morning, but if you're not feeling well, maybe we should postpone it," he said as they set off down the hallway.

Her head jerked toward him. "A ride?"

"Aye. I must check the perimeters, and I wondered if you might want to collect your bow and arrows. The storm should hit later today or tomorrow, so we cannot tarry long."

Jayna closed her eyes, and unbidden, a memory of her and Gabriel racing across the hills on her father's fastest horses came to her. She opened her eyes to find Gabriel watching her silently.

"I think I'd like that very much."

"Then you'll need this," he said as he handed her the

cloak that was draped over his arm.

She ran her hands over the fur-lined cloak. "What happened to my cloak?"

"It's being repaired," was all he said as he started down the stairs to the hall.

The great hall was nearly empty by the time they arrived. She was slightly embarrassed to have slept so long, and doubly so when she saw Mina smiling at her.

"I do apologize for sleeping so late. I normally wake with the sun," she said as she took a seat beside the lady of the castle.

"I asked the servants to let you sleep," Mina said. "I thought you might need it. Want another visit to our bathing chamber?"

Jayna smiled as she remembered the luxurious warmth of the water and the heavenly bliss of soaking for as long as she wanted. "Words cannot describe how wonderful it was. I'm sure I'll make my way there sometime this day."

"I thought you might," Mina said with a laugh. "Usually, Elle and Shannon are in there for hours."

Jayna glanced beside her, expecting to see Gabriel, yet there was only an empty spot. She looked around her, searching for him.

"He went to speak with Hugh in the solar," Mina said.

She turned to look at Mina and found Mina staring intently at her.

Mina cleared her throat and said, "Gabriel is a very handsome man."

"I suppose so," Jayna replied. She wasn't about to tell Mina Gabriel was the most handsome man she had ever, or would ever, meet. "I must thank Elle for allowing me to borrow her gowns."

Mina waved away her words. "Think nothing of it. Consider them yours."

Thankfully, food was placed in front of her then and Jayna concentrated on eating and not thinking of how nice Mina was.

She had just finished eating when Gabriel walked to the dais. "I know it's early, but I thought we would leave now. The horses are saddled and waiting," he said.

"Of course," Jayna said as she rose from her seat and reached for her cloak. She was really looking forward to being on a horse again.

"Be careful," Mina warned.

Jayna nodded and followed Gabriel to the door where he stopped and took the cloak from her.

"Allow me," he said.

Jayna lowered her gaze as he swung the cloak around her then fastened it at her neck. The brush of his warm fingers on her skin left her tingling and unable to breathe. Her body remembered his touch, recalled the way he brought her pleasure with his caresses and kiss.

She found herself leaning back into his touch as need speared her. The door banged open, jerking her out of her passion. As soon as the cloak was clasped, she stepped away from him.

Gabriel tried to control his breathing as he fought against pulling Jayna into his arms and smelling her hair once again. The smell had been familiar, just as her face had been.

Even the way his body responded when she was near was too coincidental to ignore. He might not know how he knew her, but his body did. There was no denying that.

"Ready?" he asked as he held open the door. Once she walked out, he followed, nodding to Hugh as they strolled through the bailey.

Their horses stood ready, their breaths billowing around them. He pulled on his gloves and regretted not finding any for Jayna. Just as he was about to return to the castle, Roderick walked up and handed a pair of gloves to her.

"Thank you," Jayna said and gave Roderick a smile.

For some reason that irritated Gabriel because she might have smiled at him, it hadn't been as open and inviting as the one she'd bestowed upon Roderick.

He waited until Jayna had the gloves on before he wrapped his hands around her waist and lifted her atop her mare. He didn't move to mount his own horse until he saw her take the reins properly.

A grin pulled at his lips. Just another sign she wasn't a peasant. The clatter of hooves sounded around them as Hugh and Roderick rode up beside them.

Jayna gave him a questioning look.

"It's safer with numbers," he explained as Hugh and Roderick rode ahead of them.

"Ah, the Great Evil and its creatures."

Gabriel flattened his lips. "Let's hope for your sake we don't run into any of them while we're out."

Out of the corner of his eye, he watched her as they passed through the gate. She sat straight, almost queenly, and with an ease that only a practiced horsewoman could manage.

"Do you recall where you buried your bow?" he asked.

"Over there," she said as she pointed toward the forest.

Hugh gave him a nod as they set out in the direction she had pointed. Gabriel kept a vigilant lookout for anything that looked out of the ordinary. It was eerily quiet as they entered the forest. Almost too quiet.

He put his hand on his mount's neck.

The horse, long used to the rigors of being forced to endure evil, showed no signs of unease. Gabriel blew out a breath.

"Something the matter?" Jayna asked.

He shook his head. "Just keeping an eye out for trouble."

"Are you expecting something to happen?"

"I always expect something to happen."

"That's not a very good way to live."

He shrugged, not knowing what she was looking for in way of an answer. "It's the way we live. It's what I chose."

Suddenly she stopped her mare and looked around them. Her gaze turned to him.

"What is it?"

Her face rapidly paled, and her eyes dilated. "There's something out there."

No sooner were the words out of her mouth than her mount began to prance and throw its head around. Gabriel made sure she had the horse under control before he hastily looked around the forest. He couldn't see anything, but after a deep breath he smelled it – evil.

"Jayna," he said as he turned back toward her.

She fought to keep her mare from bolting. "What's out there?"

"I don't know. We need to return to the castle. Now."

As she struggled to turn her mare, Gabriel moved his mount closer to her to give her some aid. And that's when he felt his horse begin to quiver as he sidestepped.

"Damn," he muttered.

"Gabriel!" Jayna screamed just as a shadow passed over them, her cry drowned out by loud clanging.

He barely had time to register they were under attack before her horse reared and Jayna went flying off the back. Though he couldn't explain why, his blood froze in his veins at the thought of her injured.

"Jayna!"

CHAPTER ELEVEN

"Jayna. Jayna, answer me!" Gabriel shouted as he vaulted from his mount and ran through the thick snow to her side.

By the time he reached her, she had rolled onto her stomach and slowly pushed to her hands and knees. "I'm all right. Just bruised my vanity is all," she grumbled as she gained her feet, then grimaced. "I think I might have twisted my ankle."

Gabriel let loose a breath he hadn't known he was holding. He wrapped his arm around her waist to help hold her up as he tried not to think how nicely her body molded to his. "Did you see what flew over us?"

She swallowed hard and nodded. "It was huge. And both ugly and beautiful."

"A harpy. Did you just see one?"

"One?" she repeated as she visibly shook. "Isn't one enough?"

"They usually come in threes," he said as he led her closer to the trees. "Your horse ran off, and mine will never make it back to the castle carrying both of us."

"Go and get help then. I'll stay hidden."

He searched her hazel eyes and saw fear but determination, as well. "You have no idea what it is that is out there do you?"

"I know enough to know that I must stay hidden. You're the better rider, Gabriel."

He shook his head. "Hugh and Roderick should've heard the clanging of the harpy's wings."

"Gabriel," she said to gain his attention. "I'm in no condition to run. Help me find a place to stay out of sight of the harpy. Then, you can find Hugh and Roderick."

"I'm not leaving you. You haven't seen what the harpies can do."

She leaned against the tree and sighed as her breath billowed around her. "I think it's turned colder."

Just then Gabriel spotted the mist that had rolled around them. Something wasn't right.

"Gabriel," something whispered around him.

He took a step away from Jayna as her eyes grew round. "You heard that?"

She nodded slowly.

The mist grew around them, swirling and climbing with each passing moment. Gabriel's heart thundered in his chest. The skies grew dark and the stench of evil permeated the air.

"Jayna, don't move," he warned her.

The last thing he wanted to do was mistake her for the evil while his vision was hampered by the darkening skies and thick mist. Something touched his arm and moved around his body before vanishing.

"Oh, Gabbbbriiiielllll," the voice said, louder, more sinister. "I've been waiting for you."

Gabriel reached for his bow only to remember he left it tied to his saddle. He gripped his sword instead and unsheathed it. "Show yourself."

Mocking laughter filled the air. "Oh, if only I could," the voice murmured.

It was the Great Evil. Gabriel knew it in the pit of his heart and it scared the hell out of him. "What do you want?"

"You."

"You'll never have me," he retorted angrily.

"Gabriel!" he heard Roderick shout in the distance. "Gabriel, where are you?"

He opened his mouth to answer when something suddenly grabbed him by the neck, lifted him up and threw him back against a tree. Whatever it was held tightly and squeezed.

Gabriel kicked at empty air in an attempt to break free.

"You'll never be free of me," the voice whispered in his ear. "Haven't you realized that by now?"

"By the gods!" Roderick exclaimed.

Gabriel moved his gaze downward and saw Hugh and Roderick atop their mounts staring up at him.

"Gabriel?" Hugh asked quietly.

He tried to talk, to give them some clue the evil was there, but whatever held onto him only squeezed harder. Couldn't they smell the evil? The scent was so strong it made his stomach roll.

His sword was yanked from his grip violently, and he watched as it fell to the ground in front of Hugh and Roderick. Where was Jayna? Was she scared? Why didn't Hugh look for her?

"You've searched for clues to your past, Gabriel," the evil whispered in his ears. "All you had to do was ask me. I was there. I saw it all."

Gabriel closed his eyes and growled as he struggled against the hold on him. He knew that a fall from the height he was at would most likely cause a break, or worse. But he didn't care, he just wanted away from the evil and the lies he spouted.

"Not lies," the voice sounded around him.

And just as abruptly as he was taken, the hold on him vanished. For a heartbeat, Gabriel wondered how badly the fall would hurt just before he fell.

He landed on thick snow that had fallen from the branches when he had been banged against the tree. He raised his head to the bare limbs above, thankful they had let loose the snow to cushion his fall.

"Gabriel, what the devil happened?" Roderick said as he helped him rise.

On his other side, Hugh gripped his arm and brought him to his feet. "Gabriel?" he asked softly.

The mist swarmed around them then, and the smell of evil filled their nostrils.

"The time is at hand, Shields," the voice screamed around them. "Prepare to die."

As the voice disappeared, so did the mist. Gabriel wasted little time in searching for his sword. Once he had it, he hastily sheathed it.

"Jayna!" he called.

"Gabriel," Hugh barked. "We need to talk."

He waved away Hugh's words. "Not before I find Jayna."

"I'm here, Gabriel," she said as she hobbled out from behind two trees.

He rushed to her and wrapped his arm around her waist again. Her body shivered, but he doubted it had anything to do with the cold.

Once he walked her to Hugh and Roderick, he situated her against a tree and turned to his leader.

"The harpy flew over us."

"We never heard anything," Roderick said. "It wasn't until we heard Jayna scream that we knew something was wrong."

Gabriel scratched his head. "I know what I saw. It was the harpy. It didn't attack us, just flew over us."

"And what had you pinned to the tree?" Hugh asked softly, too softly.

Gabriel turned his gaze to Hugh. He couldn't tell them all the voice had whispered in his ear. Not because it might be true, but because he didn't want the Shields doubting his loyalty in any way.

"He's after me," he finally decided to tell them. That much was the truth, he just didn't know why.

"You?" Roderick repeated and paced before him. "Why you?"

Gabriel shrugged. "I don't know. I think he's after all of us, but he wants to divide us first."

Hugh nodded. "It's a perfect tactical move, one that I would make in his position."

Gabriel sighed mentally and squeezed his eyes shut. He was suddenly very tired and cold. "We need to return. The Harpy frightened Jayna's horse and caused her to fall. She sprained her ankle."

"The mare will return to the castle," Hugh said. "I think it's safe enough now that we can all return."

But Gabriel had a nagging question he needed an answer to. "Hugh, when you rode up and saw me hanging there. Did you smell the evil?"

For a long moment, Hugh simply stared at Gabriel, his dark eyes revealing nothing. "Aye."

Relief flooded Gabriel. He could never live with himself if his brethren thought he had betrayed them.

"We didn't know what had you," Roderick said. "We didn't want to chance injuring you just to get at whatever had you."

Gabriel turned to Roderick and nodded. He then moved to Jayna when the vicious scream rent the air.

"Harpy!" Hugh bellowed as everyone dove for cover.

Gabriel started to duck when he spotted Jayna trying to limp around the tree. He pivoted and rushed to her, pushing her against the tree to shield her with his body.

"Don't move," he whispered in her ear.

Her soft breath fanned his neck as her hands gripped his jerkin beneath his cloak. "I can hear it," she murmured, her lips brushing the exposed skin at his neck.

Gabriel nearly groaned aloud as his cock throbbed to life. "I'll protect you."

Her head moved as she looked into his eyes. "I don't want to die."

With the harpy screaming around them and her metal wings clanging loudly, Gabriel knew trying to speak now would be impossible.

Instead, he moved closer to her, offering her his warmth and his body for protection.

Her arms wrapped around his waist beneath his cloak. Gabriel gripped the tree tightly as he fought the urge to turn around and attack the harpy.

"Nay!" Roderick yelled, drawing Gabriel's attention.

His fellow Shield had moved until he was in line with Gabriel's vision. And his friend knew him well enough to know just what Gabriel wanted to do. Fight.

"Not now," Roderick mouthed.

Gabriel would wait, but only because he had Jayna to protect. Or else he'd be ending it now.

"Come out, come out, wherever you are," the harpy said from above them. "It's time to die. Who would like to go first?"

"Don't go," Jayna begged him. "Please don't go."

There was an odd note in her voice, as if her very being depended on him not facing the creature.

"I won't leave you willingly," he finally agreed.

The loud banging of the harpy's wings stopped, and Gabriel could only guess that she had landed somewhere. But where?

"She's above and behind you, to your left," Jayna whispered. "She's resting on the limbs of a very old oak."

Gabriel knew to move now would be folly. The harpy had keen eyesight, but he must blend in fairly well to the surroundings for her not to have spotted him immediately. But one move, one twinge, and she would be on him instantly.

"No takers?" the harpy questioned. "It would be wise to understand that at least one of you *will* die this day. Who wants to sacrifice himself so the others can run to safety?"

Gabriel sighed as he watched Roderick and Hugh exchange glances. If anyone were to die, it would be him. Hugh and Roderick both had wives that desperately waited for their return.

"I have to face it," he whispered to Jayna. "Understand, I do not leave you willingly, but because I cannot fathom facing either Mina or Elle and telling them their husbands died to save me."

"I thought you said you were immortal?"

He smiled wryly. "Everything must die," he said as he took a step away, letting his hand linger for just a moment on her cheek before he unsheathed his sword and whirled around to face the creature.

"You want a battle," Gabriel bellowed, "I'm here. Come and get me."

"Damn you, Gabriel," he heard Hugh shout, but he was too intent on the harpy's smile of victory to think about anything else.

He braced his feet apart as he waited for the attack.

The harpy didn't let him wait for long as she spread her wings and dove toward him. While he knew the first hit would hurt, he didn't expect to feel as though a hundred horses had trampled every bone in his body.

He grunted as he landed on his back on the packed snow, sword still in hand. When he opened his eyes it was to see the harpy standing over him.

CHAPTER TWELVE

"I was told you would give me great sport. Instead, you are nothing more than a flea to flick away."

Gabriel barely saw the harpy raise her arm, her claws extended, through his haze of pain. He forced his body to move and rolled away to come up on his feet. The harpy growled in frustration, her blonde hair hanging in her bright blue eyes.

Fair of face she might be, with the upper body of a goddess, but the evil within her, and the lower half of her nothing more than a metal bird was enough to make any man forget the beauty of her face.

He wanted his bow. Badly. Instead, he gripped his sword with both hands and swung upwards. His blade bounced off the metal of her stomach but cut a long gash beneath her bare breast. She screamed and backed away as blood poured from the wound.

With his breath coming in great gasps while he struggled to clear his vision, Gabriel wrapped his left arm around his ribs and waited for what the harpy would do. He prayed that by now, Hugh and Roderick had gotten Jayna out of the forest and safely inside Stone Crest.

With one last look at Gabriel, the harpy spread her wings and soared into the air as she dodged the branches of trees. That had been easy. Too easy.

"You did it!" Jayna yelled as she hobbled out from behind the tree. The smile on her face could have lit the darkest pit of despair.

A prickling of warning was all Gabriel received before he raised his gaze to see the harpy coming back at him...at Jayna.

He raced toward Jayna, praying he got to her before the creature. He dove at her, slamming into her body as he pushed her down onto the ground with him. He rolled several times before he stopped and looked down at her.

Something warm and sticky ran down his side. "I told you to stay hidden."

She licked her lips. "I...I thought it was over."

"It's never over, not until they're dead."

She squirmed beneath him, and he gritted his teeth as he tried to keep his cock from swelling at the feel of her curves. "Don't do that," he said between clenched teeth.

In an instant, she stopped. He breathed a sigh of relief, but made the mistake of looking at her lips. They were plump, red, and slightly parted. The last thing he should be thinking about while facing death was bedding a woman.

But, damn, that was all he seemed to be able to do around her.

Jayna couldn't stop staring at Gabriel. Seeing him fight the creature, being thrown as if he weighed no more than a feather, was almost her undoing. She didn't like the fear that had pooled like lead in her belly when she thought he might die.

What was wrong with her? She had come here to kill him herself.

That's it. You want to be the one to kill him, not have him killed by some creature.

Aye, that had to be the reason.

He moved away from her, and instantly she missed his warmth. He was helping her to her feet when Hugh and Roderick came running up.

"You fool," Hugh said to Gabriel as he embraced him.

Jayna watched the exchange with interest, noting how much both Hugh and Roderick cared for Gabriel. It was also obvious by the way Gabriel returned the embrace that he cared for Hugh just as much.

"What were you thinking?" Roderick asked. "We could've all attacked at the same time."

Hugh shook his head. "Nay, Gabriel should've stayed with Jayna."

"Nay," Gabriel said, raising his voice slightly. "Do either of you forget that you have wives awaiting you?"

The stark loneliness she saw for a moment in Gabriel's silver depths stirred her very soul. But regardless of what he had become, he still had to pay for past deeds.

"Come. We must return to the castle," Hugh said after a moment of silence.

The men turned as one. In their discussion, they had forgotten about her. She swallowed the pain in her ankle as she limped after them.

She had gotten only two steps when Gabriel turned to her. "Forgive me," he said and swept her into his arms.

Her breath left her in a whoosh. She quickly wrapped her arms around his neck and looked anywhere but his face. His horse waited patiently for them with Hugh and Roderick's mounts.

He set her atop the horse then climbed up behind her. It had been so long since someone had helped her without wanting something in exchange, that for a moment, Jayna wasn't sure what to do.

"Thank you," she said.

Because of her ankle, they walked the horses back to Stone Crest, though all three men kept a look out for the creature. By the time they reached the bailey, all Jayna wanted to do was soak in the steaming water of Mina's giant tub.

"I'll need to see to your ankle," Gabriel said as he reached up to help her down from the horse. His hands slid around her waist, setting her gently on her good foot. "Should I carry you in?"

"Nay," she said, embarrassed by the attention. "I'll be fine. There's no need for you to look at it either."

"Let him," Roderick said as he and Hugh walked up. "Gabriel has a gift of healing of the like I've never seen."

She raised her gaze to Gabriel. Aye, how had she forgotten his healing abilities? It was what had led her to him in the first place.

For long moments, she and Gabriel stared at each other, until the sound of running feet reached them. Jayna turned to see Mina and Elle throw themselves at their husbands.

Envy wasn't an emotion that Jayna had very much experience in, but she felt it keenly now. More so because being with Gabriel reminded her of all that she had lost, of all that she could have had.

"What happened?" Mina asked as she stepped out of Hugh's arms. "We heard the harpy. Did it attack?"

"Aye. Or rather it attacked Gabriel and Jayna," he answered.

Suddenly, every eye in the bailey was directed at Jayna. And she didn't like it. "I'm all right. I just sprained my ankle."

Out of the corner of her eye, she saw Gabriel brace his

hand against his mount.

After all he had been through, she could imagine he was exhausted and needed rest. And she needed to get her plan in order so she could carry through with it and then leave.

"A sprain?" Elle said. "I think it's more than that if the blood on your cloak is any indication."

Jayna looked at her cloak, but she knew the blood wasn't hers. Her gaze snapped to Gabriel to see his face pale and tight with pain.

"Why didn't you tell me?" she accused as she pushed his cloak aside to look for the wound. What she saw made her weak.

Blood. Everywhere. She looked to the saddle on his horse and saw the blood there, as well.

When her gaze returned to him, he gave her a small smile. "All will be fine. I'm immortal, remember?"

"My arse," Roderick growled as he took Gabriel's arm and draped it over his shoulder. "Where's your black bag?"

"With me," he mumbled. "Always with me."

Hugh raced ahead of them. "Mina."

"I'm getting everything," Mina said as she raced into the castle.

Jayna watched them take Gabriel away, watched how everyone in their concern dropped everything to tend to him. How did someone who had done so much evil have such devotion in their lives?

"Jayna?"

She jerked her gaze away from Gabriel's retreating back to find Elle at her side. "He's going to be fine," Elle assured her.

"Of course." *He better be. I've yet to kill him.*

Elle smiled. "I can help you into the castle. I think a nice soak in the tub will do you wonders."

Aye, that's exactly where Jayna wanted to be. Why then did she feel as though she should be next to Gabriel to see if he would indeed heal?

She accepted Elle's assistance and slowly made her way into the castle and the bathing chamber. Elle helped her take off her shoes and clothes. It wasn't until she was seated in the tub and the soothing water was around her that she looked at Elle.

"Why are you being so nice?"

Elle, who had been folding Jayna's clothes, stopped and looked at her. "What do you mean? I'm nice because that is who I am."

"But you don't know me. You don't know why I'm here."

"You told us who you were and why you were here. Was it a lie?"

"What if it was?"

Elle chuckled as she went back to folding the clothes. "Ah, Jayna. Life has been hard for you, I see. It's not easy for you to trust, nor understand why someone would trust you. Maybe now is the time to try."

Jayna could only stare at the beautiful auburn haired woman.

But Elle only smiled. "Rest. I'm going to check on Gabriel, and I'll return with fresh clothes for you."

"I can wear the same gown once it's been washed. There's no need for you to keep lending me your gowns."

Elle laughed this time. "I see Mina didn't tell you."

"Tell me what," Jayna asked, not liking that Mina had lied to her.

"Your clothes are a gift from the Fae. In your chamber, the chest before your bed will be filled with all you need."

Jayna felt sick to her stomach. The Fae. "Why?" she croaked out.

"Because it is what the Fae do," she replied before leaving the chamber.

Jayna rubbed her eyes with the heels of her hands and tried to stop the tears.

The Fae, who she had never met, had given her a chest full of clothes.

And what did the Great Evil give you? Not clothes. Not food. Not even a place to live. All he gave you was revenge.

Though it was the truth, she had given her word to the Great Evil in exchange for finding Gabriel. She couldn't go back on her word now. There would be consequences.

Dire consequences.

CHAPTER THIRTEEN

Gabriel gritted his teeth as Roderick and Hugh peeled away his cloak, leather jerkin, and tunic. The door to his chamber banged open, and Val and Cole rushed in.

"What in the name of all that's sacred happened?" Cole bellowed.

Gabriel tried to shrug but regretted it as needles of pain ripped through him. Funny, he hadn't felt anything until he reached the castle. Surely if he were as injured as Hugh thought, he would have felt something as he carried Jayna.

"Where is she?" he asked Roderick.

Roderick didn't glance up from inspecting his ribs. "I assume Elle is taking care of her."

"Assume?" Gabriel thundered. He grimaced in pain and gritted his teeth until the worst of the throbbing had stopped. In a quieter voice he said, "She's injured."

Roderick's gaze sliced up to his.

But it was Hugh that spoke. "Jayna has naught but a sprained ankle. You, however, have much more severe injuries."

Gabriel wanted to roll his eyes. "Aye, and I'm immortal, so they'll heal."

"Not if we don't stop the blood."

Val threw up his hands in disgust. "For the sake of the gods, will someone tell me and Cole what happened?"

Gabriel waited for Hugh or Roderick to respond, and when they didn't, he knew he would have to. He sighed as he glanced at the two glaring Shields. "We were attacked."

"We gathered that," Cole said tightly. "We want details, Gabriel. For once, just tell us without us having to ask every little detail."

Gabriel glanced away. He didn't want to tell them anything, but he didn't have a choice. He most certainly didn't wish to tell them that the Great Evil had suspended him above the ground. Again, he didn't have a choice.

"Well?" Val prompted.

Gabriel looked into Val's pale green gaze. Val had been with him when he had discovered his immortality. And he had seen the dark side of Val, a side Val had never let any of them see before.

"I was with Jayna hunting for her hidden bow. I wanted to see if she was lying about it."

"And it afforded us an opportunity to do some searching before the storm hit," Roderick said as he poked at Gabriel's ribs.

Gabriel hissed through his teeth. "Bloody hell, Roderick."

"Sorry," he said as he sat up. "I think you have some cracked ribs."

Gabriel knew that already. He was more concerned with the fact that Hugh and Mina hadn't been able to stop the blood from the slice on his back yet. And the fact they said nothing only added to the fear growing in his belly.

He looked up and found Val and Cole watching him again, silently waiting for him to continue the story. "We had no sooner entered the woods than Jayna's horse began to dance around. Before I could reach Jayna to help, the harpy flew over us causing her horse to rear and her to fall off."

"I suppose that's how she sprained her ankle?" Cole asked.

Gabriel nodded. "Then...," he stopped, unable to talk about the mist and the voice that had called his name so eerily.

Thankfully, Roderick intervened, "Hugh and I heard Jayna scream, and we raced to find them."

"The harpy attacked you then?" Val asked.

Gabriel squeezed his eyes shut and shook his head. Even now he could still recall the stench of evil as it had surrounded him and spoke of his past.

The hands on his back ceased, and he felt more than saw Hugh straighten.

"Nay, Val. Roderick and I came upon Gabriel and the Great Evil. The evil had him. It could've killed him, and I felt sure that he would try."

Val cursed in Latin as he raked a hand through his hair.

Cole on the other hand stood still as a statue with his arms crossed over his chest. "Why didn't he kill Gabriel? If he had him, what would've stopped him?"

"I don't know," Roderick said as he rose with a sigh. "Maybe it was because the son of a bitch doesn't have a form!"

"Enough," Hugh bellowed. "Gabriel was right. The evil is trying to divide us."

"Its frustration that's dividing us," Roderick said as he stormed out of the chamber.

Gabriel could barely lift his hand to his face he was so tired. His head ached, it hurt to breath, and it was near excruciating to move his arms.

"Gabriel?"

He heard Cole's voice as if from a great distance. Slowly he opened his eyes to find him sitting in the spot Roderick had vacated.

"What is it?"

"Tired," was all Gabriel could muster. He had never felt so exhausted, so devoid of any type of momentum.

"It's the loss of blood," he heard Hugh mumbled from behind.

But I'm immortal. Gabriel wanted to shout it, but the most energy he could manage was to think it. He had seen Cole sustain greater injuries than this and be healed by morning with the help of his herbs.

With great effort, he raised his head. "My bag. I need my bag."

Instantly, Val and Cole opened the bag before him. The many small clear jars and herbs blurred before his eyes. But he didn't need his eyesight. He knew where each herb was located by heart.

He lifted his hand and pointed to the fourth jar on the left. "Two, nay three drops mixed with a cup of water."

Val raced off to do as ordered, and Gabriel moved his hand to the right. The third pocket on the second row. "Take two leaves and crush them until there is only a fine powder. Mix with water to form a paste and spread on the wound."

By the time he finished, he could barely breathe. Each breath was like a knife through his lungs. Coldness crept over him like a veil of death. He looked down at his hands and rubbed his fingers together.

"I can't feel my fingers."

"Val!" Hugh bellowed from behind him. "Mina you must hurry."

"I'm doing all that I can," she whispered.

But Gabriel knew. Something was wrong, dreadfully

wrong.

Suddenly, a cup was thrust into his hands. "Drink," Val said, his voice breathless and worried.

Gabriel lifted the cup with much difficulty and ignored the pull of his back. He drained the water and then handed the cup back to Val. "Hugh," he said.

"We're working on it, Gabriel."

"Hugh." He waited until his leader walked around to stand in front of him. "Something is wrong. I don't know what. Aimery. Call for him."

A forced smile pulled at Hugh's lips. "We won't need Aimery, my friend."

But Gabriel knew they would. There was a reason Hugh wasn't calling for Aimery, but Gabriel couldn't get his thoughts together. Darkness edged his vision as he succumbed to the healing draught.

Hugh and Cole caught Gabriel before he hit the floor. Carefully, they laid him on his side so Mina could administer the paste.

"So much blood," Mina said as she wiped at her face with the back of her hand. "Are you sure we can do this?"

Hugh could well understand her tears. They had already buried one of their own. He didn't with to bury another. Not Gabriel. "Aye. We have to."

"What do we do?" Val asked.

Hugh turned to the Roman before looking to Cole. Both men were anxious and frustrated. "We heal him."

"He's supposed to be immortal," Val argued. "I saw it with my own eyes in Scotland, Hugh. He should be healing by now."

Cole stood and gripped Val's arm. "Gabriel will be fine. If he healed once, he can do it again. Maybe there was something different about this harpy. Hugh?"

He shrugged. "In truth, I barely paid attention to her. I

was so rattled by having the Great Evil right there. He had Gabriel high up in the tree by the neck. All around us was this thick mist and the reek of evil."

"Yet he didn't hurt Gabriel."

Hugh met Cole's gaze. "The look on Gabriel's face...it was pure terror. In all the creatures we have faced, all the evil men we've fought, never once has he shown an ounce of fear."

Val shook his head and sighed. "Who knows how any of us would react if the Great Evil had us in its clutches."

"He could have feared for Jayna," Mina said as she lifted her hand, the thick, white paste on her fingers.

Hugh turned to her. "Jayna? Why do you say that?"

She spread the paste on Gabriel's back gently. "For men who see in great detail, you miss many things. Have none of you noticed how Gabriel rarely dines with us, and when he does, he never stays long?"

"Aye," Cole said. "He likes to be alone."

Mina sighed. "Nay. Each of you has found your mate. Each of you has love and happiness in your lives regardless of your pasts. Gabriel doesn't have that. He doesn't have anyone."

"We are his brethren," Val stated.

Hugh watched his wife smile sadly. "She's right," he agreed. "I wouldn't have thought it to bother Gabriel, but it makes sense."

For a long moment, he watched the rise and fall of Gabriel's chest. The wound had been deep, but it shouldn't have caused as much damage as it had.

"Do you think the evil could've taken away his immortality?" he asked softly. Val and Cole jerked their gazes to him.

"Nay," Val answered first.

Cole shrugged. "It's possible, I suppose. We all know

he wants us and the women dead. He has gone to great lengths to do that. It could be why he went after Gabriel and not you or Roderick."

"But Roderick is immortal as well," Val said.

Hugh nodded sadly. "I need to speak to Aimery."

~ ~ ~

He smiled into the darkening skies. A storm was indeed brewing, and not just the one in the clouds. His plan was working out nicely, though he would have liked more time with Gabriel. He needed to speak with him, to make him remember the past.

To remember his promise.

He had been surprised to see Gabriel with Jayna and still alive. The little minx had been fixed on revenge for so long he naturally assumed she'd seek retribution as soon as she found Gabriel.

But then Gabriel didn't remember her.

He laughed. How ironic. Jayna must have felt let down facing Gabriel after so long and he not remembering her...or the crimes he committed.

"But it won't be long now," he whispered into the air.

He gathered the mist around him. He had been angry when he'd first learned that Gabriel had joined the ranks of the Shields, aligning with the Fae. But it hadn't taken him long to discover that Gabriel had lost his memory.

That's when he'd realized just how wonderful everything could turn out.

Oh, he hadn't wanted it to reach this far. He would have much preferred to destroy Earth like he had so many other realms. Yet, now that he had a pawn such as Gabriel, things would turn out just as he wanted.

Not even the Chosen could stop him now.

CHAPTER FOURTEEN

Jayna was pacing her chamber. Well, not pacing, more like shuffling. Her ankle was better, though it was still swollen and sore.

She had heard nothing from Elle or anyone regarding Gabriel, and even asking the servants had turned up nothing. Whispers could be heard through the castle, but for what...or whom?

Could it be Gabriel? Surely not, he was supposed to be immortal. He should be fine. He should be up and walking around, tormenting her with his sexy smile and molten silver eyes that looked as though they could see straight into her soul – a soul that wanted to kill him.

She sighed and sank into a chair before the fire. All her pacing had done nothing but aggravate her ankle. She stared into the leaping flames, her mind taken to another time...another place.

"Marry me," Gabriel whispered into her ear as they stood before her father, the king.

She smiled when she really wanted to throw herself into his arms. With the barest nod of her head, his hand moved to grace the small of her back.

"I've already spoken to your father," Gabriel continued. "He's approved of our match."

"It wouldn't matter if he didn't," she whispered, which earned her a stern look from her mother.

But Jayna didn't care. It was the most joyous day of her life.

"Jayna?"

She jerked and turned in the chair to find Hugh standing beside her.

"Forgive me," he said with a slight bow of his head. "You didn't answer my knock and I worried you might be ill."

"Nay," she said with a small shake of her head. "I'm not ill."

He took the seat beside her. "You looked very deep in thought. Were you thinking of your past?"

She looked into his brown eyes as his hand swept his dark locks away from his face. There was no need to lie to him, at least not about this. "Aye."

"Good memories?"

She glanced away and licked her lips. "One of the few. It's odd, is it not?" At his questioning gaze, she said, "How memories once forgotten suddenly become all you can think of?"

"I've always thought that when those memories come to the forefront it's because they are needed in some way. To comfort perhaps?"

Jayna gave a short laugh. "Good memories should comfort, my lord, yet this one only brings pain."

"Good memories that bring pain. Just what happened to you, Jayna?"

She sighed and folded her hands in her lap. "I don't think you came to my chamber to speak of my memories, my lord. I do hope, however, that you bring tidings of

Gabriel."

At Hugh's diverted gaze, Jayna felt sick to her stomach. "Is he all right? He said he was immortal."

"I know," Hugh finally replied as he looked into the flames. "The wound was...difficult...to stop bleeding."

"But you did stop the bleeding?" She gripped the arms of the chair unknowingly.

Hugh's gaze looked down at her hands, then to her face. Jayna instantly refolded her hands in her lap. She couldn't allow any of them to know how important it was that Gabriel be all right. Let them think she was worried about him because she was fond of him. They need never know she must kill him to end her own torment.

"Aye, we finally stopped the bleeding," Hugh said quietly. "The wound traveled from his left side to his right shoulder. Along with the cut on his back, he also has cracked ribs."

Her lungs began to burn and she let loose the breath she had been holding. She sat perfectly still, waiting for whatever it was that brought Hugh to her chamber.

After a moment of silence she said, "You talk as though he is still in danger."

"Because he is." He sighed and raked his fingers through his thick hair. "Jayna, I need you to tell me what happened to Gabriel before we arrived."

All the saliva in her mouth vanished. She tried to lick her lips only to fail. A shiver ran through her, and she rose to get closer to the fire, hoping it would warm her since her thoughts would not.

"It happened so fast," she said softly.

"Tell me," Hugh urged.

Jayna closed her eyes as she wrapped her arms around herself. "The mist, there was so much of it and so quickly. I've never seen it move so quickly, as if it were alive.

Then...." She stopped the memory of the Great Evil's voice snaking fear through her.

"And then?"

She opened her eyes to find Hugh beside her. "The voice. It was...everywhere, but nowhere."

"What did it say?"

"He spoke Gabriel's name."

Hugh nodded. "And Gabriel? What did he do?"

The look of terror in his silver depths would be with her forever. "I saw fear in his eyes. The mist was all around him, swallowing him. The next thing I knew, he was being lifted high into the tree, just dangling there. Then, you arrived."

"You didn't hear anything else the voice said?"

"Nay. I'm not sure it did say anything." As soon as the words left her mouth, she wondered why she had uttered them. She knew the evil had spoken to Gabriel. Why was she protecting him?

Hugh gave an audible sigh. "You are taking all of this very well. Not many people would be so calm after all they saw today."

"Would it do any good for me to be other than I am? I've survived this long because I do not let emotion rule me."

"Hmm. I'd say you do allow emotion to rule you, Jayna, just not the emotions of most females."

She stopped him just before he reached her door. "It will come again, won't it?"

Hugh nodded solemnly as he turned toward her. "Do not venture outside of the castle walls unless you wish to die."

"I'll heed your advice, my lord."

And with that, he was gone.

Jayna's knees gave out and she crumpled to the floor.

She would be here far longer than she anticipated. But the burning question in her mind was why the Great Evil had forgotten to mention the creatures to her and his involvement in everything?

Or had he?

~ ~ ~

Lips as seductive as Rufina, the Fae queen, beckoned him. Hair as golden as the sun upon the sea glided through his hands while hazel eyes smiled up at him.

"Come, Gabriel," she called as she ran out of his arms.

He chased after her, unsure of where she was leading him, but desperately needing to know. She smiled as if she knew him, wanted him.

Gabriel couldn't help but return the smile she threw over her shoulder as she ran ahead of him. With the sun shining in the vivid blue of the sky without a cloud in sight, and the bright green grass beneath his bare feet, it felt as though he were in Heaven.

No worries weighed upon his heart, no doubts, no fears. Nothing but the need to have the beautiful woman in his arms again.

He lengthened his stride and easily caught her. She wrapped her arms around him as he swung her around, her glorious hair trailing around them like golden ribbons.

"Oh, Gabriel," she said as she tucked her head in his neck. "You make me so happy."

Gabriel's eyes snapped open. His heart raced and sweat beaded his skin. It took a moment for his eyes to adjust to the darkness for him to see he stared at the stone wall of his chamber.

It had just been a dream, but it had seemed so real. He closed his eyes and wished for sleep to claim him again. He wanted the beautiful woman and the comfort of her arms, yet the dull throbbing of his back and the ache in his ribs said that wasn't going to happen.

Gingerly, he rolled onto his back and regretted it instantly. Pain lanced through him. He shut his eyes tightly and fisted his hands in an attempt to rule over the agony.

"We had you on your side for a reason."

Gabriel opened his eyes to see Val standing over him with his mate, Nicole by his side. He tried to smile at them, but must have failed by the worry in their eyes.

"I'll be fine," he gritted out. His mouth tasted of sand, and he wanted nothing but a very large jug of ale. Several jugs in fact.

"Many times you've cared for us and insisted we follow your directions. Heed your own words, Gabriel, and do what needs to be done."

This time he did manage the smile. "Always has something to say, doesn't he?" he asked Nicole.

She glanced up at Val as she leaned into him. "He's right though."

While he was happy that they were so concerned over his welfare, Gabriel just wanted to be alone to think over his dream and wonder why the hell he hadn't healed yet.

"You've had everyone very worried."

The soft, unmistakably feminine voice made chills run over his skin.

He turned his head to the side and found Jayna sitting stiffly in a chair beside his bed.

"You should be taking care of your ankle, not sitting here worrying over me."

She glanced down at her tightly clasped hands. "It seems there is need to worry over you."

Gabriel sighed and closed his eyes. Damn but he hurt. The need to take a deep breath was great, but so would the pain be if he attempted it.

"I'll be fine," he said again.

No one had said a word after Jayna's statement.

"Aye, you will," Hugh's voice said from somewhere in the chamber.

By the heavens! Is everyone in here?

He was afraid to open his eyes, afraid to see the concern, the doubt in everyone's gaze. What kind of man was he that he would face evil creatures but wanted to run and hide from the very people he considered his family?

A soft hand touched his arm. Was it Jayna? Was she reaching out to him because she felt his pain? Curiosity made him open his eyes to find Mina's hand on him.

"We're all here for you," she said with a bright smile.

It was too much for Gabriel. He turned his head away from her. "I'm tired."

When the door finally closed, he opened his eyes. Hugh stood on one side of the bed and Aimery the other. "I can't do this now."

"You must," Aimery said.

"I've told Aimery all that happened. We think the harpy's talons may have been poisoned in order to effect you so," Hugh said.

Gabriel shook his head. "Does it really matter? I see how everyone looks at me," he said more harshly than he intended.

"You'll get better," Aimery said.

"I know." Gabriel was unable to meet either of their gazes. He was angry, angry because he shouldn't be in a bed suffering, he should be healed already.

He took a deep breath and then rolled to his side. Out of the corner of his eye, he watched as Aimery gave a swift shake of his head. Probably to stop Hugh from aiding him. With great effort, he swung his legs over the side of the bed and sat up.

"I'm going to kill that harpy myself," Gabriel said through clenched teeth. Then he raised his gaze to Aimery. "The Shields cannot afford to have a member injured. I am no good to them like this."

Aimery nodded, his flaxen hair barely moving. "I know. I was waiting for you to understand that."

Pride had often kept Gabriel from asking for help, but the evil surrounding Stone Crest could win if Gabriel didn't put aside his pride for once.

"Will you heal me?"

"Though I am not supposed to, I will."

Just as the power of the Fae thundered through him, healing his injuries, Gabriel's mind gave up one more memory long buried – of him lying on a bed, blood soaking the sheets, and Aimery along with several other Fae doing their best to keep him alive.

CHAPTER FIFTEEN

Jayna knew she should go to her own chamber, but she couldn't seem to leave the corridor outside of Gabriel's. Everyone else had departed but Hugh. She hoped that once Hugh left, she could sneak inside and talk to Gabriel.

She desperately wanted to know what the Great Evil had said to him. Had the evil whispered to Gabriel her intent? Did Gabriel know his days were numbered? If so, then she needed to finish her deed that night and leave.

"Dark are your thoughts."

The smooth voice startled Jayna and she spun around to find herself staring at what was possibly the most stunning man she had ever laid eyes on. His hair was so blonde it was nearly white and hung long and straight down his back. Several small, intricate plaits adorned his temple to fall over his shoulder. With a face that was perfect in symmetry and grace and manliness, she could do nothing but stare. And lose herself in his mystical blue eyes.

A smile pulled at his wide lips, as if he knew the reaction she had to him. Jayna blinked and jerked her gaze away from him.

"My thoughts are none of your concern, sir," she said as she tried to get herself under control.

"Ah, but they are, my dear Jayna."

Her gaze returned to him, but this time she didn't look at his face. He wore a tunic and pants, but the material was not common to her, and the silvery white of the color was odd, almost...royal. She saw no weapon on him, but by the power radiating from him, she didn't think he needed one.

"Who are you?" she asked.

"You may call me Aimery, though my title is Commander of the Fae army," he said as he crossed his arms over his chest.

A breath hissed from her lungs. She took a step back and braced her hands on the wall.

His forehead puckered in a frown. "There is no need to be afraid. I'll not harm you."

But he would if he ever discovered who she had aligned herself with and just why she was at Stone Crest. With her ankle, she couldn't run and she doubted it would do any good anyway. He was a Fae, with powers beyond her comprehension.

"What do you want with me?" she finally decided to ask.

He shrugged. "To talk for a moment."

She licked her lips and leaned into the wall to take her weight off her injured ankle. It was swelling worse than before now. She should have taken Gabriel's suggestion and kept it raised.

"You're injured as well," Aimery said, his voice as smooth as silk and as commanding as a king's.

"It's just a sprain."

"A sprain that festers." He suddenly knelt before her and held out his hand. "May I see the ankle?"

She hesitated for only a moment before she lifted her

skirts and raised her leg for his inspection. His hands closed over her ankle, and even through the thick wool of her stockings, she could feel the heat of him.

His eyes closed, and he began to move his lips but no words could be heard. Then, her body began to almost hum, as if, magic poured through her. Almost instantly the pain in her ankle ceased, and when he finally released her, she knew he had healed her sprain.

Slowly, she stood on her foot and felt not a twinge from the damaged ankle. "Thank you."

He bowed his head. "Think nothing of it."

"I understand I have the Fae to thank for the clothes as well."

He smiled. "You do not like that we've been kind?"

"It has been...awhile since anyone has been kind to me."

His unusual blue eyes grew sad. "You are in the company of very good people. They are risking their lives for the fate of all mankind. You couldn't have come to a better place."

"I agree," she said softly. But she wasn't fooled. The Fae were all-powerful, which meant, he must know her story was false.

"Tell me, Jayna," he said as he held out his arm for her. "What brings you to Stone Crest?"

Jayna wanted to run away, to hide from the prying eyes of the Fae, eyes that could see deep into her soul. She took his arm instead. "I'm sure Lord Hugh has told you my story."

"Aye, as has Gabriel. However, I'd like to hear the truth from you."

She stumbled and nearly fell to her knees, but he was quick to right her. She looked straight ahead, unsure of how to answer.

"I'll be honest," he continued. "Your mind is blocked from me. That doesn't usually happen unless someone knows how to block a Fae, or magic was used. Which was it?"

She shook her head and stopped. "I don't know what you mean," she said as she looked up at him. "My mind is blocked from you?"

"Aye. The Fae have the power to read minds. It is how I keep the Shields safe from harm. Whenever I encounter someone who has blocked their minds from me I become suspicious, as I'm sure you can understand."

She nodded slowly. "I don't know how to block my mind from you."

He studied her for a moment. "You're being honest." He held out his arm once again.

"You know that as well?" she asked as she took his arm and continued walking.

"There isn't much we can't do."

"But save this realm."

He sighed softly. "Understand, Jayna, that if it were in my power, I'd battle the Great Evil myself. I would fight him from now to eternity if it meant he left this realm and others alone. However, I don't have that authority."

"Why?"

"The Fae once dwelled on Earth. We had a great love of this place, but eventually, we had to leave."

"Why?"

He smiled down at her as he opened her chamber door and ushered her in. "There was a war long, long ago. We had no choice but to relinquish Earth to man. Because we loved it so, the Fae have always looked out for this realm, as well as man."

Jayna was riveted by the story. "It still doesn't explain why you cannot fight."

Aimery gestured to the chairs before the roaring fire. When she had taken a seat, he took the other. "Upon abandoning this realm, there were...rules set in place that kept us away. Most people of this realm think the Fae are nothing more than a myth, a story to tell children at bedtime."

"Yet you walk among them."

"What people don't believe, they don't see." He shrugged. "Though we are allowed to aid mankind, we cannot fight their battles."

"So you gathered together the Shields?"

"Exactly. They have kept Earth safe."

She thought over his words for a moment. "You say you can't fight the evil here, but you will if it comes to your realm."

A dangerous fire lit the Fae's blue eyes. "How I wish it would dare to step foot into our realm. The evil is not that brainless, however. He knows a direct battle between him and the Fae would destroy him."

"This evil, it has to know you are aiding the Shields."

Aimery laughed, but there as no mirth in the sound. "Of course he knows. For he understands, to destroy Earth, it would destroy our realm as well."

Jayna felt as if the wind had been sucked from her body. "What?"

"Since we once inhabited this realm, we are connected to it in ways that you couldn't possibly understand. The Realm of the Fae is directly linked to this realm. The Shields fight not just for this realm, but for mine as well."

"A mighty task they have undertaken."

"You only know half of it," Aimery said with a sigh. "What the Shields have endured is impossible to comprehend. They are men who know they might never live through this final battle, but willingly do it to save two realms."

Jayna found herself looking at the Shields much differently. Her mind wandered to Gabriel, it was always Gabriel.

"Gabriel can't remember his past," she said. "How can he give an oath to the Shields if he doesn't know what his past holds?"

Aimery's gaze held her prisoner for several heartbeats. "Gabriel has proven his worth time and again to the Shields. His knowledge of healing and herbs has saved each of their lives more times than I can remember. His past matters not to any of them. Or to me."

"You hold him in high regard."

"I hold each of the Shields in high regard, most especially the ones whose lives their missions have claimed. We've lost so many. I cannot lose these last remaining five."

He looked into the fire. "Gabriel is special. I wasn't the Fae who found him near one of our doorways, but I was called as soon as they discovered the extent of his injuries. In all honesty, I'm not sure how he lived. His will was strong, that I know. It was almost as if he couldn't let go of something, or something held onto him."

Jayna blinked away the hated tears. "He does sound special."

Aimery turned and smiled at her. "With all our magic and healing abilities, there are times Gabriel can heal what we cannot. His knowledge is unexplainable."

But Jayna could explain it all to them, to expose Gabriel for who he really was. Yet, she found herself unwilling, not when Aimery had such great things to say about him. She was getting another look at Gabriel, one she hadn't thought to ever hear.

"What do you think of Gabriel?"

Aimery's question startled her. It seemed she was always startled around the Fae, never knowing what to expect from the handsome commander. "He is very loyal."

"Loyal? Is that all you've gained from him during your stay here?"

"This is only my second day, and I met him at supper just last eve. It is difficult to discover the true extent of a person in so short a time."

"Not true," Aimery said as he leaned back and threaded his fingers over his stomach. "You can discern a lot from a person by a simple conversation, much like we are having now."

"If that is so, then what have you discerned from me?"

"Besides the fact that you are no commoner as you claim, that you are much, much more than that? At the very least, you're a noblewoman."

"I had reasons for telling that lie."

"I'm sure you did. However, once you tell one lie, you'll find they aren't so easy to believe anything else you say. How many other lies did you tell?"

"If I had told Hugh and the others that I was a lady, do you think he would have allowed me to stay? Nay, he would've wanted to know who my family was immediately so he could send me back."

"You don't give Hugh enough credit," Aimery said sternly. "He is a good man who puts a person's well-being before anything else. He might have sent you somewhere only to get you out of Stone Crest and the dangers surrounding this castle."

Jayna was caught. If Aimery pushed, she would have to tell him at least a partial truth or another lie. She was tired of the lies, so very tired of living the way she had. She wanted to be free of Gabriel, to be free of the revenge controlling her life. She wanted to return home, or to what was left of her home.

"Why did you leave your home?"

Jayna turned her face to the fire with a deep sigh. She decided some truth was needed. "There was a war. I lost... someone. And I was betrayed."

"So the revenge I see in your heart is what has kept you going?"

She nodded, not bothering to look at him.

"My heart bleeds for your misery, Jayna, but you must know that this revenge you seek will not stop the pain within you."

"I know, but I must carry through with it. For too long I have sought this revenge. I can't give up now."

A hand touched her shoulder and immediately the worries clouding her mind vanished. "Be at ease. And know that turning away from your revenge won't be giving up, it'll be living again."

Tears burned the backs of her eyes before they fell down her cheeks. "I wish...."

"Wish what?" Aimery asked softly.

"I wish things were different."

Aimery knelt beside her and turned her head toward him. "If you ask, I'll help you in any way that I can."

"I won't ask," she assured him.

His kind eyes then turned hard. "But know this, Jayna, if you play any of us false, the retribution will be swift."

She swallowed hard and decided to turn a question to him. "You think I came here to do someone harm?"

"I do. I just haven't discovered who it is. Yet."

She forced a smile through her tears and stood. "If you think I've come here to do someone harm, why give me clothes and a warm, safe place to stay? Why the kindness?"

Aimery stood, his sheer height causing her to tilt her head back to meet his gaze. "Because deep inside you there is goodness. We'll do whatever it takes if we can turn you away from your revenge."

He took a step away from her and bowed. "Until later," he said. Then vanished.

Jayna blinked. He was gone. She tentatively moved her arms over the spot Aimery had just been, but felt nothing. Her emotions were in a whirl around her.

She sank back down onto the chair and let the tears flow that wouldn't be held back, tears she hadn't shed since the day Gabriel betrayed her.

CHAPTER SIXTEEN

Gabriel opened his eyes and took a deep breath. Only a minor twinge of pain bothered him. Aimery's magic had healed him. Someone had laid him back down and covered him. Most likely Hugh.

He sat up and swung his legs over the bed. Cool air brushed against his bare torso. Cautiously, he poked at his ribs. There was only a slight discomfort. To test his back, he held his arms out to his side and slowly lifted them over his head.

The skin on his back pulled, and Gabriel released his arms. The wound was still healing, but healing quickly. Maybe it had just been something on the harpy's talons as Hugh said.

He needed a bath, desperately, not only to wash away the sweat that had soaked his body, but also to sink into the heated water and help with his sore muscles.

Gabriel padded barefoot to the trunk at the end of his bed for a clean tunic and pants, and then he left his chamber for the bath.

Torches flared in the hallway, and the castle was almost

ghostly quiet. He passed the balcony overlooking the great hall to see row upon row of bodies sleeping. As he continued on his way, he couldn't help thinking of the dreams that had plagued him.

The woman in the dreams was fascinating, and he would have given almost anything to see her entire face. Snatches of his first dream flashed in his mind. The woman had a wonderful, infectious laugh, one that put a smile on his face even then.

But was she real, a person from his past, or just a figment of a dream?

The answer he might never know. With a yawning sigh, he walked into the bathing chamber, stripped and sank into the heated water with a groan.

In the distance, he could hear soldiers moving around outside on the battlement, searching the skies for the gargoyle they all expected. And he couldn't wait to fit his bow in his palm again and let an arrow find its mark.

The need to battle the creatures was great, so great that it left little room for anything else. He had never felt such hatred for the creatures before. Though he suspected it had something to do with his exchange with the Great Evil. Part of him wanted to forget it ever happened, yet another part, the part that yearned for knowledge of his past, wanted to seek the evil out.

With a curse, Gabriel reached for the soap and began to scrub himself clean. It wasn't until he had dried off and put on his fresh clothes that he thought about Jayna. He silently chided himself for forgetting about her, especially after she had sat in his chamber, worry clouding her pretty hazel eyes.

On his return to his chamber, he detoured to the left and walked silently to her chamber. He knocked softly, not wanting to wake her if she slept. When she didn't answer, he reached to try the handle, just wanting to check on her to make sure her ankle was healing.

The handle moved, opening her door noiselessly. He looked to the bed but found it empty. His gaze quickly scanned the small chamber and found her sitting before the now dead fire.

Gabriel shut her door to help keep what little heat there was in her chamber, then moved to the hearth to work the still glowing embers to life. It took him a bit, but once the fire was roaring again he turned to her.

She had unbraided her hair, letting it fall all golden and loose around her like a blond mantle. Her nose was red and her eyes ringed with dark circles. She was still in her gown and fast asleep.

He shook his head and touched her hand to feel her icy skin beneath his. Gabriel stalked to the bed, yanked down the linens and then walked back for her. He gently moved her into his arms and carried her to the bed without waking her.

Once she was in her bed, he reached down to remove her shoes and noticed that her ankle no longer had any swelling. He smiled, knowing Aimery must have seen to it, and tucked her feet beneath the thick blankets.

As he pulled the blankets up to her chin he saw the streaks down her face where tears had been. Why the thought of her crying twisted his insides, he didn't know.

She stirred and buried herself deep within the covers. Her lips parted on a soft sigh, and for a moment he couldn't tear his gaze from her. There was something different about Jayna, something familiar as well, and he desperately wanted to know who she was. If she could be a link to his past, even one that was nothing more than a replica of someone he knew, he needed her.

The wind began to howl as gusts blew past the castle.

The storm would be fierce, keeping away the creatures for one more night at least.

With one last look at her, Gabriel straightened and closed the bed curtains around her. He checked her fire again then left her chamber. His feet were like bricks of ice, but it was better than not being able to move in bed.

As he walked the stairs to his chamber, he felt someone near. He slowed his steps, checking the shadows as he walked.

"Do you fear me now, brother?" Roderick said as he stepped from one of the shadows.

Gabriel sighed. "You know I don't." One look at Roderick's face and he knew something was seriously wrong. "What is it? What keeps you roaming the corridors instead of in bed with Elle?"

"Fear for her life," he said softly and turned away from Gabriel. "Have you ever had something within your grasp that you never thought possible? A love so pure and right that you knew 'twas your mate?"

Gabriel swallowed past the lump of pain in his chest. "Nay."

"I pray you don't, Gabriel," he said as he faced him once more. "The very thought that I might lose Elle has robbed me of my sleep. I need her. Without her...I am nothing."

Gabriel gripped Roderick's shoulder. "We won't let Elle or any of the Chosen die."

He gave a half grin and lowered his head. "Thank you for trying, but you cannot promise that, my brother. No one can. Is it shocking to you that I long to take my wife far from here, to a realm untouched by evil? To forget about my oath or Earth and live my life as I wish?"

"Not shocking, Roderick. I think if I had discovered my mate, I would feel the same way. But you won't leave because Elle won't let you. She also has a duty."

"I know," Roderick said and all the apprehension and agony could be heard in his voice. Suddenly he lifted his head and looked Gabriel in the eye. "You're healed?"

Gabriel shrugged and let his hand drop from Roderick's shoulder. "Aimery helped to speed it along."

"How do you feel?"

"There's still pain, but it should be gone shortly. Do not worry, Roderick. I'm ready and eager to fight."

Roderick sliced a hand through the air to stop his words. "That isn't what I mean. I know you would fight even if your blood drained from you as it did earlier today. My faith does not waver from any of the Shields."

"Then what does your faith waver on?"

"Us standing together," he said softly before walking away.

For a long moment, Gabriel simply stared after his friend. Of all of them, he never suspected this of Roderick. Roderick had shouldered so very much with the weight of his realm hanging in the balance.

Worry for Roderick and the other Shields filled Gabriel's mind. He was so caught up in his conversation with Roderick that he didn't look in his chamber as he always did when he entered.

It wasn't until he checked his fire and turned to his bed that he saw it – the puddle of clear, thick liquid near his chest at the foot of his bed.

Gabriel's gaze glanced to his bow and arrows that stood by the bed near his sword. It was too far way for him to reach. He let his gaze wander over the chamber in a lazy slow motion, as though he didn't suspect someone, or something, of being in his chamber.

When he didn't immediately see anything, he searched the chamber and came up empty. Without further ado, he pivoted and left his chamber.

He stopped before Hugh's chamber and knocked. Loudly. Within moments, Hugh stood before him bare-chested.

"Gabriel?" he asked as he rubbed his eyes. "What is it?"

"You need to come," Gabriel said as he turned and retraced his steps. There was a commotion in Hugh's chamber, which meant Mina was determined to come with them.

Gabriel stood at his door and waited for Hugh and Mina. Hugh took one look inside, then looked down at his wife and said, "Wake the others, my love."

It wasn't long before Roderick, Val and Cole stood with them. "What was so important to wake us?" Val asked. "Not that I'm not relieved to see Gabriel up and about, his regular cheerful self," he said with a grin.

Gabriel threw his friend a look. "Cole," he said and turned to the other Shield. "Do you recall the substance we found at the monastery?"

"Aye," Cole said as he stepped into Gabriel's chamber. He walked to the puddle near the chest and went on his haunches before it. After he dipped a finger into the liquid, he rubbed it between two fingers. "It's the same, Gabriel."

"What. Is. It?" Hugh asked, his entire being radiating anger.

Gabriel sighed. "With everything that has happened, Cole and I both forgot to tell of the substance we found. Neither of us thought much of it since we didn't find any sign of a creature."

"In various places throughout the monastery we found this liquid," Cole said as he moved to stand beside Gabriel. "I've never seen anything like it."

Hugh moved his gaze to Gabriel. "Is anything missing in your chamber?"

"Nay," he said. "All is accounted for."

Hugh raked a hand through his hair and walked into Gabriel's chamber to stand over the puddle. "What could it be, and why the hell is it in your chamber?"

Gabriel walked with the others to stand around the pool of liquid. "I wish I knew."

Val knelt down and leaned close to the liquid. He inhaled deeply and coughed. "There is a slight smell to it that you don't notice unless you get near it."

"Whatever it is, it got into the castle unseen," Roderick pointed out. "I've walked these halls all night and have not seen a soul other than Gabriel."

"I want to inspect the monastery tomorrow," Hugh said as he walked to the door. He stopped and turned to look at his men. "I don't care if it is storming or not. We will ride out."

Gabriel let out a breath as Hugh disappeared down the hall. There was tension among all of them, but not for reasons of the unknown liquid. It was because each of them had something precious to lose, their mates.

He looked over his comrades. Roderick was still as stone and withdrawn. Val, whose smile had come much easier since finding Nicole, had also retreated into his shell once more. Only Cole seemed the same, though unease clouded his eyes.

Silently, they filed out of his chamber and returned to their own, leaving Gabriel staring at the liquid and wondering how it had gotten in his chamber and what it meant.

CHAPTER SEVENTEEN

Aimery stared out over his beloved land from his balcony in the great Fae city. The sun showed its brilliance as it rose above the tall mountains in the east.

"It is going to be a beautiful day," Theron said as he moved to stand beside him.

Aimery bowed his head to his king. "Aye."

"What troubles you, my friend?"

Aimery turned and faced his liege who was dressed all in white save the blue cloak that hung around his shoulders. "The Great Evil spoke to Gabriel."

Theron's face drained of color at the news. "What did he say to Gabriel?"

"Only Gabriel knows, and he isn't talking."

Theron sighed and clasped his hands behind his back as he turned and walked the length of Aimery's office. "If Gabriel discovered his past he wouldn't have been able to hide it from you."

"I know."

Theron stopped walking and cocked his head to the side. "You aren't worried about him discovering his past."

"Nay," Aimery said. "He is a strong man with a strong soul. He can withstand anything."

"Then what is it?"

Aimery sighed and closed his eyes as he sank onto one of his large, soft chairs. He opened his eyes and looked to his king. "Did we do the right thing in keeping the truth from him, Theron? How many times has he asked me if I knew anything, and how many times have I lied?"

"You haven't lied," Theron said sharply. He took a deep breath and started again. "Aimery, we didn't have a choice. It was by sheer chance that we happened upon Gabriel when we did. To this day, we still don't know if the things he said while the fever raged are true."

"I think they are," Aimery replied softly.

"But we don't know for sure. There is a difference. You knew instantly he was a man for the Shields. You weren't wrong then, and you're not wrong now for keeping speculation from him."

Aimery nodded. "There's something else."

Theron shifted and crossed his arms over his chest. "I gather this also has something to do with Gabriel? Has he allowed you into his mind? Have you seen the truth for yourself?"

"Nay. I do not think Gabriel is blocking me from his mind. I think something else is."

"Maybe," Theron said and looked into the distance. "There are many beings out there that could be keeping Gabriel's mind closed."

"There's a woman," Aimery finally said. "A woman that Gabriel seems drawn to. There is much darkness in her soul and revenge in her heart, though there is no evil running through her."

"Is she from Gabriel's past?"

"I do not know. I tried to question her, but discovered

nothing."

"Then read her mind," Theron said, losing patience.

Aimery smiled, for his king was known for his emotions. "I have tried. Her mind is also blocked."

Theron's flaxen brow rose. "Coincidence?"

"Doubtful. I hesitate to interfere too much though."

"I know you care about the Shields, Aimery. It's what makes you such a fine commander. However, the growing evil might not give Gabriel the time he needs. And now you say this woman is full of revenge? Could she be after Gabriel?"

Aimery inhaled deeply and softly blew out the breath. "She is at Stone Crest for someone. Who? I do not as yet know."

"And there isn't time for you to keep watch over them either."

Aimery soared to his feet. "I must be with them. The fate of our realm is also at stake."

Theron's face hardened and his voice lowered dangerously. "I don't need reminding, Aimery. I need you to take some of your army to the west. Someone has slain a white dragon."

Aimery felt as if he'd been punched in the gut. "No Fae would dare to slay a white dragon."

"I know," Theron said and turned away, but not before Aimery saw the weariness in his king's face. "Only evil would dare to kill such a pure dragon. How evil stepped over our boundaries without us knowing it, I know not." He turned back to Aimery. "I need you to find out who did this."

Aimery nodded and waited until Theron left his office before he sat and dropped his head into his hands. Never did he think he would have to abandon the Shields. They needed him and his army.

But the Fae also needed him, for to slay a white dragon carried serious consequences to the magic of their realm. It might not be felt now, but it would soon.

Somehow, Aimery knew this was all connected to the Great Evil. He knew the evil had garnered great power, but was his magic so great that he could walk undetected into the Realm of the Fae and slay one of the most precious of their dragons?

The answer was nay. For if the Great Evil could venture into the Fae realm, there would be no reason for him not to destroy it.

He sent someone else, or something else, instead.

~ ~ ~

Gabriel shifted in his saddle as the heavy snow fell around them. His quiver of arrows and bow were slung over his shoulder. He had made a mistake the day before by leaving them on his mount. He wouldn't make the same mistake twice.

Barely visible through the falling snow were Roderick and the five women on the steps of the castle. Another of the Shields should have stayed, but Hugh wanted more protection for them.

The people of Stone Crest had been warned and were ready for any kind of attack.

The holes dug beneath their homes were stocked with food and water as well as an escape route if necessary. They were prepared.

He glanced once more to the steps. Roderick stood behind Elle, arms crossed over his chest and a fierce expression on his face. The women were safe with Roderick, for Roderick would sell his soul if it meant his Elle would be safe.

"The faster we leave, the faster we return," Val said.

Hugh nodded, and with a last wave to Mina nudged his horse toward the gate. The horses weren't any more eager than their riders to venture into the storm, but they were well trained and did as commanded.

Gabriel looked over his shoulder to find the others filing into the castle. All except one. Jayna. She stood watching him.

He turned back and followed the others out of the gate. As the gate banged closed behind them, the winds grew stronger. The horses trudged through the mounting snow, their heads bowed beneath the onslaught.

Gabriel pulled his cloak tighter. He brought up the line as they filed one by one into the forest. Hugh could find the monastery blindfolded he knew his land so well.

The only sound to be heard was the wind whistling through the bare trees. Gabriel's hair on the back of his neck started to rise and he gripped the pommel of his sword. He unsheathed his sword as he whirled his mount around.

But nothing was behind him.

"Gabriel?" Hugh called.

Gabriel let his gaze wander slowly around him. There had been something there, he would bet his soul on it.

"What is it?" Val asked as he rode up beside him.

Gabriel didn't lower his sword. "I felt something," he whispered. Yet nothing moved or attacked them. It was as if whatever it was had disappeared.

Finally, Gabriel sheathed his sword and looked at Val.

"I know I felt something behind me. We've done this for too long for me to mistake that feeling."

Val nodded. "Let's get to the monastery. There's something foul in the air today."

Gabriel followed Val and continued on. The rest of the

ride was uneventful, though Gabriel kept his senses open in case something tried to sneak up on him again.

The ruins of the monastery rose from the snow like giant fingers to the sky. For decades, the monastery had been abandoned, leaving the once marvelous structure to be occupied by wild animals and any stranger who dared to venture through the gates. Though the place was once holy, its atmosphere was that of a dark shadow creeping upon you.

Gabriel shuddered despite himself as he tethered his horse. He gave his mount a pat on his neck before following the others through the gate.

A flash of movement out of the corner of his eye spun Gabriel around as he withdrew an arrow and notched it, aiming it in the direction he had seen the movement.

"There's something out there," he whispered to the others.

One by one they drew their weapons. Hugh notched his crossbow, a deadly weapon he used with incredible skill. Beside him, Cole held his impressive double-headed war axe, a weapon that could cleave a man's skull in two. Val let his gaze wander as he fingered his halberd, a weapon he used with lethal accuracy.

"I don't see anything," Hugh said.

"I know," Gabriel replied. "But it's out there. I've seen it out of the corner of my eye twice since we entered these woods."

Hugh swore viciously. "Into the monastery. Now."

The four walked carefully into the monastery, their weapons always at the ready. Once inside, Hugh moved to the right as Cole quickly stepped through the doorway and then to the left so his back was against the wall.

Val and Gabriel were the last two in. While Gabriel kept his gaze outside, waiting for an attack, he was back to back with Val who stood at the ready inside the monastery.

Gabriel didn't put down his bow until he heard Hugh say the room was clear of creatures. He inhaled deeply and pivoted so that he faced his comrades.

"I know what I saw."

Cole raised a hand. "I never doubted you, Gabriel. Did you see anything about it? Was it human or creature?"

"I didn't see it clearly," he said.

Hugh stepped forward then. "Cole, set up watch at the door. I want to make sure we aren't surprised by any creatures while we're here."

With a small nod of his head, Cole moved to his position by the door. "Val."

"Aye," the Roman answered.

Hugh pointed above him. "Check the upper levels."

Gabriel watched Val run up the stairs with nary a sound and waited.

"Lead me to these puddles you and Cole found earlier."

He turned to Hugh then Gabriel motioned around the vast room. "Look around, Hugh. They're everywhere. In every level Cole and I checked, we found the same substance."

Hugh cursed again as he rested his crossbow on his shoulder and looked around the room. "I've never seen anything like it."

"There is much more of it below," Cole said over his shoulder. "Whatever it is, it prefers the dank, dark chambers below the earth."

Gabriel gazed at the substance that dotted crumpled bookshelves, stairs, overturned tables and chairs, and even the earth. "You can tell the ones that are older," he said as he leaned closer to a pool of the liquid. "It starts to turn a milky white and harden."

"Whatever it is," Val said from above them, "it's nasty.

I never cared for the monastery, and I care for it even less now."

Hugh sighed and glanced up at Val. "Did you find anything?"

"Nothing. Not a trace of a wild animal or a whisper of a ghost," Val said as he started down the stairs. "It's odd, don't you think? Before we found traces of animals. Now there's nothing."

"That is odd," Hugh agreed.

Gabriel shifted feet and shook his head. "I would say whatever did this belongs to the Great Evil, but I don't smell any evil."

"Nor do I," Cole said. "With as many piles of that liquid that are around here, if it was evil, we would smell it all the way back to Stone Crest."

Hugh nodded. "Aye. If it's not evil, and I know it isn't an animal from these parts, what could it be?"

"Maybe Aimery will know," Val offered as he rubbed his hands together. "It's damn cold. Let's return to Stone Crest and call for Aimery. He can look over the liquid in Gabriel's chamber then."

Gabriel let his gaze wander the monastery again. There was no sign of the creatures, no stench of evil, but he *knew* something was there.

And he would bet his prized bow made of magical Fae wood that it was something other than the Fae army, something other than an animal.

Deep down, he feared that whatever it was might very well be there to harm them.

CHAPTER EIGHTEEN

Jayna stood on the steps of the castle long after the gate closed behind Gabriel. Anxiety writhed in her stomach, and she didn't know if it was because she was more concerned about the Shields encountering the harpy again...or the Great Evil.

Thick snowflakes landed on her lashes and hindered her vision, but she didn't move. The heavy cloak did little to keep her warm, and it wasn't long until her toes and fingers began to grow numb.

She inhaled deeply, the cold slicing into her lungs and making her shiver. She gazed around the empty bailey. Besides the guards atop the battlements, she could have been the only person on Earth. She had worried for so long about finding food, clothing, and a safe place to sleep. Being at Stone Crest, being welcomed and loved, had made Jayna realize just what she had left behind when she set her course for revenge.

But without the Great Evil's constant meddling, her thirst for revenge had slackened.

Your thirst hasn't slacked. Dare you forget what Gabriel did?

How he betrayed you?

Jayna blinked away sudden tears as she thought of her family, her beloved family who she had cherished deeply. They were gone, all gone. And all because of Gabriel.

The sound of footfalls crunching on snow jerked her out of her memories. She was appalled to find more tears had escaped her eyes. She lifted her hand to dash away the hated moisture only to find it had frozen to her face.

"It's not a fit day for man or beast," Roderick said as he stopped beside her. "It feels as though we are the only people left on Earth everything is so quiet." He sighed and crossed his arms over his chest as he turned to look at her.

"They will return, Jayna. You needn't stay out here waiting for Gabriel."

She swiveled her head to stare at the tall, golden warrior beside her. "I don't wait for Gabriel. I like the peace out here."

Roderick's dark blue eyes narrowed slightly before they turned compassionate. "Peace. It means something different to everyone."

"Aye." Jayna wasn't sure what Roderick spoke of, but he looked as though he needed to speak and she suddenly found that she didn't want to be alone.

"What does it mean to you?"

She thought over his words a moment. "Peace to me is ridding myself of ghosts."

"Ghosts?" Roderick asked, his head cocked to the side. "You are too young to have ghosts."

Jayna chuckled. "I've learned that one is never too young to have ghosts, my lord." She looked out over the bailey, thoughts of her family filling her mind. "One can be young, happy, innocent, trusting and...in love." She returned her gaze to Roderick. "Then, in less time than a heartbeat, it can all be taken away."

"Is this why you seek revenge?"

She nodded.

He closed his eyes briefly. "Put aside your revenge, Jayna. It will not slay the ghosts that haunt you."

"If you knew who had killed your family, would you go after them? Would you have your revenge?"

His arms dropped to his side and he took a step toward her, his eyes widening. "Is that what happened to you?"

Jayna hastily shook her head. "Would you?"

For a long moment, Roderick stared at her. "Aye," he finally answered. "I would."

"You asked me what my peace was, my lord. What is yours?"

Roderick closed his eyes and lifted his face to the cloud laden sky. "I would take my wife and return to Thales. The Great Evil would be vanquished once and for all, and the threat hovering over my realm and this one would end."

"You must love Elle very much."

His face lowered and his eyes opened to look at her. "I cannot begin to describe my love for her. But you must understand how I feel. You said you were in love."

"Real love wouldn't have betrayed me, my lord. What I thought was love was only a shimmer of the true emotion you hold within you."

"What a pair we are," Roderick said with a smile.

It was infectious, and Jayna found herself returning the smile.

"Come," he said and offered his arm. "Let us return inside where Elle will see that you are indeed all right. She worries deeply for you."

Jayna's toe caught on a step and the world tilted toward her. Her heart pounded roughly against her chest. *Elle worries deeply for you.* Roderick's words repeated over and over in her mind.

Hands, big and strong, gripped her shoulders and righted her. She raised her gaze to find Roderick staring down at her with his dark blue eyes.

"Jayna?"

"There is ice on the steps," she said weakly, praying he believed the lie.

After a moment, he nodded his head and took her arm to steady her as they climbed the remainder of the steps to the door.

As soon as she stepped inside, the warmth of the castle enveloped her. No sooner had she handed her cloak to Roderick than Elle and Shannon raced up to her, leading her to the blazing fire.

Jayna found the lump in her throat growing and tears stinging the backs of her eyes again. She blinked away the tears and smiled as Elle and Shannon talked.

Jayna didn't even try to keep up with their conversation. She was too busy wondering how they would feel about her once she killed Gabriel.

CHAPTER NINETEEN

Jayna knew the moment Gabriel and the others entered the bailey. It was as if her body was attuned to Gabriel's in a way that defied description.

Before they entered the great hall, Jayna rose and moved to the shadows. She watched as Hugh, Cole, Val, and Gabriel filed into the castle, all of them looking grim. Whatever they had set out looking for, they must have found it.

She released her breath when she realized Gabriel didn't have any injuries.

Get a hold of yourself, Jayna. He's immortal, remember?

He might be, but it wouldn't be the same if she killed a man who was already weak from another wound. She wanted him hail and hearty when she plunged the dagger in his heart.

She fingered the dagger up her sleeve and knew it was time to take a step closer to finishing her mission. She turned on her heel and hurried to her chamber. She needed to make herself as alluring to Gabriel as she could.

There had been a time all she had to do was smile at him and he was by her side. But this Gabriel was different. This Gabriel would need more coaxing.

~ ~ ~

Gabriel dusted the snow from his feet and held out his hands before the hearth.

The storm had only worsened by the time they returned to Stone Crest, and had they not known the land as well as they did, they could have become lost.

Lost. He knew that word well. He had been lost for so long he didn't know any other way. The image of the woman in his dream flashed in his mind.

He desperately needed to know if she was someone from his past. How he longed to see her entire face, to know that the smile she showed him was for him.

With a curse, he surged to his feet. It was only because the other Shields had found their mates that the loneliness was more visible. He might envy the others finding their women, but he would never wish it otherwise. If he were destined to walk alone, then he would.

"Gabriel."

He turned to find Roderick behind him. By the way Roderick's lips were flattened and his forehead frowned, something was wrong. "What is it?"

"Have you learned anything else from Jayna?"

He shook his head. "Nothing more than what Mina and Hugh were told. Jayna is very careful not to say more than she has before. She keeps her secrets close."

"Aye," Roderick said softly as he rubbed his chin with his thumb and forefinger. He dropped his hand then. "She spoke of wanting peace from her ghosts today."

"Ghosts?" Gabriel repeated.

"Ghosts. She has admitted to several of us now that she does seek revenge. With the threat of the Great Evil, we need to know where she stands."

Gabriel sighed. He knew what it was Roderick wanted. It was the same thing Hugh had asked of him. Seduction. The worst part about it was that he was looking forward to seducing Jayna. There was something intriguing about her, something that made Gabriel want to be near her at all times. And the more he was around her, the more the feeling grew.

"She'll talk once you've bedded her," Roderick said.

Gabriel ran a hand down his face as he sighed. "You make it sound so easy, my friend. Cole was the charmer of women, not me. I cannot woo her with just a smile. Besides, she does have feelings. I haven't used a female before, and I'd prefer to not start now."

Roderick took a step closer to him. "Gabriel, I'm begging you. I like Jayna, but if she is in any way connected with the Great Evil, she must not remain here. I cannot jeopardize Elle's life."

"All right," he reluctantly agreed. Gabriel could see just how much it meant to Roderick, and because the Shields were his brethren, his family, he would do whatever they asked.

Roderick let out a loud sigh. "Thank you."

"Don't thank me yet, brother. I haven't bedded her," he said as he walked away.

"You will."

Gabriel hesitated at Roderick's words before he wearily walked up the stairs to his chamber. There was so much confusion at Stone Crest. The Chosen had no idea how to bring down the Great Evil as they were supposed to. The Shields had no idea how they were going to battle the harpy and the gargoyle. No one knew why Jayna was at the castle, or if she meant one of them harm. And now the problem with the clear substance in his chamber as well as the monastery.

He sighed loudly. Too much disorder and not near enough answers. He sensed that the odds weren't in their favor of winning, but hadn't the Great Evil alluded to that very thing in Scotland?

The Shields had fought the creatures for so long, managing to win when it seemed doom was inevitable, but now...now was different. It seemed the entire world held its breath, waiting for the final hammer stroke that would end all as they knew it.

Gabriel had a difficult time believing that all the work the Shields had done was for naught. If they could find at least one answer in all the whirlwind, then it would help right some of the chaos.

Maybe.

~ ~ ~

Gabriel ran his hands through his still damp hair. He was nervous. Nervous!

Of all the emotions he thought he might feel at the prospect of seducing Jayna, being nervous wasn't one of them. Though he didn't proclaim to be a lover of Cole's proportions, he'd had his fair share of women.

"Damnation," he growled and stormed from his chamber. If he sat and worried about it any longer, he wouldn't carry through with it.

He told himself it was because Jayna could be an innocent, and by duping her with a seduction, he would be hurting her. That was partly it, but the other part, the part that urged him to sink into her body, told him their joining would be right.

His steps slowed as he came to the stairs. If he ventured down, he would find the other Shields in the great hall, but if he ventured down and to the right, he would find himself in front of Jayna's chamber.

Just the thought of her chamber led him to think of her bed, of him gently laying her on the bed and kissing her sweet flesh. He could see her beautiful hazel eyes grow dark with desire and her body quiver with need as he brought her to her release.

A soft touch on his arm brought him out of his thoughts. And he found himself staring down at none other than Jayna.

"You look deep in thought, my lord," she said, her husky voice moving over him like the warmth of the sun.

"Aye," he answered.

She lowered her gaze demurely and then she smiled up at him. "I am glad to see that you are indeed immortal. You had everyone worried."

"Everyone?" He didn't know what was wrong with him that he repeated everything she said.

Her dusky pink lips turned up at the corners. "You had me worried."

The thought of her concerned for him sent a jolt through him. "You don't even know me."

"Odd isn't it?" she asked. "I can't help how I feel, though."

Her words tugged to a memory long forgotten. He stood before a golden throne, a tall man wearing a jeweled crown stared down at him, his dark eyes unfriendly and disapproving.

"I cannot help how I feel, sire. I love her."

"-rial?"

He jerked and stepped back. He could still feel the sting of anger and fear of rejection from that memory. He had spoken to a king about a woman he loved. But what king? What realm?

What woman?

"Gabriel?"

He looked down at the soft hands wrapped around his arm. His gaze moved up her slim arms to her face and the concern clouding her beautiful hazel depths.

"You have beautiful eyes," he said suddenly. "Has anyone ever told you that?"

She swallowed and released him. "One other person."

An awkward silence followed. Gabriel wasn't good with wooing women, he didn't know the flowery words to tell them.

"What happened to you a moment ago?"

He blinked and leaned against the wall. "Something you said made me remember something."

"Really?" she asked. Though her voice sounded happy, her expression was guarded, almost as if she was afraid of what he had remembered.

He shrugged. "The memory didn't tell me any more than I already know."

Nay. It told me much more. It told me that I had loved. Deeply.

"I was wondering if you would give me more of a tour of the castle?" Jayna looked at him with wide eyes, her expression hopeful.

Since Gabriel had been searching for a way to be alone with her, he readily grasped her offer. "Of course. How about some of the splendid views of the towers?"

"Lead the way."

Gabriel took her hand and tucked it in the crook of his arm. He shortened his steps and turned her down the corridor.

"Isn't this the way to Lord Hugh and Lady Mina's chamber?"

He smiled down at her. "You've a good memory. Aye, their chamber is at the end of the hall. However, we're going a different route."

She asked no more questions as they walked silently along the hallway. It was a comfortable silence, like old friends content to be in each other's company as they walked.

Or lovers looking for a secluded spot.

He mentally shook himself and turned her to the left just after his chamber. "The stairway is narrow and very steep in parts."

"I'll manage," she said over her shoulder. Her smile and the excitement lighting her eyes made it all worthwhile.

He followed her up the stairs, trying in vain to wrench his gaze away from the alluring sway of her hips. He could just imagine running his hands along her bottom and the curve of her hips, the indention of her waist.

White-hot desire flooded him, his rod becoming hard and aching with just a thought. Gabriel clenched his teeth together and tried to focus on anything other than Jayna. But it was impossible.

She was...well, she was different. She wasn't like any woman he had ever met. Her spirit, her courage and her beauty were unmatched by anyone. He saw the darkness in her as well, which only made him want her all the more, because she didn't try to hide the darkness. She accepted it as part of herself.

Suddenly, she stopped and Gabriel found himself a few steps below her, their faces just breaths apart.

"I'm not a commoner."

He smiled. He didn't know why she had confessed to her lie, but he was terribly glad that she had. "I know."

"And you're not going to make me leave?"

There was something in her eyes. Was it hope? Did she

want to leave? Gabriel shook his head. "We've all known from the very beginning that you weren't a commoner. A blind man could see it in the way you walk, the way you carry yourself, and most importantly, by how you speak."

After a moment's hesitation, she continued up the narrow stairway. Gabriel was disappointed. He thought she might have divulged more of her reasons for coming to Stone Crest, though he kept a small vein of hope that it was just by chance that she had happened upon the castle.

It wasn't long before they came to the north tower. The square room overlooked most of the castle, though it wasn't the tallest of the towers.

He came up behind her as she slowly entered the tower, her gaze taking in the nearly empty chamber. Only a few chairs and a small table occupied this tower.

"Not what you expected?" he asked.

She tossed a grin over her shoulder. "The castle is very grand, and I do suppose I expected something more for the towers. Almost like a sanctuary of sorts for Mina and Hugh."

"There are other towers. This one is used mostly by the knights since it has a direct view of the road leading to Stone Crest."

"Ah. Which explains only the chairs and table." She ran her hand along the table as she walked around it. "You don't seem at all concerned that I lied," she said softly.

Gabriel turned from the window and crossed his arms over his chest as he regarded her. "It isn't that I'm not concerned that you felt the need to lie, which makes us wary of you. What concerns me more than anything right now is defeating the evil and anything that stands in the way of us succeeding."

"I understand." Her eyes had taken on a faraway look, as though she remembered something very dear to her. She blinked and focused her eyes on him. "Did you find what you went to search for this morn?"

"Hugh wanted a look at something Cole and I had found a few days ago."

She lowered her gaze and took a step toward him. "I've seen many things in my life, Gabriel, and I hate to admit it, but those creatures terrified me."

"We've an entire castle to protect from the creatures. You'll be safe as long as you stay inside."

She gradually raised her gaze to his. Sadness flashed briefly in her eyes. "Aye, I should be safe."

Gabriel didn't know what propelled him toward Jayna. Maybe it was the loneliness that seemed to radiate from her like the glow of the moon, or maybe it was because he didn't want to deny himself another moment. But whatever it was, one moment he was leaning against the wall and the next he stood before her gazing into her lovely hazel eyes.

"It's odd, you know," he found himself saying as his hand came up to rub the ends of her braid between his fingers. Her golden locks were made to be loose and flowing about her.

Her entire body stilled. "What is?"

"How familiar you are to me. It's as if I know you, though that cannot possibly be true. If I did know you, it might explain why I can't seem to keep my hands from you."

In answer, she simply smiled. Her eyes that had once seemed like great pools of despair were now focused on him like a falcon eyeing its prey.

"Why try to explain our feelings," she said, her voice low and husky as she raised a hand and placed it on his arm. "I've learned the best thing to do is just *feel*."

Gabriel stared at her parted lips. Her lashes lowered, and his breathing quickened. By the heavens, it was near torture not to take her lips. Then he remembered her words.

Just feel.

He dipped his head and captured her lips with his own. It was as if the world had awakened then, shaking off its gray mantel and shining brightly. Yet, he couldn't be parted from Jayna to enjoy it. The need to taste more of her, feel more of her was stronger than his need to breathe.

His mouth moved over hers, gently at first then more insistent as his desire for her grew. His hands slid around her trim waist then moved up her sides until he felt the weight of her breasts touch the outside of his hands.

The yearning, nay *need*, to feel her body beneath his nearly brought him to his knees. Never had he experienced such longing before and it both frightened and intrigued him.

A soft sigh escaped her when he slid his tongue along her plump lips. It was all the encouragement he needed. He pulled her against him, needing her to feel how desperately he wanted her.

Her arms wrapped around his neck as her fingers threaded through his hair. Gabriel's skin shivered as chills raced through him. But still he needed more.

He slipped his tongue between her lips and was rewarded with a soft moan of pleasure. The more he tasted her, the more he wanted. She was like fine wine, heady and addictive.

Their kisses turned frantic as need drove their bodies closer. And when she rubbed against his throbbing cock, it was all Gabriel could do not to lay her back on the table and take her right then, his desire was so great.

But he also wanted to see her splendid flesh devoid of clothing. He wanted to trace every inch of her with his lips, to kiss her sex and watch her writhe with pleasure, to feel the heat of her on his fingers. But most of all, he wanted an entire night to get to know her body.

Somehow, he managed to break the kiss. When he looked down into her eyes, he was amazed to see the hunger and desire darkening her gaze.

"I want you," he said once his breathing was back under control. "You have no idea how much I want you."

"I want you, too." She said it as if she herself was amazed with the realization.

He smiled and ran a finger along her high cheekbone down to her jaw. "I want you naked on my bed. I want to run my hands along your flesh, to see all your womanly curves and explore your body. I want an entire night of nothing but loving you."

His words affected her deeply. Her eyes misted over and her throat worked as she tried to swallow. "I'm yours, Gabriel."

I'm yours, Gabriel.

CHAPTER TWENTY

Jayna didn't even try to stop the words as they tumbled from her mouth. What he'd said to her touched her more deeply than anything had for a very long time.

She wasn't sure what surprised her more, how much he desired her, or how much she desired him. So when he took her hand and hastily left the tower, she willingly followed him. It had been too long since she her body had been awakened.

By Gabriel.

Again.

But she refused to think about it. She was following her own advice. Just feel.

It was easy to do that with Gabriel. He made her feel like a woman, a beautiful, loved woman. And she would allow herself to feel that, if only for a little while. After everything Gabriel had done to her, she deserved this little slice of bliss.

Her breasts ached for Gabriel's touch, her sex throbbed with need and her soul...her soul cried for a tender touch, a lover's touch.

They practically ran down the stairs to Gabriel's chamber. He pulled her inside and then turned to bar the door. The massive bed beckoned her, promising untold pleasure in Gabriel's arms.

She closed her eyes and still felt his lips moving over hers. The feel of his thick arousal pressed against her belly had brought a rush of liquid between her thighs.

Warm fingers stroked her neck as he came up behind her, molding his body to hers again. "Jayna," he whispered in her ear as his mouth kissed her skin.

She moved her head to the side as his hot tongue did delicious things to her body. Desire strummed through her, making her forget everything but the man behind her and the need in her body.

"By the gods you're beautiful."

His words, though murmured, sent a bolt of longing through her. Memories of her past began to stir, pushing past the fog of desire.

Nay!

Jayna turned to face Gabriel. His molten silver eyes flared with longing as she ran her hands from the flat planes of his stomach to his muscled chest.

"Make me forget. Please."

His gaze bored into hers as if he were trying to read her soul. A soft smile pulled up one corner of his mouth as his hands cupped either side of her face.

Time seemed to beat to almost a halt. Nothing existed but her and him – and the desire they shared.

His mouth teased her skin with light kisses and soft licks of his tongue. But his hands moved over her body as if she might disappear at any moment.

Yet it wasn't enough for her. For too long she had been alone. For too long she had only memories of Gabriel before he betrayed her. And now, he stood before her as he once was, before she saw him in his true form.

It was too much for her. She desperately needed the past, to feel like the girl she used to be. She needed to forget about betrayals, loss, and revenge.

She needed Gabriel.

With a little shove, she pushed his leather jerkin over his shoulders and he let it drop to the floor. To her surprise, her hands shook as she reached for his dark red tunic. Her fingers scraped his skin as she tugged the tunic higher.

Her breath caught in her throat as Gabriel pulled the tunic over his head and stood before her. She had seen him while he lay wounded, but she hadn't had a chance to really *look* at him as she did now.

He was more magnificent than she remembered.

Her hands rose to move over his sculpted torso, to feel the muscles beneath her hands. Gabriel had always been handsome, but his body had never looked like this. The training and battles he had faced while a Shield had shaped him into a splendid figure of a man.

"My turn." Gabriel's voice was hoarse, as if it pained him to speak.

She was about to ask him what he meant when his hands began to bunch her skirt at her waist. Her heart raced as her gown was drawn over her head and the rest of her underclothes soon followed.

The cool air of the chamber raced across her bare skin, but the heat from Gabriel's gaze warmed her. When his hands reached toward her, she was ready, anxious to feel him against her again. Yet, he didn't take her into his arms. He began to unbraid her hair until it hung in waves around her. She turned and stepped toward the bed when she suddenly found herself in his arms.

"I've wanted to carry you to my bed since the night I

first saw you."

For some reason, Jayna found it difficult to breathe. She became lost in the wonderful silver eyes staring at her. Her surroundings melted away again, leaving only her and Gabriel. And the bed.

Gently he laid her atop the bed and stretched out beside her. Jayna could feel his gaze on her, could feel the desire strumming through him.

And it only quickened her blood.

She squeezed her legs together and nearly cried out from the longing. As much as she wanted his hands on her, Jayna wasn't going to beg. Patience was a virtue she had learned very early in life, though it was being sorely tested now.

He rose up on his knees and straddled her legs. Then, finally, his warm, large hands touched her. Her skin burned as he gripped her hips and began placing kisses along her stomach, stopping to lick her bellybutton.

She squirmed, wanting more. Needing more.

Her hands dug into the covers as his moved up her side to her waist, then higher until he was...almost...touching her breasts.

A moan rushed past her lips as his hands cupped her breasts and massaged them as his mouth continued to follow his hands. When his hot mouth closed over her aching nipple, Jayna's back arched off the bed as pleasure spiked to her core.

The pleasure was intense and all-consuming. She was drowning in it but didn't care. She yearned to throw off her cloak of worries and revenge and just be Jayna, the woman that used to laugh and smile easily.

While his mouth and tongue did delectable things to one breast, his fingers gently pinched her other nipple, sending a cry of satisfaction from her throat. With each flick of his tongue, each tweak of her nipple, spasms of need pulsed in her sex.

"Gabriel," she whispered as she ground her hips against his chest.

His hand left her breast to travel down her side, over her hip to her thigh. His mouth soon followed, leaving a trail of hot kisses and warm breath over her skin, heightening her senses even more.

When he moved her legs apart with his knee, she opened for him, silently giving him her consent that she wanted more. Much more. His hands moved over her legs, touching her as a skilled lover would, a lover that knew just what would leave her trembling and begging for more.

She bit her lip as his fingers traced the line of her inner thigh until he reached her sex. She held her breath, waiting for him to touch her, to bring her some release. But his hands continued on. Again and again he teased her, tormented her with feather light kisses and near touches.

Then, finally, he touched her. Jayna moaned as his tongue flicked across her swollen pearl. With his hot breath tickling her skin, his tongue swirled around her pearl, bringing her to new heights of pleasure. Deep inside she could feel the pressure building like a slow crescendo.

Gabriel had never felt anything so *right* in his life. With each lick, kiss...touch Jayna became more and more familiar to him. He no longer tried to remember the past as he gave in to the desire humming in his veins. All that mattered was Jayna and the pleasure he was giving her.

He didn't question how he knew exactly where to touch her or how to touch her that would drive her wild. Her soft whimpers had become moans, and it wasn't long before cries of pleasure left her delicious lips.

Gabriel could spend eternity loving her body and still it wouldn't be enough. Just holding her, touching her brought him more pleasure than a thousand women. She was special somehow.

He continued to move his tongue over her tiny pearl that had grown hard and swollen. She was near release, but he wasn't ready for her to peak yet. He dipped a finger inside of her to feel her hot, tight sheath, and he couldn't stop the moan that fell from his lips.

His cock yearned to sink into her, and it was all he could do to hold back. Her body responded as if she had been waiting for his touch. He could feel her begin to tighten around his finger, her climax nearly upon her.

Gabriel raised his head to look at her. Her hands were fisted in the blankets at her side, her golden hair spread around her, and her mouth parted slightly as she moaned her pleasure. She was intoxicating to watch.

He added a second finger inside her, stretching her as best he could until he could stand it no more. He removed his fingers and leaned over her, his rod touching the entrance of her sex.

Her beautiful hazel eyes opened, and she smiled up at him. His heart nearly burst from his chest at her smile. He leaned down and took her lips in a fierce kiss as he slowly entered her.

Gentle hands moved to his back and gripped him as he pushed inside of her. When he was fully seated, she wrapped her legs around his waist and Gabriel knew true heaven then, for it was Jayna, the angel in his arms.

He began to move, sliding in and out of her with a tempo she quickly matched. Their desire soon spurred them on as each sought to find their release.

Gabriel was so close that he feared he would spend himself before Jayna reached her climax, but then she suddenly stiffened as her body convulsed around him.

He let go then, giving over to the passion that

consumed his body. As he poured his seed into her, he felt her arms tighten around him.

"Oh, Gabriel," she whispered in his ear.

And then he knew.

Everything.

CHAPTER TWENTY-ONE

Gabriel waited until Jayna was asleep before he rose naked from the bed and walked to the dying fire. He stoked the embers until flames once more rose high in the hearth.

He reached for his pants that had been discarded in their hurry to undress and slipped them on. Then he collapsed in a chair before the fire and faced the truth.

All his memories had returned.

Every last damn one of them.

And they were exactly as he had feared.

He knew why Jayna was at Stone Crest. He knew why she sought revenge. Because of him, because he had betrayed her. He leaned forward and dropped his head into his hands.

But you aren't that man anymore.

Nay, he wasn't, but it didn't absolve him of his sins, especially not the ones toward Jayna.

Nothing will ever right the wrong done to her. Nothing.

He sighed and raised his gaze to the dancing flames before him. All the answers he had sought he now had. He knew who he was, where he came from, and if he had left someone behind. That someone had been Jayna.

"Sweet Jayna," he murmured.

And now that he had his memories back, he wanted them gone. He wanted to pretend he didn't know he was such a monster, a betrayer of lovers...a murderer.

To think he had thought about urging Jayna to give up her revenge after they had made love. In truth, he wanted her to carry out her revenge. It was what he deserved. He just hoped she waited until after the Great Evil was defeated, for the Shields would need him.

The Shields. Aimery.

What was he to tell them? He knew if he told them the truth, there was a possibility they would see him for what he had become and not what he once was. But then again, they could very well consider him a part of the evil and kill him on the spot. And they needed him.

So he would keep silent.

And do his best to stay away from the Great Evil. It was amazing Hugh and the others hadn't figured out why the evil was after him, but he prayed they stayed ignorant of the facts, for he didn't think he could face the men he called family if they knew all he had done.

His head snapped up as he heard movement behind him. He rose and walked to stand beside the bed. Jayna slept peacefully, her beautiful lips slightly parted and her chest rising and falling slowly. Her blonde locks were spread around her like a golden crown.

She was beauty personified. The one woman who had been able to capture his heart. The only woman he had ever loved. A smile pulled at his lips as he recalled the joy they had shared, the simple pleasure of being together.

The smile soon faded, however, when he remembered her beautiful hazel eyes growing wide with realization, then the hatred that shown in them as she looked upon what his betrayal had done.

If he could take it all back he would. But there was no changing the past. Even though the Fae had taught them how to shift through time, Gabriel wasn't fool enough to try and change his past. The consequences for his actions would be more severe than he was paying now.

"Jayna. My sweet Jayna," he whispered as he ran a finger down her smooth cheek.

He turned on his heel and quickly finished dressing before he walked from his chamber. He stopped just short of reaching the great hall. His emotions were all mucked up, and his worries of his fellow Shields discovering the depth of his treachery made him want to return to his chamber.

But he had played the coward long enough.

Gabriel took a deep breath and was about to continue down the stairs when he heard a voice behind him. He turned and found Nicole descending the stairs.

"I haven't seen you all day," she said, her Scottish accent thick as she looked him over.

Gabriel swallowed and gave a swift nod. "Aye. We've been busy."

She laughed. "You mean you've been busy trying to discern just how much Jayna has lied to us. Have you discovered anything?"

For a long moment, Gabriel simply stared at her. The urge to tell someone of his deeds, of his awful past, was great. His shoulders grew heavy as his burdened settled upon him. "I've learned a little," he finally answered.

"Gabriel," she said and took a step closer to him, her gaze searching his. "What is it? What's wrong."

He forced a smile. "Do not worry over me, Nicole. It's just the strain of finishing this mission."

Her violet eyes grew sad. "We all grow worried. I know

the other Shields are trying to be patient with us, and we are trying the best we can to figure out just what we are supposed to do."

Gabriel held up his hand for her to stop. "There is no need for you to explain to me," he said softly. "When the time comes, I've faith the Chosen will know exactly what to do to destroy the Great Evil."

A slow smile spread over her face. "You're a very kind man, Gabriel. I hope you find the answers to your past. Maybe then you'll find peace."

He watched her walk away knowing that peace would only be his when his final breath left his body.

~ ~ ~

Aimery was more than frustrated as he arrived at *Cranon Megeg*. The city was small compared to most in the Realm of the Fae, but very influential people made their homes in the quiet city.

A whip of cool air passed over him. He looked to the mountains surrounding the picturesque city.

Cranon Megeg was in the northern mountains where many dragons made their homes. It was the chosen place of the white dragons.

"My lord."

Aimery turned and found a dozen of his soldiers standing behind him waiting for orders. He sighed. "Begin to question everyone. I want as many details of who killed the dragon as we can get."

The troops swiftly began carrying out their orders. Aimery raised his hand and motioned for the others to take their places. Some would guard each entrance to the city while others would scout the perimeter for signs of where the murderer had entered and left. The rest followed him to the dragon.

Aimery could hardly believe his eyes as he stared at the fallen dragon on the outskirts of *Cranon Megeg*. Even in death, the beautiful white dragon was a spectacle to behold. It was one of the largest dragons, as well as the purest. It held more magic inside of it than an entire city of Fae. The death of a white dragon did not bode well for the magic of the Fae realm.

Slowly, Aimery walked around the enormous dragon. One wing had been totally ripped off while the other was bent at an odd angel. He looked at the ground and noted how deep the groove was where the dragon came to lay.

"He was killed mid-flight," he said sadly to himself.

Aimery continued around the dragon until he stood looking at the animal's underside. It was too heavy for them to roll it on its side to see what weapon was used to bring it down, and Aimery didn't wish to disturb the dragon any more than he had to.

He knelt by the dragon's great head and bowed his own. They had lost so many dragons recently, that any more could greatly affect the Fae's lives.

The boots of a soldier stopped near him. Aimery took a deep breath and turned to him. "Do you have news, lieutenant?"

"Aye, my lord."

"Well? Tell me you found someone who saw the murderer?"

"We did, my lord."

Aimery sighed, but before he could ask the soldier who it was a woman burst through the small crowd and soldiers. She pointed a finger at him, her blue eyes blazing with fury.

"You want to know who killed the dragon?" she shouted. "It was him. Aimery killed the dragon."

Aimery stepped back he was so taken aback by her

words. "I would never."

"I saw you," she screamed. "I saw you with my own eyes."

With his heart pounding in his chest, Aimery moved and placed his hand on the dragon's forehead and closed his eyes. He concentrated all his magic toward the dragon.

Then, slowly an image of the dragon flying through the air flashed in his mind. It was as if he saw through the dragon's eyes, and through them he saw himself standing not twenty paces away with an arrow aimed at the dragon.

Aimery yanked his hand away and stumbled back. He knew he didn't do it, but he also realized he couldn't convince the growing crowd of that either.

His entire body jerked as he heard Hugh call out to him. For a moment he almost left, but he knew to go to Hugh now would make him look guilty. And he had to prove his innocence.

"Theron," he called silently. *"Theron, I need you now."*

Almost instantly the Fae king stood by his side. "What is it? Did you find who killed the dragon?"

Aimery slowly raised his gaze to his king. "I'm being told I killed it."

"What?" Theron asked softly. He licked his lips and looked around him. "Aimery, what is going on?"

Aimery stepped aside and motioned to the dragon. "See for yourself."

Theron hesitated but an instant before he moved to the dragon and placed his hand on its forehead. His face contorted with pain, then he dropped his hand and raised his gaze to Aimery.

"I didn't do it," Aimery said before Theron could speak. "I know what you saw for I saw it myself, but I tell you honestly, it wasn't me."

The crowd began to grow restless and the woman who

accused Aimery walked nearer. "What are you going to do King Theron? Killing a dragon is punishable by death."

Soon the entire crowd called for Aimery's death. He sighed and turned to Theron. His king and the man he had called friend for centuries wouldn't meet his eye.

"Take me before they kill me now," he said to Theron. "I know I didn't do it, but I cannot prove that if I'm dead."

Theron glanced at him before he motioned for the soldiers to surround Aimery. Then he turned and faced the crowd. "Thank you all for aiding us in finding the killer of the white dragon. Aimery will be punished according to our law."

All Aimery could think about was the Shields. They would need him soon now. He could leave and go to them, but it would only make matters worse on his realm. He had no choice but to return to *Caer Rhoemyr* with Theron.

CHAPTER TWENTY-TWO

Jayna slowly came awake, stretching beneath the blankets. She smiled and rolled over to search for Gabriel, only to find she was alone in the bed.

She gripped the blankets to her chest and sat up as she searched the chamber. The fire popped in the hearth, but other than her breathing, there was no sound in the chamber. She was alone.

At first she found she was disappointed to know Gabriel had left, but in the end she realized it was probably for the best. Memories of their lovemaking flooded her.

It had been better than she remembered, more sensual, more emotional...more everything.

He had brought her body to life with the simplest of touches, and for a man who didn't remember her, his body had known her. He had known how to touch her, how to love her.

Jayna sighed. It would be so easy to forget the past, forget the revenge and find a new life with the new Gabriel. But eventually, he would regain his memory. Then what? Would he continue to be the man he had become? Or would he revert to the betrayer?

It wasn't a chance she could take. And her family needed to be avenged. She *needed* retribution.

She still couldn't believe how easy she had fallen into his arms. She had told herself it was because she needed to seduce him, but the truth was she needed him.

And she hated herself for it.

She threw off the covers and jumped from the bed to hurry and dress. If she were lucky, she could return to the tower and claim her dagger she had hidden there.

As quickly as she could she dressed and stuffed her feet in her shoes. Her hair would have to wait until she returned to her chamber, but she doubted she would see anyone before then.

She inched open Gabriel's door and peered into the hallway. When she didn't see anyone, she slipped out of the chamber and closed the door behind her then she raced down the hall to the stairs that would take her up to the tower.

With her skirts in her hand, she ran up the stairs, her breath coming faster with each step until her sides ached and her lungs burned. But she didn't stop until she reached the tower.

They had left the door open in their haste, which allowed her time to see if anyone was inside before she walked through the threshold.

She let out a breath of relief when she spotted her dagger on the table. There hadn't been another place to put it, and Gabriel had been too intent on her face to realize she had removed a weapon to lie in plain sight in front of him.

Jayna rushed to the table and swiftly put the dagger up her sleeve. She sighed and turned to find Val in the doorway.

"My lord," she said as she tried to figure out a way around him without causing suspicion.

"I followed you up here hoping to have a quiet word with you."

She had always thought Val a friendly sort, but she realized she had been wrong. She saw the steel in his pale green gaze. He was first and foremost a warrior, and she would be good to remember that.

"About what?" she asked, amazed her voice didn't shake.

He glanced at the floor. "Gabriel."

Her curiosity was piqued now. Of all the things she expected, Gabriel wasn't one of them. "What about him?"

"Don't hurt him."

She opened her mouth, but no sound came out she was so shocked. "Wh...what?"

"I know he's told you much of his life as a Shield as well as some of his past, at least what he can remember. The Shields, well, we're a ragged group of men, but we are all the family some of us have."

"You care very deeply for him."

Val nodded. "Gabriel has saved each of us. He would gladly give up his life for any of us. All of us would like nothing more than to give him the memories he has lost."

"What if those memories would only make his life worse?"

Val narrowed his pale green eyes at her. "Do you know something?"

Jayna shrugged. She liked the Roman, and knew he was only trying to help a friend. "I'm merely asking a question I wonder if any of you have considered. Sometimes it is best if we can forget the past."

"Yet it is the past that shapes us, my lady."

She smiled. "Ah, I see Gabriel told you of my

confession."

"We all knew it to be a lie." He walked farther into the tower until only the table separated them. "You say that it is best to sometimes forget the past. There were times I prayed that I could forget the memories that haunted me. Do you know why I stopped begging for that?"

Jayna shook her head. The tower seemed to shrink as Val dominated the chamber.

"I never told any of the Shields of my past. Not a single one of them knew of the nightmares that haunted me, of the pain I suffered every day. It wasn't until Gabriel and I were in Scotland searching for Nicole, that I had no choice but to tell Gabriel my secrets."

"Why did you have to tell him?"

Val chuckled, his hands behind his back. "History was about to repeat itself, you see. I had vowed to protect Nicole with my very life. The Great Evil was using my past and my sins to weaken me. And it worked."

"Yet you live."

"Only because of Gabriel. He didn't bat an eye when I told him of my past and the sins I carried. He simply told me I couldn't carry the weight of the dead around forever."

The weight of the dead. Aye, she had carried the weight of the dead for some time now. How much longer could she continue?

"Each of us Shields came to the group with specialties. Some of us are immortal, some with great battle skills, and then there was Gabriel. A warrior who could heal all but the dead. I've seen him heal wounds I knew would kill. How he does it, none of us knows. He doesn't even know."

"Why are you telling me this?"

Val sighed. "Gabriel has been alone for a very long time. I see how he looks at you. Whether you know it or not, you have the power to break him as few have."

Jayna swallowed and tried to lick her dry lips. "I am merely a traveler, my lord."

"You are far more than that. I ask you, on behalf of the Shields, do not trifle with Gabriel's heart. He deserves a strong woman, and if you aren't it, leave him be."

With that, he turned on his heel and left the tower. Jayna stared at the doorway long after Val had departed, yet she didn't move. His words had touched her.

At one time, she felt just as Val did toward Gabriel. She would have given her life for him had he but asked.

But what the Shields are doing is worthy. Even you know that despite being aligned with the Great Evil. How can you, in good conscious kill Gabriel, which would inadvertently destroy the Shields?

In one answer, she couldn't.

She had seen what evil could do to a realm, and she had no desire to see another evil take over another realm. But what to do? Wait until after the Great Evil was defeated?

He would never allow that.

Or would he? He hadn't contacted her once she had walked inside Stone Crest's walls. If she stayed within she would be safe from him.

Her heart squeezed painfully as she recalled the look in Gabriel's eyes when he had filled her. She wiped away a tear the fell upon her cheek.

When had things become so complicated? And how was she going to get out of this mess?

Jayna walked to the window of the tower and looked over the land of Stone Crest covered thick with snow. The storm continued to howl keeping both man and beast inside.

It kept the evil at bay for a moment longer.

~ ~ ~

Gabriel felt the night fall around him like a blanket of darkness. He had no need to look out the windows into the storm to see that the moon had risen, he knew it just as he knew the Great Evil crept around the castle.

None of the Shields had suspected anything when he had walked into the great hall. He had told them of Jayna's confession of lying of being a commoner, of which none of them was surprised.

But the rest...the rest he kept to himself.

Now, he sat with a mug of ale in his hand staring into the fire of the hearth. Its flames danced around the popping wood, yet he didn't see any of it.

All he saw was the glow of Jayna's skin as his hands moved over her, loving her, kissing her, learning her again. He could still feel the tremors of her climax.

He closed his eyes and relived the moment he had entered her, her tight sheath surrounding him, opening for him. And her hazel eyes watching him, silently begging him to take her.

When his cock began to grow hard, Gabriel opened his eyes and slumped lower in his chair. Out of the corner of his eye he saw Val and Nicole watching him. He briefly met their gaze before looking at Roderick and Elle, Hugh and Mina, and Cole and Shannon. All of them watched him.

"Do I have horns growing out of my skull?" he asked harshly. "Or hooves for feet?"

Val chuckled. "Nay."

"Then why do you all watch me as a hawk watches a mouse?"

Hugh was the first to speak. "Because we can see something bothers you."

Gabriel rose to his feet. "You want to know what bothers me? I'll tell you. I seduced a woman because we needed information."

"Did you both enjoy it?" Shannon asked.

Gabriel swung his gaze to the brunette sitting on Cole's lap. "Aye, if it's any of your concern."

She smiled. "What are you more angry with, Gabriel? The fact that we asked you to seduce Jayna, or that you wanted to seduce her?"

For a moment, all he could do was stare at her before he slumped back into his chair. "Both. Equally."

"Has seducing her changed things for you?" Roderick asked.

Gabriel ran a hand down his face. "A lot of things have changed."

He desperately needed to change the subject before they asked the right question and he was forced to give them answers he wasn't ready for. He looked to the women. "Did you make any progress today?"

Mina shook her head. "None. I don't know what we're doing wrong. None of us can remember what we are supposed to do."

"Maybe we aren't supposed to know until its time." All eyes turned to Elle who sat twiddling her thumbs. She shrugged and gave a small smile. "It's what I'm hoping for at least."

Gabriel nodded. "You might have the right of it."

"I called to Aimery today," Hugh said into the silence. He looked to each of his men. "He never responded."

"Aimery always comes," Val argued.

Hugh shrugged. "He didn't this time. I'm not sure what it means, though I suspect something must have kept him from coming here."

"But what?" Roderick asked.

"Only Aimery knows," Hugh responded.

Gabriel leaned forward so that his elbows rested on his knees and blew out a breath. Too many things were going wrong. The feeling in his gut wasn't a good one, and he feared that all their fighting had been for naught.

Cole rose to his feet and paced in front of the giant hearth. "Call for him again, Hugh. Hell, why don't we all call for him?"

Together, the Shields called for Aimery. Heartbeats later the Fae commander still didn't appear.

"Something has happened," Roderick said tightly. "Aimery would never leave us like this."

Hugh shook his head, his face weary. "Nay, he would not. Yet, we cannot find the answers since none of us can venture into the Fae realm without aid."

"We can do this," Gabriel said as he set his empty goblet on a table and stood. "We've battled countless creatures, each stronger than the last. We can do this."

He met Hugh's gaze, praying that Hugh would not let his hope dwindle.

Hugh gave a brief nod as he too gained his feet. "We've no other choice but to go it alone. The worst of the storm should pass tonight. Cole, you and Roderick will ride out and see if you can discover if the Fae are still guarding Stone Crest."

"And if they've left?" Roderick asked.

"We'll deal with that as well," Hugh said. "Gabriel is right, we can do this."

Cole crossed his arms over his chest and rocked back on his heels. "We're sealing our doom, Hugh."

Hugh turned and looked at Cole. "Aye, but we all knew that when we joined the Shields."

"You still have us," Mina said as she stood and took Hugh's hand. "The Chosen haven't been hunted for nothing. The Evil knows we can defeat him."

Gabriel saw the spark of interest flare in the other Shields' eyes. They were all ready for a battle.

CHAPTER TWENTY-THREE

"What in the name of all that is magical is going on?" Rufina demanded as she walked into the chamber where her husband held Aimery.

Neither man spoke, so Rufina walked to Theron and glared at him. "What is this nonsense that I hear of you holding Aimery prisoner to be executed?"

Theron wouldn't meet her eyes as he turned away. "He killed a white dragon."

Rufina turned to Aimery who stood in the middle of the chamber. The look of utter despair in Aimery's eyes squeezed her heart. She walked to the Fae commander and saw that her husband had bound him, as well.

"Aimery, tell me what happened?" she urged.

His head bowed slightly. "My queen, it appears as though I was the one that killed the dragon."

"I don't believe it."

Aimery's head jerked up, and he searched her eyes. "Why?"

She smiled then and rubbed her hand over her swollen stomach that held the future heir to the throne. "We have known each other for countless centuries, my friend. I know you would sooner rip out your own heart than harm a dragon."

A small smile of thanks pulled at Aimery's lips.

Rufina turned to her husband then. By his rigid posture and refusal to look her in the eye, she knew he was having a difficult time. With a deep breath, she moved to him and placed her head upon his shoulder.

"Talk to me, my love."

"I don't know what to say," he said, his voice rough with emotion.

"What are you thinking?"

"I'm thinking that I may very well have to kill my closest friend."

Rufina lifted her head and turned Theron to face her. "Nay. Aimery says he didn't do it, and I believe him."

"I wish I could believe him as well, but I saw it." His blue eyes held such anguish that, for a moment, she couldn't breath.

"You...saw it? You looked into the dragon?"

He nodded solemnly. She clasped her hands in front of her as her mind sorted out the details. It was a great risk looking into a dragon's last thoughts. It had been known to kill or drive people insane. Only in dire circumstances did anyone dare look.

She swiveled her head to Aimery. "Did you look?"

He nodded gravely.

"Dragon's breath," she cursed as she began to pace the small chamber. "Aimery, for the love of magic, why didn't you leave?"

"Would it not have labeled me a murderer if I had?"

"Aren't you labeled that anyway?" she retorted and regretted it instantly. "You cannot be here. The Shields need you."

"I know. They have been calling to me," he said as he tested the invisible bonds on his wrists.

Theron spun around and stalked to Aimery. "Why haven't you told me before now?"

"You didn't ask," Aimery said between clenched teeth.

"Enough," Rufina said as she stepped between the two of them. "Aimery, tell me what happened?"

He sighed long and low. "I arrived and sent troops to speak to the people while I went to inspect the dragon. I could tell by the way it landed and its torn wings that it had been killed in mid-flight. I got no farther before a woman rushed out and said she had seen me kill it. No one asked questions after that as they began to demand my death. I knew I didn't do it, but I needed to see what the dragon had seen."

"So you looked into its thoughts," Rufina supplied.

"Aye. It was me who stood there with an arrow notched and waiting. I knew then that I needed Theron."

"So he called to me," Theron said. "I arrived immediately to find a growing crowd around Aimery and the dragon. When he told me they said he did it, I checked the dragon myself and saw just as he had. It was Aimery."

Rufina rubbed her temples as her head began to ache. "There is something afoot here. What amazes me is that neither of you sees it."

"I know what I saw," Theron shouted. "How do you think I feel knowing the man who has been like a brother to me, who leads the Fae army, killed a dragon?"

"I didn't kill it," Aimery said, though his voice held no conviction.

Rufina took Theron's hand and led him from the chamber. She didn't stop until she reached their bedchamber, then she whirled on him as her anger bubbled up.

"What has gotten into you? That's Aimery back there."

Theron sank onto their bed and dropped his head into his hands. "You aren't telling me anything I don't already know. I've been trying to figure out how the dragon was killed."

That stopped Rufina in her tracks. She watched as her husband raised his head, his eyes heavy with worry. "You don't think he did it."

"Nay. At least, our Aimery didn't do it. Whether that's our Aimery in there or not, I have no idea and I can't allow myself to think it might be our Aimery."

"So you're holding him until you can discern who is who."

"Exactly." He rose and walked to the table near the door to pour himself a glass of Fae wine. "I just pray if that is our Aimery I've bound that he'll forgive me."

Rufina walked to her husband and wound her hands around him as she pressed herself against his back. "I have no doubt he will forgive you. You are thinking of him, and our Aimery will realize that."

"Which brings me to my next thought," he said softly. "No Fae, or friend of ours, would dare to kill a dragon."

Rufina dropped her arms as Theron turned towards her. "You think evil broke through your walls?"

"I think something used one of our doorways."

"If it was evil we would have been alerted, Theron. You know as well as I that anytime our doorways are used, we are aware of it."

"Ah, yes, the doorways we are aware of. But then again, as a Fae, we are able to go from realm to realm without the doorways. The doorways are for humans or others that don't have magic."

The full force of what Theron said shot through Rufina turning her blood to ice. "By all that's magical, Theron.

What are we to do? If they kill any more dragons, especially white dragons, then our magic could suffer greatly."

"I know," he said as he took her hand and led her to the bed. He sat and pulled her down beside him. "I don't think they'll come to kill another dragon. If my hunch is right, this has something to do with the Great Evil. He wants Aimery away from the Shields."

Understanding dawned within Rufina. "What better way to do that than to have the Fae imprison Aimery?"

Rufina felt the icy fingers of defeat began to crawl towards her. "It's going to be very difficult to triumph over the evil when we have our boundaries but he doesn't."

For the first time that afternoon, Theron smiled. "We have boundaries, but the Shields do not."

~ ~ ~

Jayna, coward that she was, chose to have her dinner in her chamber. She didn't think she could face Gabriel, at least not yet. Though part of her wondered if he would come to her that night, if his body would yearn for her as hers yearned for him.

"I'm such a fool," she murmured as she pushed her food around her trencher.

She had only been at Stone Crest a short time, but she had quickly come to like the camaraderie and laughter at mealtime. She had eaten alone for so long that it had become a habit for her, one that she hated to the very depths of her bones.

A knock sounded at her door. Figuring it to be a servant come to retrieve the food, she bid them enter, and turned to find Gabriel walking toward her.

"Are you feeling well?" he asked as he leaned against the wall by her door.

She shrugged. In truth, she wasn't feeling well at all, but none of his herbs could cure what ailed her. "Fine."

"Will you tell me why you are hiding in your chamber? Is it me? If it is, then I'll remove myself from the dais so you can enjoy your meals with the others."

She gaped at him. How had he known how much she loved eating with the others? She turned back to the fire. "It isn't you. I just needed to be alone."

"I'm sorry I had to leave you this afternoon." His words, spoken softly touched her heart.

"I know."

"Tell me what bothers you," he urged.

Jayna watched as he took the seat opposite her. Gabriel had always been a good listener. How many times had she come to him with a problem, large or small, and he had always helped her see a solution? She missed having that bond with someone. She missed sharing her troubles with him.

She licked her lips and decided to tell him part of it. Maybe that would help her out of the depression she was sinking in.

"Being at Stone Crest makes me remember my family and friends. It brings to mind just how much was taken from me."

Was it her imagination or had something like pain flashed in Gabriel's silver depths? She decided it must have been a flash from the fire, and thought no more about it.

"Can you never return to them?" he asked.

She shook her head. "There is nothing left to return to. All was destroyed."

"And you know who did it?"

The words were spoken as a question, his tone even, but by the way he gripped the arms of the chair, she knew better. "I do."

"Do you know why they destroyed your home?"

"Does it really matter?" she countered. "Innocents were killed. Children. Entire families. Someone must pay for this."

He nodded and turned his gaze to the fire. "Aye, someone must pay."

She looked at her food unsure of what to say after his comment. It was almost like it saddened him.

"Have you eaten?" she asked.

He shook his head. "I find I do not crave any food at the moment." His gaze swung to her. "My appetite is for something else entirely."

All the moisture left her mouth to pool between her legs at his words. There was no mistaking what he meant, no mistaking the heat in his silver depths, no mistaking the bulge in his pants.

"It seems my appetite is the same as yours," she found herself saying.

Suddenly, Gabriel rose and held out his hand. He pulled her up against him and swept his hands through her hair. "What is it about you that lures me so? Do you hold some kind of magic?" he teased.

"No magic," she answered as her hands moved over his sculpted chest and shoulders. "Only my body."

"It's enough," he said just before his mouth claimed hers in a kiss that scorched her very soul. The kiss was as demanding as it was gentle, sensual as it was arousing. His lips and tongue knew just how much to give...and how much to take.

He left her body pulsing with desire and weak with need. When she didn't think she could stand on her own feet another moment, he broke the kiss and spun her around so that her back was to him. With one arm around her waist and the other holding her hair away from her neck, he proceeded to nip, lick, and kiss the sensitive skin on her neck.

Chills raced over her skin, heightening her desire. She arched her back, pushing her bottom against his arousal, and heard him groan.

"By the gods, Jayna, you'll make me spill my seed now," he moaned against her skin.

Urgency filled both of them as they scrambled to remove their clothes. Jayna felt her blood heat as she could sense Gabriel's gaze on her as she yanked off her gown and underclothes. Her thick wool stockings and shoes flew off, and she turned to find Gabriel in all his naked glory staring at her.

She moved to him and ran her hands all over his body kissing his chest and flicking her tongue over his nipples. Her hands drifted lower and gently ran along the length of his rod. She heard his intake of breath and smiled against his skin.

Slowly, she kissed her way down his chest to his stomach to his hips. She fell to her knees as her hands moved around to trace over his taut bottom. His hands buried themselves in her hair, and when her hands cupped his sac he whispered her name as his fingers tightened in her hair.

The feel of his sac in her hand made her sex pulse hungrily. Her gaze rose to Gabriel's to find him watching her. She kept her gaze locked with his as she took his rod in her hand and ran her tongue around its thick head.

His head dropped back as a low moan rushed from his mouth. Jayna closed her eyes as she took the tip of him in her mouth, loving how hot, hard, and smooth he was, almost like velvet. She had never been able to get enough of Gabriel, and even after he had committed such grave crimes against her, her body still yearned for him.

"Enough. I'll spill," he cried as he pulled from her mouth then carried her to the bed.

Before she could wrap her arms around him, he turned her onto her stomach and began to place kisses along her back, his hands roaming everywhere, touching every inch of her.

Her breasts swelled as his hands grazed her nipples. She cried out and arched against him. Instantly, his hand closed over a breast, gently massaging it. His fingers tweaked and pulled against her nipple, sending flames of pleasure to her throbbing sex.

His hands left her breasts, and she bit her lip to keep from crying out as his finger delved into the heat of her.

"Open for me," he bade, and immediately she opened her legs.

He murmured something that she didn't hear, but she didn't care, his hands were almost on her sex, almost touching her pearl. She tensed, waiting for him to touch her, to give her the release she so desperately needed.

But he didn't. Instead, he lifted her hips in the air and settled himself behind her. The tip of his rod moved over her bottom and down the slit to her sex, leaving a trail of liquid in its wake.

Jayna was nearly delirious with need. Her sex clenched urgently, her pleasure building with each heartbeat. "Please, Gabriel."

"Not yet," he whispered as the tip of his rod dipped into her sex.

She tried to move back against him, but he pulled out too quickly. He reached around and found her nipples, gently pulling and tweaking them as he rubbed his rod against her bottom.

Jayna buried her face in the blankets while Gabriel's rod continued to tease her and his finger stroked her pearl. She rotated her hips against him, urging him to take her now. Yet, he continued his assault on her body, alternating fast, hurried strokes over her pearl to slow swirls of his finger.

It left her body shaking with need. Just when she didn't think she could stand it a moment longer, his hands gripped her hips as his rod filled her. His fullness made her catch her breath, and when he began to slowly move within her, Jayna could feel her climax building swiftly.

But he didn't let her find a tempo. He would stop and start at will, teasing her even more and prolonging her pleasure until it was almost unbearable.

One hand was unrelenting in its exploration of her body. It would dip down and tease her pearl or tweak her nipple, or, as it was now, playing with her bottom. He would run the finger along her spine, down her lower back to the slit in between the cheeks of her bottom, each time, taking longer and longer on her bottom.

Jayna was delirious with need. Her body had never experienced anything so lovely, so devastating, and she feared it might end just as much as she feared it might never end.

Suddenly, Gabriel let out a low growl and began to move within her, his thick cock thrusting faster with each glorious stroke. Jayna was near to climax as he continued to pump into her, and in the next heartbeat, the orgasm claimed her. Ripples of pleasure pulsed within her, building and building until she thought it would never end.

Dimly she felt Gabriel grip her and thrust deeply as he howled her name, spilling his seed into her. Something deep and profound wrapped around them, cocooning them in a place meant only for them.

With her body sated, Jayna found she could hardly keep her eyes open. She didn't wish to sleep, though, she wanted more of Gabriel. She wanted to see his molten silver eyes darken, to run her fingers through his brown hair...to feel his rod in her mouth again.

Next time, next time she would bring him to release with her mouth, she thought as she drifted off to sleep.

CHAPTER TWENTY-FOUR

Gabriel couldn't wipe the smile from his face. To think, just a few moments ago he had thought the world was crashing around him, but then he had tasted Jayna's body and all seemed right again.

He turned and looked at her. She had fallen asleep with a smile. The arrogant male in him rose up, proud of his skills. But he knew it was more than that. He and Jayna were connected in ways most people would never understand, and in truth, there were times he didn't understand it. It was just one of the mistakes he had made.

As gently as he could, he rolled her onto her back so she wouldn't get a crick in her neck. He pulled the blankets from underneath her and covered them.

His mind began to drift to his memories, of a place of spectacular beauty, of unimaginable peace. A place he had known instantly was where he belonged. A place that was now gone thanks to him.

He recalled days of him and Jayna lolling about naked on the grassy hills overlooking the river. Many days they had spent exploring each other's bodies in the fresh, clear waters of the river.

One of the games they had played was how quickly he could catch her before she reached the water. And when he had caught her he had kissed her lips and her left wrist.

Left wrist.

There had been a reason he had kissed that wrist, but try as he might, he couldn't remember anything about it, just that he had done it.

He reached over and lifted her left hand in his. He studied her skin, but there was nothing there, no mole, no birthmark, nothing. But he had known for sure there had been something he had kissed.

His thumb ran back and forth over the skin as he struggled to remember. It was the one place he kissed even in public. It had special meaning to him, and the symbol meant something to her.

Symbol.

Gabriel froze. It couldn't be, he thought to himself. He looked closer and just faintly made out a mark, and then he knew for certain.

"By the gods," he whispered.

And before his eyes, the mark grew darker, as if some invisible shield had been placed over it was now gone.

"The fifth Chosen. Jayna is the fifth Chosen." He couldn't believe it. It didn't make sense, but then not much to do with the Great Evil made sense.

He gently shook her. "Jayna, you must wake. Jayna."

"Aye," she murmured sleepily. "What is it, Gabriel?"

"Open your eyes."

He knew he sounded worried and more forceful than he intended, but it was of great importance that he spoke to her about the symbol.

Jayna opened her eyes and studied him. "What?"

"Do you have a mark on you, a symbol?"

She went to nod then stopped. Her brow furrowed. "I...I don't know."

"You almost said you did, didn't you?"

She grinned. "Aye. Odd isn't it? You would think I would know my own body."

"Then what is this?" he asked and held up her wrist.

Her eyes grew round and her lips parted as she looked at the mark. "It's the same mark that is on Mina and the others."

"Aye."

"What is it doing on me?"

"I was hoping you could tell me that."

She shook her head. "I don't have any memory of it."

But Gabriel knew otherwise. Somehow the Great Evil had managed to hide it, and in doing so had managed to erase the knowledge of it from Jayna's mind.

"You're scaring me," Jayna said softly.

Gabrielle gathered her in his arms. "I don't mean to. This find though, it's of utmost importance to the Shields."

"I know."

But he could tell by the way her voice shook that she wanted no part in any of it. He wanted to ask her how she had really come to be at Stone Crest. A part of him feared that she was somehow connected to the Great Evil. Yet, the coward in him wasn't ready for her to know he had regained his memory.

What they had now, it was almost what they had shared before he had betrayed her. It was a part of his past that was good and pure, and he didn't wish to destroy the fragile bond they had forged.

Though, he wasn't dim-witted. He knew there was a great chance she had allowed him to seduce her so she could exact her revenge. It was what he would do.

He leaned back and held her head between his hands.

"Like it or not, you are now in the thick of this. You are no longer an innocent bystander."

"I cannot help them," she whispered.

"You can. The more Chosen we have, the quicker the Great Evil can be destroyed. Countless realms will be released from his hold and countless more will never know the fear and devastation that follows him. Please."

Her beautiful hazel gaze searched his until she let out a small sigh. "All right."

Gabriel closed his eyes tight as he hugged her to his chest. He knew his grip was tighter than needed, but he hadn't wanted to force her to help them.

He released her and jumped from the bed. "I thought this time we would be allowed to spend several hours loving each other, but we must seek the others."

Jayna left the bed more leisurely. Her movements were measured as if she already regretted agreeing to help them. He watched her out of the corner of his eyes as he hurriedly dressed. As he strapped on his sword, he turned to face her.

She stood looking down at her wrist, her fingers lightly running over the mark.

He walked to her and knelt before her where he picked up one of her wool stockings and began to pull it over her foot.

"Gabriel," she whispered, her voice low and seductive. Gently, she took her foot from his hands and smiled. "You do not need to dress me."

"I know," he said as he gained his feet. "I can't take the doubt from your mind, but I can vow to protect you with my life."

Her gaze lowered, as if his words pained her somehow. And he imagined that they did. Why should she believe him? Even though he wasn't the same man who had betrayed her, the fact was that he hadn't earned her trust yet.

She gave him a small smile, quickly pulled on her woolen hose and slid her feet into her shoes. "I'm ready," she said before grabbing a pale yellow ribbon that matched her dress to tie back her hair.

Gabriel liked it flowing around her, but he knew how she hated to have her hair in her way. He smiled despite himself as a memory of them swimming and her hair coming free of the braid to get in her eyes. She was magnificent when she was angry and her eyes blazed.

He walked her into the great hall where the meal had already been cleaned and put away. He found the others before the fire, staring into its red orange flames as if seeking answers.

The closer they walked to the small group, the more he felt Jayna shake. "All will be well," he whispered in her ear.

"Nothing will be well," she retorted.

Before he could question her, she looked into his eyes and shook her head. "Leave it. Please."

He nodded reluctantly. There was something in her tone, something that told him if she helped the Shields, she was forfeiting her life. Instinctively he thought of a connection between her and the evil, but he couldn't help her until he knew for sure. And if he couldn't outright ask her, he would have to do it in other ways.

"Jayna," Elle cried out happily as they approached. "Are you feeling better?"

Gabriel watched as Jayna straightened her spine and nodded.

"I've found something," he said as he pulled Jayna into the center of their semi-circle. He glanced at her and noticed that though she still trembled, outwardly, she looked like the princess she was.

"Well," Cole prompted.

Gabriel took a deep breath to tell them, but before he could get the words out, Jayna spoke.

"It seems as though I'm one of you," she said and raised her hand where her left wrist faced them.

There was a collective gasp before Elle jumped up and rushed to engulf Jayna in a hug. "I'm ever so glad," Elle said with a bright smile.

Jayna wished she could share in Elle's joy, but, in fact, she had most certainly sealed her doom. The Great Evil must have wiped her memory of the mark when he hid the mark from her. Though he hadn't asked her to side with him, she had no doubt once he realized she knew of the symbol he would demand that she align to the side of evil.

Beside her, Gabriel stood as still as a statue. His vow to protect her should have had no effect on her, yet it had. Greatly. She glanced at him to find him watching her.

She took a deep breath and turned to Hugh and the questions she prayed she could answer without lying.

Hugh's dark gaze moved from her to Gabriel. "When did you find the mark?"

"Just this night," Gabriel answered. "We came down as soon as I realized what it was."

Hugh nodded, seemingly satisfied. His gaze returned to Jayna. "I assumed you knew of the symbol on Mina and the others."

"I did."

"Then how come you didn't announce your mark?"

She swallowed. "Because I didn't know I had it." She chewed her lip, wondering what the next question was. She was still unsure how Gabriel had known about it, but she was too afraid to ask him.

Hugh rose to his feet and circled her. "I find it odd that you didn't know of the mark on your wrist."

She locked gazes with him. "I had forgotten about it."

"She's not lying," Gabriel interrupted before Hugh could speak. "I think the Great Evil had a part in hiding the symbol."

Val stood and walked to them. He looked down at her wrist, then at Gabriel. "How so?"

Gabriel shrugged his massive shoulders. "The skin looked...different, changed almost. I couldn't make out what was on her skin, but I knew it was something."

"He asked me if I had any kind of mark," Jayna added. "I was about to tell him aye when something told me to say nay."

Gabriel nodded. "I knew then something had been done to her. So I kept prying until she remembered. When she remembered, it was revealed."

Hugh sighed and sunk into his chair. Jayna watched as the others simply stared at her as they tried to digest the story.

"As odd as it sounds, it is the truth."

"We know," Mina said, her blue-green eyes soft with understanding. "All of us have seen too many odd things to find anything amiss in your story. Besides, Gabriel never lies."

Jayna's head jerked to Gabriel to find him watching her again. His molten silver eyes were hooded as though he were afraid she might look too deep into his soul. A lock of his dark hair fell over his forehead and before she could catch herself, she reached up and pushed it back.

Almost immediately Gabriel's hand rose up to cover hers. His eyes darkened, and for a moment she thought he might kiss her, but then he dropped his hand and stepped away from her.

Jayna swallowed and turned to find Hugh regarding her intently. *He doesn't trust me.*

And should he?

"Well, Jayna. It looks as though Fate brought you to Stone Crest after all," Hugh said ominously.

CHAPTER TWENTY-FIVE

Gabriel didn't try to seek the sleep his body desperately needed. Dreams of Jayna and his betrayal would only haunt him. After all this time, he finally understood why his dreams were plagued with nightmares, for only the evilest of men could do what he had done to Jayna and not carry it around with him forever. Instead, he sat in front of the hearth with an untouched goblet of ale in his hand.

He wanted nothing more than to drown his sorrows in the ale, but bigger things than his past counted on him. So, the drunken state he so desired would have to wait for another night.

If it ever came.

He had never held any delusions that he would come out of this fight alive. He expected death, and, in fact, had wished for it on several occasions. But now, now that Jayna was with him again, he prayed for life.

He squeezed his eyes closed as he continued to war with himself.

"The ale will do no good if you do not drink it."

Gabriel was so surprised by the voice that he jumped

up, spilling the ale in his attempt to unsheathe his sword. "Aimery?"

The Fae commander bowed his flaxen head every so slightly and turned his amazing, swirling blue eyes to Gabriel. "What is amiss?"

Gabriel sighed and shook his head. "Nothing. And everything."

Aimery moved to the chair opposite Gabriel and slowly sat, his fine clothes never seeming to wrinkle or look other than perfect. "Tell me," he urged gently.

For many years, Aimery had listened as Gabriel shared his fears and his hopes. If Gabriel could trust anyone, he knew he could trust Aimery.

"Jayna is one of the Chosen."

Aimery's pale eyebrows rose. "So, we have five Chosen now. That is good."

"Aye."

"Tell me, Gabriel," Aimery said as he sat back and crossed his arms over his chest. "How did you figure out Jayna was one of the Chosen?"

For a long moment, he stared at the Fae. "Aimery, I remember my past. I remember everything, including how I came to be at the Fae's doorway."

Aimery's smile vanished as his arms dropped. "Since I still cannot see into your mind, I gather the memories aren't good."

Gabriel couldn't voice the words, so shook his head in answer.

"It was your memories that helped you see Jayna's mark?"

"Aye. I think the Great Evil hid it somehow, for even Jayna had forgotten it. Makes me wonder what else the Great Evil has managed to fool us with."

"Have you told the others that your memory has

returned?"

"Nay," Gabriel answered. "They will ask questions, and...I'm not ready for them to know the truth, to know that Jayna is here to seek revenge on me. For betraying her."

"Hugh will not take the news well."

"I know he won't." Gabriel didn't like that Aimery was saying the words he had feared to even think. He rose and moved to the hearth. The feel of the fire helped warm his skin, but nothing could warm his soul.

"I think you should keep it from them for now. Don't tell the others until you have no other choice."

Gabriel looked over his shoulder to Aimery. "And Jayna? Should I tell her?"

"Nay."

And in a blink Aimery was gone.

Gabriel ran a hand through his hair and wished the storm would hurry and pass so they could get on with the battle. He didn't like deceiving the only family he knew, the people who had given him their trust.

Trust. He'd had Jayna's trust and he had betrayed her. If he kept silent to the Shields, he would betray them, as well. Every instinct in his body urged him to go to the Shields, to tell them everything.

But Aimery had advised him against it, and he always listened to Aimery. Never once had Aimery steered him wrong in any way. So, he would heed Aimery's words, and he would pray that once the Shields did learn the truth that they didn't kill him on the spot.

With a sigh of resignation, Gabriel turned to reach for his goblet when something caught his eye near the window. The goblet forgotten, he strode to the window and felt his heart plummet to his feet.

There, on the stones of the window was more of the

clear substance. He simply stared at it as it ran down the stones to puddle on the floor.

"What is doing this?" he asked himself.

Another inspection of his chamber found nothing, just as he expected. With his mind in a whirlwind, Gabriel slowly backed out of his chamber. There was something in his chamber he had no doubt. Whether it was good or evil he didn't know yet.

He didn't know how long he stood in the hallway staring into his open chamber before Hugh came upon him.

"Are you afraid of your chamber," Hugh teased.

"Aye."

Gabriel glanced over at his leader to see Hugh wearing a wide smile.

There must have been something in Gabriel's gaze though because Hugh's smile faded quickly. "What is it?"

Gabriel pointed to the window. "It was here again."

Hugh glanced at him before he slowly walked into the chamber to the window. Gabriel heard him curse as he got to his feet and walked back into the hallway.

"I wish I knew what it was."

"Me as well," Gabriel agreed. "Why only my chamber though? I haven't seen traces of that liquid other than the monastery."

Hugh leaned back against the stone wall and crossed his arms over his chest. "I wish I had an answer for you, my friend. There is so much going on that I don't know which way is right, which is good. One wrong decision and all could be lost."

"We've always managed to come out ahead of the evil. I have no doubt we will again."

Hugh snorted. "If only I had your same faith. I fear that the time has come where the Great Evil will show us just how much power he has."

Gabriel didn't like how Hugh had seemed to lose hope, as if he was just waiting for the time the evil would win. "We have the Chosen. Aimery promised us they were the key to the evil's destruction."

"Ah, Aimery. I would feel better if I could talk to him."

"He was here," Gabriel said as his confusion grew as to why Aimery would visit him and not Hugh as well grew.

Hugh's frown increased. "Aimery was here? With you?"

Gabriel nodded. "Not but a few moments ago. I assumed he had seen you first."

"Nay."

That one word, spoken softly and deeply, disturbed Gabriel. "Hugh, he had to have had a reason for not seeking you out."

"You sound like Val," he said as he shook his head in disgust. "Aimery has always come when we've called for him. Always. Why did he not come now?"

Gabriel shrugged since he lacked any words of comfort. "He does know about Jayna though. I told him."

"There is that at least." Hugh ran a hand down his face with a sigh. "I won't admit it to Mina, but I fear we will not win this battle. The Shields are strong, but how strong against the Great Evil I don't know."

Gabriel gripped Hugh's shoulder. "You've never led us astray yet. I have faith that we will win this. Don't lose hope, Hugh, for if you do, we'll all know it."

"Aye," Hugh said softly, his gaze thoughtful as he looked into Gabriel's chamber. He blinked then turned to Gabriel. "I had better return to Mina. She'll come looking for me soon."

Gabriel nodded and watched as Hugh walked to his chamber. As long as he'd known Hugh, as many times as they'd fought side by side, he'd never seen Hugh lose hope.

Not even when it seemed that all hope was gone. Hugh had never given up. It's what made him a great leader.

The fact that Hugh had doubts began to concern Gabriel. He knew Roderick already worried for their failure. If Hugh cracked, as well...it didn't bode well for the Shields.

~ ~ ~

He had waited too long for the end. He had planned down to the very detail, and not even the meddlesome Shields and the Fae had been able to stop him. Oh, they had managed to trip him up every now and again, but they had never stopped him.

And they wouldn't be able to now either.

With his latest idea, the Shields and Fae would be hit so fast and so hard they wouldn't be able to do anything other than stand there as their realms crumbled around them.

But there was one thing he hadn't counted on. Jayna. Her revenge made her invaluable to him. It had made her unique, and it had kept her going when others would have sat down and died.

She had no idea how long he had kept her running in circles after Gabriel. In truth, he could have led her to him long ago, but the longer she searched for Gabriel, the more her need for revenge grew. And he fed off the rage in her.

Because of that rage and need for retribution, he had assumed she would walk into Stone Crest and try to kill Gabriel immediately. Yet, she hadn't.

When he'd had Gabriel in the woods, he should have spoken to Jayna as well, but he had been so giddy in finding Gabriel all to himself he had completely forgotten that there was someone else with them.

Though entering Stone Crest would be risky, he might have to in order to give Jayna the final push she needed.

Her death and the turning of Gabriel were critical to his plan.

He laughed as he recalled the look of horror on Gabriel's face when they had spoken. It had been invaluable, and he couldn't help but wonder if Gabriel had remembered all yet.

"Ah, Gabriel. You were my finest weapon. It's time you came home."

CHAPTER TWENTY-SIX

Jayna sat with the other Chosen after their morning meal. She had wanted to speak with Gabriel, but she hadn't had the nerve to seek him out during the night. Then, first thing that morn, he and the other Shields mounted up and headed to the forest.

A shiver raced through her spine as she recalled the Great Evil and his words to Gabriel.

"Jayna?"

She jerked her gaze up to find Nicole looking at her expectantly. "Aye?"

"Is everything all right? You seem to be elsewhere this morn."

She forced a smile. "Forgive me. I'm just a little dumbfounded to discover I am one of you. What is it that you need me to do?"

Mina scooted forward in her chair. "First, I need you to tell me all that you know of the Chosen."

Jayna blinked, then swallowed. "In truth, Mina, I don't recall anything. It wasn't until the mark appeared on my wrist that I remembered having it. Even now I struggle with trying to understand how I could have forgotten such a mark was on my body."

Aye, the Great Evil took care of that, you stupid fool.

"For as long as I can remember I've always had it," she continued. "It was always a part of me."

"Hmmm," Shannon said as she tapped her chin with a finger. "That explains why the evil hid it from her and us. Having a fifth Chosen will only make us stronger."

Elle rolled her eyes. "Only if we figure out what we're supposed to be doing. I'm not a fool. I know just how upset Roderick is over us not knowing what to do. He's...anxious about the battle."

"They all are," Mina said softly. "The best we can do is try and sift through our memories to see if we can recall anything."

Shannon rose to her feet and moved to the window. "Easier said than done, especially since we were infants when we were sent to this realm."

Jayna hid her shocked expression at Shannon's words. Her heart began to pound fiercely in her chest as she toyed with the idea of telling them where she was from.

"Our parents wouldn't have sent us here unless we had some knowledge of how to destroy the evil," Nicole argued.

Elle nodded slowly. "I agree with Nicole, but I have to admit, I'm beginning to worry about whether or not we can actually annihilate the evil."

Jayna had listened in rapt silence. "What if we aren't supposed to know what to do?" she said cautiously.

Four sets of eyes turned to her then. Mina furrowed her brow. "I don't understand what you mean."

"What if our parents knew that there might be a chance that the evil found us? If he were able to discern what we did to destroy him, he would then be able to protect himself?"

"My God," Shannon said breathlessly. "I think she may have it."

Jayna grew uncomfortable as they all smiled at her. She shrugged. "It was just a thought."

Mina smiled. "But a good one, I think. Well, if Jayna is correct, we'll have to trust our parents and ourselves. It also means that, until the battle, we'll have to deceive the men into believing we're making headway.

Elle snorted. "There's no way I can lie to Roderick. He always knows when I try to lie to him."

"Same with Cole," Shannon agreed.

Mina sighed. "All right. Then does anyone have any other suggestions?"

"I might," Nicole said in her thick Scottish accent. "We keep the men occupied in bed as much as possible."

For half a heartbeat, the solar grew quiet before they all burst out laughing.

Jayna hadn't laughed so hard in ages and it felt wonderful.

She let her gaze roam over the four unique and vibrant women.

They were risking their lives in order to save their realm. Her respect for them continued to grow with each moment she was with them. Their men might be powerful warriors of the Fae, but each woman was strong enough to stand beside her mate.

Jayna suddenly found herself wanting to be with Gabriel. She was so very tired of being alone, and he was a connection to her family, to her realm.

For so long she had been intent on one thing – Gabriel. Yet now that she was with him, learning him all over again, she found that she remembered more and more memories of her family.

The worst part of all is that she didn't know if she could kill Gabriel now, not after seeing the man he had become and what he fought for. And the others, they had welcomed her, clothed her, and fed her.

But it didn't matter what she wanted to do anymore. She had made a promise to the evil, a vow to find and kill Gabriel. She knew better than to try and go back on her word with the evil. He would never let her rest if she didn't carry out the vow she made.

Jayna closed her eyes as tears threatened. How she wished she had listened to her mother and let the anger go instead of it festering and growing inside of her. Now, she was no better than when Gabriel betrayed her.

She had turned into the very thing she hunted.

CHAPTER TWENTY-SEVEN

Gabriel watched his breath billow around his face, the cold numbing his lips and his fingers. The storm had finally passed sometime during the night, the snow blanketing the ground thick and heavy. Most of the clouds had departed with the storm allowing the rays of the morning sun to penetrate the grayness of the morning.

They had taken a great chance that morn, as all five of the Shields left Stone Crest to seek out the Fae army that was supposed to guard them.

The air was thick with moisture and the animals quiet. It was as if the very air knew that a great battle would soon take place, a battle that could either save or destroy realms.

"I hate when it's this eerie," Val whispered from beside him.

Gabriel nodded. Hugh rode in the lead as Cole and Roderick rode behind him and Val. They all knew that if the Fae didn't want to show themselves they didn't have to, but they were hoping for the best.

His eyes itched from lack of sleep, and he wanted nothing more than to find Jayna and take her back to her chamber to make slow, sweet love to her then fall asleep in her arms. He had been tempted to go to her last eve when he hadn't been able to return to his chamber, but he decided against it.

The more he was around Jayna, the more he wanted to tell her how sorry he was and that he understood why she had hunted him.

Each of the Shields gripped their weapons as they rode into the forest. It was the perfect opportunity for the harpy to attack, and they fully expected her to.

They said not a word as they slowly made their way through the forest, the horses having a difficult time in the deep snow. When they reached the edge of Hugh's land where the Fae were supposed to stand guard, Hugh dismounted and motioned for the others to do the same.

Gabriel exchanged a look with Val as they tied their horses to a tree. He reached for an arrow and notched it in his bow. He had a bad feeling about venturing so far from the castle, but they'd had no choice. The Fae wouldn't leave their posts unless Aimery ordered them too.

"Fae army show yourselves!" Hugh shouted into the stillness of the morning.

When nothing happened, Hugh turned to his men and with a slight nod. He reached for his deadly crossbow on his mount and notched one of his unique arrows. Then, he rested the crossbow over his shoulder and motioned with his hand for the men to spread out.

Gabriel and Val moved back toward the forest. Cole and Roderick moved in the opposite direction while Hugh ventured forward. They hadn't moved two paces before something hit Val in the back knocking him to the ground.

Gabriel glanced at Val before falling to his knee and taking aim with his bow.

There was nothing to see, no creature, man, or Fae

moved. "Val?"

"Aye," the Roman answered as he jumped to his feet and readied his halberd. "What was it? Why didn't you shoot your arrow?"

Gabriel blew out a breath. "I don't know. I saw nothing."

"Well, I sure as hell felt it," Val said as he moved his shoulders around. Then he stilled as a flock of birds suddenly took flight, their cries echoing around the forest. "Gabriel."

But Gabriel already knew. They were being hunted. By something they couldn't see. "We shouldn't have left the castle," he murmured as he jumped to his feet. "Hugh. Cole. Roderick, get back to the castle. Now!" he bellowed as he and Val raced to their mounts.

The thick snow hampered their efforts to get to their horses. Gabriel was nearly to his mount when he felt what he was sure was a foot in his abdomen. He bent over, grasping for breath as something else landed hard and heavy on his back, knocking him on his stomach.

"Gabriel," he heard Val shout, but he wasn't able to breathe much less answer.

He forced himself to his hands and knees to see his bow lying within reach. He lunged toward it, rolling onto his back as he notched the arrow and waited.

He didn't have long to wait as something landed on his jaw. Gabriel hissed in pain as he took aim and let his arrow fly. To his utter amazement the arrow stopped midair and just hovered there for a moment before it jerked back a little then fell to the ground.

"Gabriel," Val said as he came up to him. "What the hell happened?"

With his gaze on his arrow, Gabriel gained his feet and slowly walked to where they arrow lay. On the tip of the double-headed arrow was a dark substance and he didn't need to lean down to smell the evil of it.

"By the gods," Roderick stated as he, Cole, and Hugh came running up. "Gabriel, are you all right? I saw you flying through the air as if someone was beating you, but I never saw a thing."

"Because there was nothing to see," Gabriel said as he went down on his haunches beside his arrow. "Whatever it was got in some good punches, but I managed to nick him."

They all stared at the arrow in silence for a moment. Hugh was the first to speak. "By the amount of blood on that tip, I'd say you more than nicked him."

"That's not blood," Cole said. "At least not blood like I've ever seen."

Roderick reached down and picked up the arrow. "It's some kind of blood, and its evil. We don't really need to know more than that."

Gabriel sighed as he straightened and reached for the arrow. "It got to me and Val without us ever seeing it. I think the Great Evil is cloaking it."

"Nay," said a voice behind them.

They turned as one to find Theron, king of the Fae, standing before them. He stood tall and regal in his robes of white trimmed with blue and silver. His long nearly white hair was pulled away from his face and hung down to the middle of his back. His unusual Fae eyes swirled blue, as he looked the small group over, though his face was devoid of expression.

Gabriel and Cole bowed low while the others inclined their heads.

"Thank God," Hugh said as he briefly closed his eyes. "We've been calling for Aimery."

Theron nodded. "I know. Aimery is...busy at the

moment with an important matter in our realm."

Cole stepped forward. "What did you mean when you said the evil wasn't cloaking the creature?"

"Simple," Theron said as he crossed his arms over his chest. "Whatever attacked you wasn't cloaked. I would've been able to see that. I saw nothing."

That in itself worried Gabriel tremendously. He felt someone's gaze on him and turned to find Cole watching him. Since both spent a considerable amount of time in the Realm of the Fae they knew better than the others just what Theron wasn't saying.

Gabriel looked to Theron. "Is the Fae army still here?"

"Aye," Theron said after the briefest of moments. "To stay out here is to invite the creatures to attack. Return to the castle. The true battle will be here soon enough."

There was something in Theron's tone that told Gabriel all was not as it seemed. He turned toward his mount only to find Cole beside him.

"Something is going on."

Gabriel nodded. "Aye, but what?" he whispered. He didn't wish to worry the others until they had proof.

Cole shrugged as they reached their horses. Hugh had already mounted and began to ride through the forest. Val and Roderick were close behind him.

Gabriel took one more look at the arrow in his hand. How he wished he could have seen what he aimed at.

"Listen close," Theron said as he stopped between Gabriel and Cole's horses. "Keep to the castle. Do not venture out until you have no other recourse."

"What is going on?" Cole demanded.

Theron glanced down. "I cannot say as of yet. Aimery will be here as soon as he can. He said each of you would know what to do."

"Why didn't you tell the others this?" Gabriel asked.

"Because Hugh feels as though he must lead no matter what. Roderick is afraid of losing Elle almost as much as he fears the Shields will lose. As for Val, he needs to see the proof before he will act. He would ask too many questions. I need to know that you two will heed my orders."

Gabriel nodded. "We will do what we must to succeed."

With a nod, Theron vanished.

"Bloody hell," Cole muttered as he mounted. "I don't like the ominous feeling I got from Theron's words."

Gabriel swung his leg over the horse and settled in the saddle. "Me either, but we don't have much of a choice."

"Not if we want to live."

They nudged their horses into a walk and hurried to follow the others. Several times, Gabriel could feel eyes on him, yet no matter how hard he looked he saw nothing. But something was out there. He'd bet his Fae crafted bow on it.

The castle and gate came into view and Gabriel let out a relieved sigh. They were nearing the gate when it began to slowly open. Then, they heard the unmistakable scream of the harpy just before the banging of her wings silenced all.

"Into the castle," Hugh cried as he spurred his horse into a run.

Gabriel reached for two arrows as he turned his horse toward the approaching harpy. He notched the arrows then sighted down them until he found the harpy. With measured precision, he let loose the arrows and watched as they sunk into the Harpy.

The creature screamed in pain before she jerked the arrows from her body and tossed them to the ground. Gabriel grabbed his horse's reins and turned the horse toward the castle. The others had made it through safely.

Gabriel raced through the crack in the gate just before

it banged closed behind him. The people of Stone Crest had been warned of an attack, so most had kept to their homes unless they had no other choice but to venture out. Those few ran swiftly to their cottages and the safety of the tunnels beneath.

"It's coming!" Roderick shouted as he handed his horse to a stable boy.

Gabriel glanced over his shoulder to see the harpy flying over the castle, her talons slicing through two of the guards on the battlements.

Hugh stood ahead of him and readied his crossbow and fired, giving everyone a few more moments to find safety. Gabriel felt a rush of excitement as he always did when battling creatures of darkness. The Shields may not hold special powers like the Fae, but they had managed to always win against the evil. This time would be no different.

Gabriel leaned over his horse as he approached Hugh. He was just about to jump from his mount when he saw Hugh's eyes narrow and his face clench.

Then he saw the harpy's talons as she sunk them into Hugh's chest and lifted him from the ground.

"Nay," Gabriel bellowed as he quickly reached for another arrow. He notched and fired arrow after arrow hoping to get the harpy to release Hugh before she flew off with him.

He had no idea how many arrows he had gone through when he saw the harpy stop mid-flight and turn toward him. She screamed her anger into the air just before she released Hugh and flew off.

With a growl, he swung his leg over his horse's neck and slid to the ground at a run. He reached for the black bag he carried with him at all times, his heart pumping wildly in his chest. He found Hugh surrounded by Val, Cole, and Roderick who was trying hard to keep Mina away from her husband.

Gabriel dropped to his knees beside Hugh to find his leader unconscious and bleeding badly.

"The fall he took," Cole said softly. "I'm afraid to see just how many bones are broken."

Gabriel gave a vicious jerk of his head. "Don't touch him," he said between clenched teeth.

If he got to Hugh in time he could save him.

He just prayed he got there in time.

CHAPTER TWENTY-EIGHT

"Hugh," Mina screamed tearfully. "Hugh, don't leave me. I need you."

Gabriel briefly closed his eyes and tried to regain some composure. He looked up at the other Shields to find them looking at Hugh as if he were already dead.

"Cole," Gabriel barked. "I need some bandages. Now," he bellowed when Cole didn't move.

Once Cole raced off to get the bandages, Gabriel turned to Val. "Get me some hot water. As much as you can carry. I'll also need some cool water. And have servants continue to bring them to me."

Val jumped up and ran to the castle, leaving Gabriel alone. He could hear Mina sobbing behind him, and he knew he would gladly give his life if Hugh would only live.

The cold ground didn't deter Gabriel as he spread open his black bag then reached to Hugh's chest to feel a very weak heartbeat. "Hang on, Hugh. I'm coming for you."

Suddenly, a soft hand touched his shoulder and he looked up to find Jayna beside him. "Tell me what to do," she urged.

"Take his hand," Gabriel commanded. "And put your other hand over a wound, pressing hard to staunch the flow of blood."

She did as he requested without question. He jerked out his dagger and split Hugh's tunic open. He swallowed then leaned over to look at how deep the wounds in Hugh's chest were. The harpy's talons had sunk deep, nearly all the way through Hugh, puncturing a lung.

Thankfully, Cole and Val returned quickly. Gabriel dunked a cloth in the hot water and began to wipe off the blood that continued to flow.

"Put your hands over the wounds," he ordered Cole and Val.

Time seemed to stand still as Gabriel took vial after vial from his bag. He mixed some herbs together then sprinkled them over Hugh's body where a thin line of smoke began to waft skyward as it touched his skin.

He then grabbed a goblet Val had brought and scooped up water. Another vial was taken out and herbs dumped into the goblet. Gabriel swirled the cool water with his fingers to mix the herb.

"Remove your hands," he told the others just before he dumped the water over Hugh's wounds.

Hugh groaned and stiffened as the herb dropped into the wounds. A hissing noise filled the air as the herb began its journey inside Hugh to stop the bleeding.

While that herb was working, Gabriel took two leaves from a vial and tore them into tiny pieces into the empty goblet. Then he took a vial with an orange liquid in it and poured four drops into the goblet. Next, he reached for a small white flower with five petals.

He looked at the flower then glanced at Mina. Her gaze hadn't left Hugh since she had run to him. Tears coursed unheeded down her face as she allowed Roderick to hold her.

Gabriel knew if he used the flower he would have to go out and look for another. He was never without one, because the flower, if used with the other herbs correctly, could bring a person back from the brink of death.

He tore each of the petals from the flower and dropped them into the goblet. With the stem and leaves still in his hand, he took his dagger and used it to cut open a small wound in his palm. Blood rushed out and he let it cover the stem and leaves before throwing it in the goblet.

Gabriel then poured a small amount of water into the goblet. He held his hands over the goblet and closed his eyes as he felt his knowledge of healing flow through him. Mumbling the ancient words of his people, he used his power to mix the contents of the goblet, but knowing it would take more than his blood, he allowed a small amount of his life essence to leave his body through his hands and into the goblet.

That small amount of life essence felt as though a minion of creatures had trampled him. His body began to ache and exhaustion began to sweep through his body. But he refused to give in until he was finished with Hugh.

"What is that?" Cole asked.

"Ask later," Gabriel answered. "Hold him still. This will hurt."

Once Val, Cole, and Jayna had a hold of Hugh, Gabriel lifted the goblet over Hugh's body and emptied it into Hugh's wounds.

Hugh let out a vicious scream as he tried to buck his holders off his body.

Gabriel cringed as he heard bones that had been fractured begin to break. More work had yet to be done on Hugh, but the bones could be healed once the bleeding was stopped and the damage to the inside of Hugh's body was repaired.

Finally, Hugh stopped moving.

"Is he dead?" Val asked softly.

Gabriel shook his head. "Nay. The mixture I gave him was repairing the damage the harpy's talons had done. When you have that much damage in the body, it can be very painful to heal."

He sighed as he saw the wounds began to heal before his eyes. Once again, his people's healing had helped him save a friend.

Cole looked up. "Is it done, then? Can we move him to the castle?"

"We're not nearly done. You were right about the fall. It was from a great distance, which did break bones. It fractured others, but in his attempt to dislodge you, he broke those as well."

Mina let out a painful cry as she wrenched out of Roderick's arms and ran to Hugh. Her hands shook as she touched Hugh's face. "My Hugh," she whispered as she kissed his forehead. She raised her gaze to Gabriel. "Please, help him."

"I will, to the best of my abilities."

She nodded and wiped at her tears. "I will get our chamber ready. What else do you need?"

"Prayers," Gabriel said. He waited until Mina left before he looked to the Shields. "I've healed bones for each of you, but healing one or two bones is different than an entire body."

Roderick moved beside Jayna and looked at Gabriel. "Is his back broken?"

Gabriel slowly nodded. "I would much prefer if Aimery were here to lend his Fae magic."

"You can do this," Val said. "I've seen you work miracles on all of us, Gabriel.

Gabriel rose to his feet to find most of the guards standing behind him. "Get back to your posts. The harpy will likely return." He turned to the others. "I also gave Hugh something for the pain, as well as something to keep him unconscious, though moving him will likely cause him more pain than I would want."

"He's strong," Cole said. "He survived the attack and the fall. He'll grit his way through the move as well."

Gabriel nodded. "All right. Let's get him inside."

Carefully, all five of them lifted Hugh. He groaned and they stilled instantly.

"Slowly," Gabriel reminded them.

Moving as steadily as a snail they walked into the castle. The narrow stairs posed a greater concern.

Roderick shook his head. "We cannot get him up the stairs without causing more pain."

Elle came running down the stairs. "Mina has readied the chamber."

"I don't think we can get him to his chamber," Val said.

Elle glanced at Hugh then looked at Roderick. She gave a quick nod before lifting her skirts and running back up the stairs.

"To the solar," Jayna said. "We can make him comfortable in there."

Gabriel gave her a small smile as they moved to the solar. No sooner had they walked into the room than Mina glided in behind them.

"Hold him for just a moment," she ordered. "I don't want my husband on the cold stone floor."

Gabriel watched as servants rushed into the room and set up the day bed. More servants came in with blankets stacked high in their arms. Mina, Elle, Shannon and Nicole readied the day bed with blankets and pillows.

Mina smoothed the last blanket and stepped back.

"Now you may lay him down."

Despite being as gentle as they could, moving Hugh even an inch caused him considerable pain. He moaned as they laid him upon the day bed.

"My bag," Gabriel said as he turned to retrieve it.

Jayna stepped forward. "I thought you might have forgotten it."

Gabriel reached out and ran a hand down her face. He knew then that he had to tell her his memory had returned. He had betrayed her too many times to continue doing so.

"Thank you."

She smiled and moved to stand beside Mina.

Gabriel sighed and opened the bag again. His supply of herbs was terribly low, and he feared that many he needed wouldn't be found at Stone Crest, especially with the snow piled as high as it was.

"What do you need now?" Cole asked. "I brought the bandages."

"Good," he said. "Once I set the bones, we'll need to wrap Hugh's chest."

Jayna had always loved to watch Gabriel heal. Many times he had told her he had no special powers, but she wasn't a fool. He might know more about herbs than most, but it was much more than that. Gabriel did work magic when he healed. It might not be as great as the Fae's, but it was still great.

Yet, she saw the hesitation in his gaze. He feared not being able to fully heal Hugh. But she knew just what he was capable of. As much as she hated to admit it, she had come to respect Hugh and the other Shields. With the evil they had to face, they needed every warrior.

It was time for her to tell Gabriel who he really was. She opened her mouth to do just that when Mina gripped her hand, causing Jayna to recall that she and Gabriel weren't alone.

She swallowed her words and gave Gabriel a reassuring smile. He inclined his head before he turned to the black bag that never left his side. His fingers lightly ran over the many vials and herbs, most she didn't even know the names of, much less their usage.

Gabriel's skill was unbelievable, his knowledge superior to most. It was one of the reasons she had been so devastated when he betrayed her. Of all the people she might have suspected, Gabriel wouldn't have been one of them. The love they had shared had been strong and their future bright.

She mentally gave herself a shake as Mina's hand tightened on hers. She clasped her other hand around Mina's, hoping that she might give her some comfort.

Her gaze followed Gabriel's hand as he chose two herbs and dusted some of the powder in his hands. He then rubbed his hands together and moved to Hugh's feet.

"Take his boots off. Carefully," Gabriel cautioned Roderick and Val. With mind-numbing slowness, Roderick and Val tugged Hugh's boots off. Gabriel raised his gaze to Mina. "I need him bare."

Mina licked her lips and reached for a blanket that she handed to Elle and Jayna. She then looked to Cole. "Will you help me?"

"Of course," Cole said and moved to the other side of Hugh.

Jayna held her breath as inch by inch they pulled Hugh's pants lower. When they reached his hips, she and Elle opened the blanket and draped it across Hugh's body. She turned to Mina to find her face pale and her hands shaking.

Confused, she turned to Hugh's face to see him moving his head from side to side.

"Let me," Elle said to Mina. "Take Hugh's hand and speak to him. He needs you now," she urged as she pulled Mina's hands from Hugh's pants.

Reluctantly Mina released her hold and moved to take Hugh's hands. Cole gave Jayna a small nod and they began to work on pulling the pants down his thighs. It wasn't long before Hugh began to moan in pain.

Cole stood and moved away, raking his hand through his blond hair. "Its not working, Gabriel. He's in too much pain."

"Take your dagger then," Gabriel directed. "Cut his pants away from him, but do what you must so I can ease his pain."

In a heartbeat, Cole drew out his dagger and sliced open Hugh's pants on either leg. Jayna gathered the ruined leather and tossed it aside.

She moved so Gabriel could approach Hugh, and watched mesmerized as Gabriel ran his herb-coated hands over Hugh, starting at his feet and working his way up. Gabriel's silver eyes were closed and incoherent words tumbled from his mouth.

Everyone held their breath as Gabriel worked up one leg then the other before moving to each arm. Finally, he stood over Hugh's torso and ran a hand over each hip, rib, collarbone, and neck. Moment by moment Hugh seemed to relax more as if his pain slowly receded.

Gabriel finally straightened, his face pale, lips pinched and hands shaking. Jayna knew he couldn't last much longer.

"Gabriel," she called, but he just shook his head.

He reached for more of the herbs to sprinkle on his hands and then raised his gaze to Mina. "We must turn him on his side so I can see to his back."

"His back?" Mina repeated and swallowed loudly. "Was

every bone broken?"

Gabriel sighed sadly. "Just about." He looked over his shoulder at the other Shields, who quickly moved to Hugh. At his nod, the Shields gripped Hugh and slowly turned him onto his side.

Hugh let out a loud, painful moan. Gabriel didn't seem to hear it though, as he once again closed his eyes and worked his magic.

Jayna could practically feel the magic from Gabriel as he slowly moved his hands down Hugh's back. A couple of times he lingered over one spot a little longer and Jayna knew the break must have been significant for Gabriel to take such time.

At last, Gabriel dropped his hands and stepped away to sink into a nearby chair. "It is done," he said hoarsely.

CHAPTER TWENTY-NINE

"Is he healed?" Mina asked.

Jayna watched as Gabriel raised weary filled eyes to Mina. "I don't know. I've done the best I can."

Mina sank to her knees beside Hugh as she began to cry. Jayna moved out of the way as Nicole, Elle, and Shannon comforted her. She turned to Gabriel to see him staring at his hands as if he were wondering if he had done all he could. Without thinking, she moved to him and knelt before him.

His beautiful silver depths were filled with fear and doubt. She lifted a hand to his lips when he began to speak. "Shhh," she whispered. "Do not doubt your skill. You saved him from certain death."

"Did I?"

She scoffed at him. "Your exhaustion is making you testy. Not another word," she said as she rose to her feet and poured him a goblet of water from a jug the servants had brought in. She went to hand him the goblet but his hands shook too much for him to take it.

"Let me," she urged as she brought the goblet to his

lips. He drained the entire contents and licked his lips. "More?" she asked, and at his nod turned back to the jug.

Val moved to her side. He made as if to pour himself a goblet of ale, but leaned down and whispered, "What is wrong with him?"

"He's weak. What he did for Hugh took a lot out of him. He needs to regain his strength."

"Tell us what to do."

She shrugged. "I don't know. Rest maybe."

Val glanced over his shoulder at Gabriel then turned to her. "Will you take care of him?"

"Aye."

Jayna wondered at how quickly she had agreed to take care of Gabriel. In fact, it was the perfect time to kill him in his weakened state. Yet, as she glanced at Hugh and the other Shields and their mates, she knew she couldn't do it. Not now at least.

Maybe not ever.

That thought nearly stopped her in her tracks. How could she have come from such a revenge-driven life to a woman willing to forgive the unforgivable?

Because you want a future.

Maybe that was it. She really didn't know why, and at the moment, didn't wish to delve further. She held the goblet to Gabriel's lips as he again drained it. After she set the goblet down, she took his arm and draped it over her shoulder.

"As much as I'd love to take you to my bed, I don't think I'm up for it," he mumbled near her ear.

Despite the dire circumstances, Jayna found herself smiling. "As if I want to be in your bed, my lord. Now, on your feet. We must get you to your chamber."

"Nay," he nearly bellowed causing everyone in the solar to turn to him. He shook his head and closed his eyes.

"Not my chamber."

"All right. We'll go to mine," she said as she looked to Val who gave her a nod.

Though she had no idea why Gabriel didn't want to return to his chamber, she could tell by the way he responded that there was something there he didn't wish to face.

The Great Evil maybe? Nay, she thought after a moment. If the evil had entered Stone Crest she knew he would have sought her out, as well.

She managed to get him to his feet then staggered under his weight. Suddenly, the majority of Gabriel's weight was lifted from her. She looked over and found Val on the other side of Gabriel. Together they walked Gabriel up the stairs and to her chamber. She lost count of the many times Gabriel stumbled, his strength rapidly leaving him until they were all but dragging him to the bed.

"I'll get him on the bed," Val said.

Jayna quickly moved away as Val lifted Gabriel and tossed him on the bed, not that Gabriel noticed since he seemed to have fallen asleep. She moved to tug off his boots and make him more comfortable.

When she finished covering him, she was surprised to turn around and find Val still in her chamber and a fire roaring in the hearth. "Thank you."

He inclined his head slightly and his gaze moved to Gabriel. "He's healed all of us so many times, and each time I watch in amazement as he does it. Yet, today was different. He was different."

Jayna swallowed and looked away.

"What was different?"

Reluctantly she met Val's gaze. "I couldn't possibly know."

He nodded at her answer. "He cares greatly for you. It's

in his eyes as he watches you."

"I think you read too much into it, my lord."

"I disagree. Each of the Shields has found their mate in one of the Chosen. Why should Gabriel be any different?"

"Because he deserves better than me," she answered honestly. "I live my life for revenge, a revenge I must carry out. I have no choice in the matter."

He stared at her a moment, his pale green eyes sympathetic. "We all have a choice, Jayna. I'll return later to see how he is," he said before he turned on his heel and left the chamber.

Jayna sighed as she moved to close the door behind him. Val's words disturbed her greatly. She knew without a doubt that Gabriel was a part of her, her mate as Val declared. But she also knew that the time when she and Gabriel could have had a future was long past.

Even if she could forgive him for his treachery and betrayal, she could never forgive herself for her hunt for retribution, or aligning herself with the evil that now threatened this realm.

She returned to the bed to check on Gabriel. He was still pale, but she knew rest would gain him his strength. Until then, she would watch over him and keep him safe from whatever he feared so greatly in his chamber.

~ ~ ~

Theron waited for Rufina's response. "Well," he prompted.

"I think your brain must have been addled recently," she retorted hotly as she paced the floor in front of their bed.

Theron rested his elbows on his knees and gazed at the spacious chamber. It was easily three times the size of most chambers, with high ceilings and many windows, as well as arches that connected other rooms and doorways. The walls were painted a soft shade of blue with intricate knotwork painted in silver and white.

Their canopied bed was hung with sheer silver cloth and a silver bed cover that matched the design on the wall. A small table with two chairs sat before the fireplace. On the opposite side of the room was a table with a mirror hung behind it where Rufina did her toilet.

He ran his hands over the smooth blue and silver Fae material that covered the bench he sat on before their bed. It was a favorite piece of furniture, and one he liked to sit on as he watched Rufina dress, one that he would sit on and watch their child play.

A sigh escaped him as he raised his gaze to his wife. "Do we have any other choice?"

"Aye," she snapped and turned to face him, her blue eyes alight with anger. Her long, flaxen hair hung past her waist and was held back from her face with a silver knotwork clip. The skirts of her silver gown swirled about her feet as she pivoted again, slower than usual with the added weight of the baby growing inside of her.

When she didn't give him any other options, he stood. "I don't believe it was Aimery," he admitted.

"Then you cannot kill him."

Her voice was soft, urgent, and he knew she worried for their future. He opened his arms and she moved to him. He held her tight as she trembled.

He kissed her temple as his hands roamed over her slender hips and small waist. The desire he felt for her had only grown over the millennia, not diminished. Even now with the turmoil around them, he wanted her with a ferocity that startled him.

She lifted her face to his. "At least tell Aimery of your

plans."

"Nay. I cannot chance anything."

"You are doing exactly what the Great Evil wants. Without Aimery, the Shields are vulnerable."

Theron smiled. "Not as vulnerable as you might think."

"What are you up to?"

The smile dropped as Theron turned to pace their chamber. "I'm trying to save our realm and Earth. The Shields cannot do it alone against such power as the Great Evil. Already he has deceived them, and us."

"How so?" she asked as she sat on the bench he had vacated.

"There is only one being who could have entered our realm without detection. One being who could have made himself look like Aimery."

Rufina slowly stood, her blue eyes wide. "By all that's magical. It cannot be. They were all destroyed."

"Aye, and so were half the creatures the Great Evil has managed to unearth and send to the Shields."

"Shapeshifters are near impossible to catch."

"Unfortunately, I know."

Rufina shook her head. "I don't understand. You know it wasn't Aimery who killed the dragon, yet you would kill him anyway."

"I'm not going to kill him, my love," he said with a smile.

"Theron, I think I might kill you myself," she said between clenched teeth. "Did you not just a few moments ago tell me you had to kill Aimery?"

Theron chuckled. "I did. However," he hurried to say when she went to speak. "You never let me finish. I'm not going to actually kill him. I'm just going to make it look as though Aimery is dead."

"And then what?" she asked, tapping her foot in

frustration.

"I'm going to send him to the Shields. He'll be away from our realm and the other Fae will think punishment has been meted out."

"And when he returns?"

Theron sighed as he pulled Rufina back into his arms. "That, my love, I will determine if we survive all of this."

"We'll survive it. We have to."

CHAPTER THIRTY

Gabriel came awake to feel a soft body beside him. He turned his head to find that Jayna had climbed into bed with him. She was on her side, her hand curled under her head and her long golden locks free of the braids. He picked up a strand of her hair and rubbed it between his fingers, loving the silken feel of it.

He lifted his arm to his face and tried to fist his hand. He managed it but only with great force. It would take several more hours before he regained his strength fully.

"Has your strength returned?" Jayna asked sleepily just before she yawned.

"Slowly," he said. "How did you get me up here?"

"Val."

He looked at the top of the canopy and took a deep breath. "And Hugh? Has there been any word?"

"You've slept most of the day away," she said as she sat up. "Val has been by thrice to check on you. He said Hugh is resting, but he hasn't woken yet."

"Good. It isn't time for him to wake. He needs to stay in the healing sleep as long as he can." He turned his head to look at her. "Did the harpy return?""

She shook her head. "Val said the guards grow more fearful by the hour. In truth, so do I. Why would the harpy attack, then leave before it could do more damage?"

"I've wondered that myself."

"Val also said the harpies always travel in threes. He doesn't understand where the others are."

Gabriel shrugged. "Val was one of the most revered generals of Rome. If he has a suspicion, I listen to it." He thought for a moment then said, "Maybe it's a trap. Maybe the harpy wants us to think there is only one, so when we do attack, we'll be surrounded by them."

"You aren't seriously thinking of venturing out of the castle again?"

"Theron, the king of the Fae, asked us to stay in the castle, but we were attacked by more than the harpy today. There was something in the forest, something that none of us could see. It attacked Val first, knocking him to the ground then it came at me. Somehow, I managed to wound it with my bow, but I think whatever it was will be back."

She threaded her fingers with his. "If you cannot see it, what makes you think it isn't already in the castle?"

"I don't know that for sure. The odds continue to stack against us. It's no wonder Roderick is losing hope."

She shook her head, her golden strands tickling his hand. "He hasn't lost hope. He is just worried that something will happen to him where he cannot protect Elle, or worse, that something happens to her. He sees a future for them, and he wants it. Desperately."

Gabriel sighed. "And Roderick deserves it. He will inherit his kingdom one day. His family already lost one son, they shouldn't have to lose another."

"Nay, they shouldn't." She turned her face from him and grew quiet.

He knew she was thinking of her family and all she had lost, and he didn't want her to dredge up painful memories. "What are your plans?"

"For what?" she asked as her fingers played with the edge of a blanket.

"Today. Tomorrow. Next month, next year."

She chuckled and threw him a teasing look. "Well, for the rest of today I will be with you. I promised Val that I would stay by your side until you regained your strength."

Knowing she would be with him the rest of the night made his heart squeeze painfully. How he wanted to erase the past and start anew, to have a future with Jayna. Their passion had been great, their love immeasurable, their bond unbreakable.

Until he had betrayed her.

"As for tomorrow," she continued. "I think I'll keep watch over you just to make sure that you don't stumble and fall," she teased. "As for the rest...." She trailed off and her smile slowly vanished. "I don't know what the future holds. Mayhap I won't survive the coming battle."

"You'll survive it," he vowed. "I'll make sure of it."

She leaned forward and cupped his check. "You don't even know me. You know I've lied, that I've come for revenge."

"Aye. I know all those things." This was the perfect opportunity for him to admit his memory had returned, but he found he couldn't do it. He didn't want to shatter what they had become. "I know that my body wants yours, that it cannot get enough of you."

Her hazel eyes darkened as her hand drifted to his chest. "I cannot deny that I want you as well."

It was all Gabriel needed to hear. He pulled her onto his chest and claimed her lips, pouring all his fears, his desires and his longing into the kiss.

His hands roamed over her lithe body, tugging her skirts up even as she pulled at his tunic. The need to feel his flesh on her flesh was nearly overwhelming. He broke the kiss and sat up, but before he could reach for Jayna, she began to yank off her clothing.

A smile pulled at Gabriel's lips as he saw the desire in her eyes. He wasted no time divesting himself of his clothes. When he turned around, Jayna was kneeling on the bed. Strands of her glorious hair had fallen over her shoulders to hide her breasts. Yet, he could make out the pink of her nipples through her golden locks.

"By the stars you are beautiful," he said as he reached for her.

She went willingly into his embrace as her arms wound around his neck and her fingers plunged into his hair. He moaned as her nails gently raked across the skin of his neck, bringing chills of pleasure across his body.

He reached his hand up and cupped her full breast, the weight in his palm bringing his already hard rod to a driving need. His fingers tweaked her nipple then rolled it between two fingers.

Jayna rubbed her hips against him in response. She reached between their bodies and took his rod in her hand. Gabriel dropped his head back as the pleasure swept through him. And when her nails softly glided over his hot, aching rod, he thought he might spill his seed right then.

He went to reach for her and found his arms shaking. Silently he cursed his weakness, but Jayna had seen him shake.

"Lay back," she ordered.

Gabriel did as she asked and smiled when she settled between his legs, her hands and lips roaming over his chest, hips, and thighs. Every once in awhile he'd feel her hand rub against his rod or his sac and he'd tense, waiting for her to take him in hand.

After what seemed like an eternity of her teasing his body with her sweet tongue and soft touch, her hand closed around his rod just before the tip of her tongue licked the head.

"Sweet Mary," he exclaimed as passion so deep went through him he forgot everything but Jayna.

He could only grip the blankets as she closed her lips over his cock. Intense pleasure scorched through him, leaving him breathless and yearning for more. Her hand closed over the base of his rod, adding a hint of pressure while her mouth sucked him sweetly.

It was too much. Gabriel knew he wouldn't last more than a few more heartbeats, and he wanted to feel her sheath surround him before he spilled his seed in her.

"Nay," he whispered as she increased her tempo. He leaned up and took her by the shoulders to pull her over his chest. She smiled as she straddled his hips and poised her sex over his aching rod.

Gabriel closed her eyes and moaned as she slowly sank atop his arousal. His hands gripped her hips and his breath rushed from his lungs when she finally took all of him.

Jayna's entire body was on fire. For Gabriel. It had always been so with them, and she had no doubt that it always would. She arched her back and dropped her head back as she rocked her hips against him.

His fingers pressed almost painfully into her hips as his desire grew. She felt him throb within her and it only heightened her arousal. When his hands released her hips she waited anxiously for him to take her breasts.

He didn't leave her waiting for long.

His fingers knew just where to touch, just how much pressure to apply to her sensitive nipples. Her need for him was great and her climax was building faster than it ever had. She could not get enough of him, and she feared it would be her downfall.

She raised her head to find him staring at her. She met his gaze and smiled as his silver eyes darkened when she rotated her hips.

"You minx. I'll spill now if you're not careful," he cautioned her.

She chuckled as she splayed her hands on his muscular chest and bent to flick her tongue over one of his nipples. "I'm nearly there myself."

He growled low in his throat just before his hands came up to either side of her face and held her still as he kissed her. The kiss was erotic, passionate and full of promises if she would only allow herself to trust him.

But the trust that had once been unshakable was now questionable. She feared what he might do to her again given the chance.

Jayna ended the kiss and straightened as she used her thigh muscles to raise herself over his rod, then slowly lowered herself. She repeated the process several times, each time going a little higher and faster until Gabriel reached for her hands and threaded his fingers with hers.

She let herself go then, embracing the growing climax that would soon explode within her. Her hips rocked against him, her breasts bounced, and then his finger flicked over her pearl and she screamed as her orgasm claimed her.

Jayna closed her eyes as pure bliss raced through her body, her sex clenching Gabriel's rod with each tremor that flooded her.

Then, she felt him stiffen beneath her, felt his seed fill her. And she was content.

She didn't push Gabriel's hands away as he pulled her down onto his chest. His hands were gentle as they pushed her hair from her face and lightly traced her back.

Given the choice, she could have gladly stayed there forever. She had finally found a small amount of peace and it felt wonderful.

Too bad it wouldn't last.

CHAPTER THIRTY-ONE

Aimery pulled at his bonds, though he knew they wouldn't budge. It was something he did every hour or so, hoping against hope that somehow his magic would free him. He gave another yank and stared in amazement at his hand now in front of him.

His bonds had been released. He pulled at his other hand and also found it free. But was it a trick? Had Theron moved up the execution? Were there guards, his men, waiting outside the chamber for him even now?

Aimery moved away from the hated wall where he had been held for the last day and sat at the open window overlooking *Caer Rhoemyr.*

"City of Kings," he murmured into the fading sunset as he heard the door to the chamber open then close. He knew Theron stood behind him. They had been friends for millennia, had trusted each other with their lives, and had fought beside each other.

Though Aimery was saddened by the turn of events, he couldn't fault Theron for doing his duty. Someone had to pay for the dragon's death, and by all accounts and purposes, it was Aimery that had killed the dragon.

Too bad he couldn't find the impostor and impose his retribution.

"You always did like looking over *Caer Rhoemyr*," Theron said as he moved to stand beside him.

"It's a magnificent city. The grand architecture of the buildings, the beautiful landscaping, the blue stone and knotwork of the Fae everywhere to behold. You cannot walk into the city and not know you are in the Realm of the Fae."

Theron sighed and turned to him. "Aimery, I have a plan. It's a simple plan, but one that could very well work if you agree."

Aimery looked at him. "You always did have an amazing way of finding plans."

For the first time in days Theron smiled. "You must leave at once. Go to the Shields, for they need you desperately. The creature that made its way here to pose as you has also been attacking the Shields."

"And just what creature are they fighting? I thought it was only the harpy and the gargoyle?"

"A Shapeshifter."

Aimery turned and swore viciously. He spun back around to Theron. "Have any of the Shields been hurt?"

"Aye. Hugh, though Gabriel managed to save his life. Your army was poised to step in and help, but they said Gabriel had it all in hand."

"So Hugh will live?"

"It appears so, though you might want to take a look for yourself."

Aimery crossed his arms over his chest as he leaned back against the wall. "If I leave, what will happen?"

"I will say that I went through with the execution. Since you were commander of the Fae armies, you are given some privileges, which means –"

"A private execution," Aimery finished with a smile. "Brilliant, Theron."

Theron strode to Aimery and clasped him on the shoulder. "Just finish this. I want you returned here with all haste. Your army on Earth awaits you. Go, my friend. And be safe."

Aimery nodded. "Thank you."

"Thank me when you return in victory."

Aimery wasted no more time in returning to the Shields.

Theron sighed as he slumped into the chair once Aimery was gone. The door to the chamber opened, and he looked up to find Rufina. "He's gone?"

"Just," he answered. "I pray he's able to succeed."

Rufina walked to him and wrapped her arms around his neck. "Give Aimery some faith, my love. He will succeed. And we'll have our commander back as well."

"If only we were able to help the Shields more. But the blood rules," he said as he rose and ran a hand down his face.

"I say we go to Earth."

Theron looked at his wife, unable to believe what he had heard. "What?"

She smiled at him. "You heard me. How many times has the Great Evil broken the rules to suit his purposes?"

"Too many to count."

"Exactly. He's doing this to destroy us, my love. I suggest we go and watch. If it appears that the Shields need a little help, well...we help."

Theron leaned down to kiss her. "You're brilliant."

She shrugged her dainty shoulder. "It's why you married me.

~ ~ ~

Gabriel wanted to stay in his chamber for the rest of the night, but he knew he needed to check on Hugh. Not to mention he and Jayna needed to eat. Once she left his chamber to take a bath, he washed and changed. He was just strapping on his sword when he heard someone give a shout.

He raced out of his chamber to the great hall to find Cole, Val and Roderick. "What is it?" he asked.

"The gargoyle," Cole said, his lip raised in a sneer. "I should have known the damn thing would attack this night."

"We best get ready," Val said. "The guards have already hidden themselves."

Gabriel nodded and strode to the solar where Hugh sat up while Mina fed him some broth. "How are you feeling?"

"Better thanks to you," Hugh said. "I hear you saved my life."

Gabriel shrugged. "The Shields need a leader."

"The gargoyle has returned."

"Nay," Gabriel said as Roderick walked in behind him. "A gargoyle has returned. It isn't the same one. We defeated one, we can defeat another."

"Not if we cannot venture out during the day," Roderick said.

Gabriel only smiled. "We'll have to come up with a plan then. Just like we did for tonight. The gargoyle will have nothing to eat since everyone is safely tucked inside somewhere until dawn."

Roderick shook his head, though a smile pulled at his lips. "What has you in such a good mood?"

"I'm thinking it has something to do with Jayna," Hugh teased.

"It most likely does," Gabriel admitted. "Nonetheless, let's focus on keeping the gargoyle guessing."

Roderick clapped him on the shoulder as he turned on his heel. "I'll go take my place in the tower. I think I'll use Hugh's crossbow to give the little bugger some pain."

Gabriel was about to turn to leave when Aimery appeared beside him. "Aimery."

The Fae nodded to Gabriel, then turned to Hugh. "Are you in pain?"

"Some," Hugh admitted. "I was told that every bone in my body was broken. I'm just thankful I'm able to move my fingers and toes."

Aimery nodded as he moved closer. "You were lucky Gabriel knows as much as he does. Let me relieve you of some pain," he said as he held his hands over Hugh.

Gabriel loved to watch the Fae use their magic, though Aimery wasn't supposed to help them. Something was definitely going on for Aimery to help heal them twice. As Aimery took away Hugh's pain, a white light surrounded his hands, illuminating them. Almost immediately, Hugh's face relaxed.

"Thank you," Hugh said.

Aimery waved away his words. "The time is at hand. I'm sure you have all wondered where I've been. I was held on my realm for several days because it was thought that I killed a dragon."

"You could never," Mina said softly.

Aimery inclined his head to her then looked to Gabriel and Hugh as he walked around the solar. "Theron and Rufina discovered exactly what it was that killed the dragon. There is only one creature that can make itself look like anyone it chooses. A creature so evil that it was hunted to extinction. Or so we thought."

"What is it?" Gabriel asked. He had a sick feeling in his

gut that the Aimery he had spoken with in his chamber was not Aimery at all.

"A shapeshifter. In order to take the shape of an animal or person, it need only touch a part of you."

"By the saints," Mina exclaimed as she covered her mouth in horror.

Gabriel met Hugh's gaze. "That's what's been attacking us in the forest. It has to be. Can the shapeshifters make themselves invisible?"

"Aye," Aimery answered. "They can be just about anything they want. You can tell a shapeshifter has shifted because it leaves an almost clear liquid puddle in its wake."

"That was what was in my chamber, what we found in the monastery," Gabriel said as he sank onto a chair in disbelief.

"Then it looks as though the Great Evil has a very powerful weapon," Val said from the doorway. "What do we do?"

Aimery sighed. "We must be careful. For all we know, the shapeshifter could be in this room."

"I'm not liking this," Hugh grumbled. He tried to swing his legs to the ground, but Gabriel quickly stopped him.

"I might have healed you, and Aimery might have taken away your pain, but it will be several weeks before you're able to move about like before."

"What bloody hell use am I then?" Hugh thundered.

Gabriel looked him in the eye. "You tell us what to do."

With a loud sigh, Hugh laid back down. "I don't have a choice do I?"

"Nay," everyone answered in unison.

Aimery glanced around the solar. "Where are Val and Roderick?"

"In the towers using their weapons to strike at the gargoyle," Cole answered.

"We need to make sure at least two of us are together at all times. No one is to be left alone," Aimery said.

"Where are the other Chosen?"

"Jayna went to take a bath," Gabriel answered.

"Jayna?" Aimery repeated.

Gabriel nodded. "Aye. She's a Chosen."

Aimery's smile was slow.

Mina set aside the empty bowl. "Elle was in the bathing chamber a little while ago. Maybe she and Jayna are together."

"Gabriel, you and Cole go find everyone and bring them in here. We need to formulate a plan," Hugh ordered.

Gabriel rose and followed Cole out of the solar as they hurried to the bathing chamber.

"Jayna?" Gabriel called as they neared it.

"Aye," she said with a laugh. "I'm nearly done, though you can join me if you like."

Gabriel heard Cole chuckle. "I cannot," he answered. "Is Elle with you?"

"Nay. Is something wrong?"

He heard the splash of water and knew she had gotten out. "Of sorts. Please hurry out."

Just a few moments later she stood in front of them, the ends of her hair damp and her face flushed from the heat of the water. "What is it?"

"We'll explain once we find the others," Cole said.

Jayna didn't argue as they turned and started up the stairs. Gabriel was surprised when he felt her hand take his. He glanced at her and gave her a reassuring smile, though he didn't think it helped her.

CHAPTER THIRTY-TWO

It took nearly half an hour before they found everyone else and returned to the solar. By the time Aimery explained everything, there was complete silence as everyone took in the new situation.

"My God," Elle said. "How do we face something that can turn at will? How do I know it's really Roderick who climbs into bed with me at night?"

Roderick wrapped an arm around her. "Ask me something only you and I would know, something private. If I answer, you know it's me. If I don't, then I think it's safe to say it's the shapeshifter."

"All right," Elle said as she nodded. "That sounds like a good plan."

"It does," Aimery said. "Everyone is paired up, so come up with private questions. And keep them private."

Gabriel found his gaze drawn to Jayna. Her gaze searched his, as if she wondered if she could trust him or not. He reached for her hand and pulled her closer to him, uncaring that the others noticed. He might be too much of a coward to tell her and the others the truth, but he would protect her with his last breath if necessary.

"Now that we've got that sorted," Cole said. "What's next? The gargoyle even now circles the castle. Are we not going to go out and meet it?"

Roderick shook his head. "To venture out would be folly. We must stay protected."

"I don't see how that will work." Val kissed Nicole on the forehead and raised his gaze to the others. "If the Chosen must destroy the evil, they must be in a situation where they can do what is needed."

Gabriel glanced at Jayna to see her gaze lowered. "Do the Chosen even know what to do?"

For several tense moments, none of the women spoke. Finally, Mina took a deep breath and said, "We could lie to you and say that we do indeed know what to do. But that isn't the case. Whatever our parents imparted to us is locked away. Our only hope is that it is a part of us somehow. That by being in a situation where we face the evil, we'll know what to do."

"You put our realm as well as the Fae realm at risk on hope?" Val asked incredulously.

"Can you think of another way?" Mina asked. "Do you think we've sat around and stitched or gossiped these past days? Nay, Val. We've all tried in vain to know what we are supposed to do. The truth is, we don't."

"She's right," Aimery said softly. "Not a single one of them knows what it is they are supposed to do."

"Wonderful," Roderick mumbled as he moved away from Elle and sat in a nearby chair.

Elle shook her head sadly as she looked at her husband. "You would lose faith in me so easily?"

"It's not you I lose faith in," Roderick said as he reached to take her hand. "The odds continue to stack against us. We move through time to find the Chosen who can destroy the evil, yet you don't know what to do. I have complete faith that each of you will try to do whatever it is you think you must do. But will it be the right thing?"

Silence filled the solar once again as each turned to their thoughts.

Elle knelt before Roderick and raised her face to him. "There was a time when you asked me to give you my complete trust even though I didn't know you. You know me, and I'm asking the same of you. If you lose faith now, then we are surely doomed."

"I want a future for us," he growled as he lowered his chin to his chest.

"As do I. Help me ensure that we get it," she urged.

Finally, Roderick raised his gaze. "I'll do whatever you ask of me."

A smile pulled at her lips then. "I want the warrior who fought to keep me from the harpies. I want the warrior who stole my heart and soul."

"You've always had him," Roderick whispered before he pulled her into his arms.

"Now that that's settled," Hugh said. "Let's form a plan. As much as I'd love to tell you that we should stay inside the castle, I think the evil will end up driving us out somehow."

"How?" Nicole asked.

Val pulled her against him with a sigh. "After all you saw in Scotland, how could you ask that?"

"Val's right," Gabriel said. "The evil will do what he must to get us out of the castle. He wants the Chosen dead."

Cole cursed. "If we are driven from the castle, we cannot fight the creatures and keep the Chosen safe."

"True," Aimery agreed. "Which is where my Fae army comes in."

Hugh shook his head. "I didn't think you could interfere."

Aimery shrugged. "The time has passed for the rules to be followed. If we stand aside and let the evil do what he will, then two realms will be destroyed, and more to soon follow. I cannot allow that."

"There will be punishment for you," Gabriel warned.

Aimery turned his swirling blue eyes to him. "And I will gladly accept it."

"You risk much, my friend," Hugh said softly. "We thank you."

Aimery inclined his head with a smile. "It is my pleasure. I have been waiting for a long time to fight this evil."

Roderick cleared his throat. "I think our two choices are the monastery or the old Druid ruins."

"The ruins," Aimery said. "You don't want to be near the monastery. It might have been holy once, but too much evil has transpired there."

Mina twisted her hands. "Even though the gargoyle was called up from the grounds of the ruins?"

Aimery nodded. "If you must leave the castle, make for the ruins. There is magic still in the stones. We'll use it to our advantage."

"We'll need horses for that," Gabriel said. "The distance is too great to run, even if there wasn't snow."

Hugh sighed and ran a shaky hand down his face. "Agreed. Getting to the barn and saddling the horses is going to be a problem."

"Leave that to me," Val said.

Cole smiled as he glanced at Val. "And me. Between me and Val, we'll get the horses ready."

Gabriel felt better and better about the situation as they talked. Yet, it was hard to ignore Jayna and her obvious unease.

"What is it?"

Her gaze jerked to his. There was fear in her beautiful hazel eyes. Her lips parted as if she were about to say something, then she licked her lips. "Nothing. I'm just nervous."

She was lying. Jayna had never been very good at lying, especially when she didn't want to lie. "Trust is a hard thing to come by."

"Aye." Her gaze dropped from his as she played with her sleeve.

Gabriel inhaled deeply and turned back to the group. Where he found Aimery staring at him.

~ ~ ~

Jayna had never felt so mixed up in all her life. She knew what she had to do, what she had vowed to do, but how could she when the realm was about to be destroyed? Just as hers had been.

She couldn't simply stand by and watch her new friends lose everything. More disturbing was the fact that she realized the Great Evil had been a part of the destruction of her world. How could she have been so blind?

Because you saw what Gabriel did and you wanted your revenge. At all costs.

At all costs. She sighed inwardly. She had sold herself to the very evil she should be fighting. All because she wanted her retribution. By all that was holy, what had she become?

But she knew that answer. She had become the very thing Gabriel had been.

Her gaze turned to him as it often did. His features were strong, just as he was. It was what had drawn her to him in the first place. He was a warrior skilled in the ancient healing arts. Yet, his smile had come easy, his silver eyes expressive as they raked over her body.

How she missed those days. But dwell on them she could not. It was time to take a stand, time to make a choice. She had no doubt Gabriel would help her leave Stone Crest if she wished, but she would not abandon her new friends.

She would help them.

When a warm hand closed over hers, she jerked and found Gabriel before her. "You were lost in your own thoughts."

She nodded and yearned to wrap her arms around his neck, to feel his warmth seep into her. "There is much to think about."

"You know we'll protect you. I will protect you."

A smile pulled at her lips at the promise she heard in his words. "I know. We all have a part to play in this. What do we do now?"

He took her hand and led her from the solar. "We must stay on guard. The gargoyle will continue to fly around the castle and try to come in, as well."

"I don't hear him anymore."

Gabriel chuckled. "That is a trap. He sits atop one of the towers and watches, waiting for someone to venture out. The people of Stone Crest know to stay hidden until dawn."

"And with the dawn it could very well bring the harpy."

"Most likely," he said as he led her up the stairs. "We have no idea how long we'll be able to stay in the castle. I fear that the Great Evil will drive us from here somehow."

She laughed. "Surely that isn't possible."

Suddenly, Gabriel stopped and turned to face her. "I've seen him do things that could never be done. I've seen him turn a good person bad. He turned Nicole's brother into an evil gryphon so powerful that it nearly killed us."

"Why didn't the gryphon kill you?"

Gabriel sighed. "No matter how much magic the Great Evil used on the gryphon, there was no ridding him of the love he had for his sister. That is what saved Nicole. And killed the gryphon."

It all seemed too much then. She couldn't go another minute without telling Gabriel the truth. He needed to know. "Gabriel, there is something I must tell you."

He put a finger to her lips. "You don't know who might be listening. Save your confessions for later when we know we are alone."

"When will that be? I must tell you this." To have finally resolved to do the right thing, then been kept from it made Jayna want to pull her hair out.

He shrugged. "I don't know. Maybe never."

"I'm ready for this to be over."

"It will happen soon. Very soon," he murmured as he turned and led her to her chamber.

He built up the fire while she closed and locked the door.

"Now I know why you didn't want to return to your chamber. The shapeshifter was there."

Gabriel nodded. "At least twice."

"Facing a gargoyle or a harpy is frightening enough, but facing a creature that you cannot see or know is terrifying. How do we fight something like that?"

Gabriel looked at her over his shoulder, his silver eyes sparkling with ire. "We draw it out."

CHAPTER THIRTY-THREE

Gabriel wasn't sure what woke him. He had been dozing in a chair by the fire for most of the night, though he longed to crawl in bed with Jayna. But getting in bed with her would mean he would make love to her, and he couldn't allow his defenses down for even a moment. Not until the evil was defeated.

He slowly sat up and stretched his back. That's when he heard a noise in the hallway. In a heartbeat, he was on his feet, his sword in his hand.

"What is it?" Jayna whispered from the bed.

He held up a hand for her to stay still. Slowly, he moved toward the door, his boots making not a sound. With his heart thumping in his chest, he reached for the latch of the door and pulled it open to find...nothing.

But there had been something there, he was sure of it. He felt something beside him and turned his head to find Jayna fully dressed. "I told you to stay put."

"Aye, but when you opened the door and didn't charge forward, I knew it was safe," she retorted as she pulled her hair away from her face to tie it with a ribbon at the base of her neck.

Gabriel sheathed his sword and slung his bow and quiver of arrows over his shoulder. "Something isn't right."

He closed his eyes and let his senses wander as Aimery had taught him. That's when he felt it. "There's something in the castle," he said as he took her hand and pulled her from the chamber.

"Wait. What do you mean something is in the castle? The gargoyle never tried to get in last night."

Gabriel didn't bother to answer her. He knew he was practically running, but he had to find the rest of the Shields. Their plan was about to be put into motion.

Suddenly something barreled into him from behind, throwing Gabriel to the floor. He immediately let go of Jayna's hand, but it was too late, she was pulled down next to him anyway.

He quickly rolled onto his back and pulled the dagger from his boot. As he jumped to his feet, he glanced at Jayna to see her slowly sitting up.

"Are you hurt?"

Her hand gently touched her forehead. "Just shaken."

"We have to go. It'll be back." He reached for Jayna's hand and kept his senses open. The shapeshifter would return, and the next time Gabriel would be ready for him.

They had gone a few steps when Jayna lifted her skirts in her free hand and lengthened her stride to keep up with him. "That was him, wasn't it?"

Gabriel gave a quick nod as they reached the stairway. He glanced down into the great hall and found it as deserted as the hallway.

"I'm not liking this at all," he murmured. "We'll have to make a run for it."

"For what?" Jayna's voice held an edge of fear in it, but it also held a note of determination.

He smiled down at her. "A surprise."

She pulled her hand free of his and hiked up her skirts. "What I wouldn't do for some pants right now," she grumbled. "It isn't easy keeping up with your long legs with the skirts about my legs."

"Just make sure you stay with me. It'll try to separate us."

She gave a very unladylike snort. "I'm not letting you out of my sight."

Gabriel stared down into the eyes of the woman who held his heart, the woman who could give him the world. She was everything to him. He cupped the back of her head and bent down to give her a quick kiss. "You're amazing."

She gave him a wink and a seductive smile. "I know."

"Are you ready?"

She pulled something from within the sleeve of her gown. He looked at the dagger and grinned. Now that was the woman he had known before. Jayna had always been prepared for any situation.

"I am now," she said as she once more gathered her skirts in her hands.

Gabriel tried to keep his strides shorter so Jayna could keep up, yet the urgency that drove him urged him faster. Jayna's ragged breathing and their footsteps beating on the stone floor as they ran were the only sounds in the castle.

He counted the tower hallways as they ran past. It was vitally important that he get the correct one. It was the fifth stairwell, and he slowed as he neared.

"Run up as fast as you can," he urged Jayna as he pushed her up the stairs.

He started up after her but had only gone a few steps before something grabbed his feet. His head hit the steps with a resounding thud that left his head exploding with pain and his jaw aching.

Still clutching his dagger, Gabriel rolled onto his back and slashed at the empty air. Not once did his blade touch anything. He looked over his shoulder to find that Jayna had stopped and waited for him.

With a groan, he rolled onto his stomach and straightened. They ran up the winding staircase to the next floor, and when they reached the landing, Gabriel looked down the stairs and sensed the shapeshifter was near. Very near.

"Surely you aren't done now? Weren't your orders to kill?" he mocked the creature.

A blast of cold air hit him in the face just before a blow landed in his stomach. Gabriel fell to one knee as he struggled to get his breath back. A scream behind him made him forget his pain as he looked to see Jayna thrown against the wall.

Gabriel flipped his dagger in his hand so that he held the blade and waited to throw it. He used the wall to help him gain his feet. Before he could throw his dagger, Jayna was yanked away from the wall just before being slammed back against it.

"Enough," Gabriel bellowed.

Jayna hung limply in the air against the wall, her head hanging to the side and her beautiful golden tresses tangled around her.

"She's easy bait. Why not try your hand at me?" Gabriel taunted. "After all, I did manage to nick you in the forest with my arrow."

To his relief, Jayna slumped to the ground. It left him just a moment to prepare as a force was propelled into him. Gabriel wrapped his arms around the shapeshifter and turned so that the creature took the brunt of the fall.

The impact jarred Gabriel's teeth as they hit the ground. When he opened his eyes it was to find Aimery looking up at him.

An evil smile spread over Aimery's face. "My the secrets you have, Gabriel. They could destroy the Shields if they ever got out."

Gabriel reared his hand back and punched the shapeshifter in the kidneys. Before his eyes, he changed from Aimery to Jayna.

"Would you hit a woman?" it asked.

For a moment, Gabriel didn't know what to do. He knew it wasn't really Jayna below him, but it was her face that stared up at him, her beautiful hazel eyes that beseeched him.

"I...I...." Gabriel shook his head before jumped to his feet. "No more tricks."

"Tricks," the shapeshifter asked in Jayna's sweet voice. "This isn't a trick. Now, put the dagger away. We both know you won't hit a woman."

"Nay, but I will," Jayna said just before she punched the shapeshifter in the face.

Gabriel could have cheerfully kissed her, but instead, he took her hand and turned to run down the hall.

"Where are we going?" Jayna asked.

Gabriel looked over his shoulder to see the shapeshifter had once again returned to his invisible self. "You'll see."

They were nearly there, just a few more steps to the tower stairs when Gabriel felt the shapeshifter coming toward them. He pushed Jayna to the floor and raced up the stairs. The door to the tower came into view the same time icy cold fingers began to claw at him.

Gabriel fell to the stairs as soon as he felt the shapeshifter attack. A loud whoosh over his head told Gabriel the creature had fallen for the trick, putting him right into the arms of Stone Crest's ghost.

The air stilled, and it grew eerily quiet before the door

to the tower began to rattle, the boards moving as if they were about to come apart. An unnatural scream rent the air as the shapeshifter realized what had captured it.

Gabriel didn't stay to see what would transpire between the creature and the ghost. He rushed down the stairs to find Jayna staring up at him, her face white and her eyes round with alarm.

"What is happening?" she asked, her voice shaking slightly.

Gabriel glanced up at the tower. "That is the ghost that haunts Stone Crest."

"Brilliant." The smile she gave him was honest and open, one that said she trusted him completely.

"We won't have much time. Let's get to the stables and hope we find the others as we go."

She gave a quick nodded and followed him. To Gabriel's disappointment, they hadn't run into any of the others by the time they reached the great hall. He glanced to the solar to find the doors shut.

He took his bow and reached for an arrow. As he notched the arrow he slowly walked to the solar until he stood before it. He motioned with his head for Jayna to throw open the doors. There was no telling what he would find inside, and he hoped it wasn't Hugh's dead body.

The door flew open, and he sighted down his bow. Just as he was about to release the arrow, he spotted a crossbow pointed at him.

CHAPTER THIRTY-FOUR

"Hold," Val shouted as he came running out of the solar.

Gabriel lowered his bow and let out a pent up breath. "I nearly killed you," he said to Hugh as he walked into the solar.

"And I nearly killed you." Hugh allowed Mina to help him resume his seat before the door. "We've been waiting hours for you."

Elle rushed to Jayna. "What happened?"

"The shapeshifter attacked us," Jayna said and pushed her hair from her face.

"He did a lot more than that," Gabriel said. "He changed into Aimery then into Jayna right before my eyes." He shook his head as a chill raced down his spine.

Cole stood in the doorway and clucked his tongue. "Out of all the creatures, I hate this one the most."

"Aye," Roderick agreed. "Where is the nasty bugger now?"

Jayna chuckled and moved to stand beside Gabriel. "He had a little run in with your ghost, Mina."

There was a moment of stunned silence before everyone laughed.

"I knew that ghost would come in handy one day," Hugh said.

Gabriel put his arrow back into his quiver before he slung his bow over his shoulder. "The ghost won't hold the shapeshifter for long. I think it's time we make a run for it to the ruins."

Val and Cole gave a quick nod before they raced from the solar and out of the castle.

"By the way, where is everyone?" Gabriel asked Hugh. "It's dawn, and I'd have thought your people would have come out by now."

Hugh glanced at Mina before answering. "We're not sure where everyone is. I fear the worst."

Tension radiated from the solar. Roderick stood guard at the doors while Mina, Elle, Nicole, and Shannon stood off to the side waiting.

"Where is your bow, Elle?" Gabriel asked. "Mina? Your weapon?"

Mina hurried to the opposite side of the solar and opened a large chest. "We put them in here."

"Good. Get them." He took the second of his four daggers from his other boot and handed it to Jayna. "Keep it hidden until you need it."

Jayna wished her heart would slow enough for her to regain the calm she always had. She was still shaken from being knocked against the wall a couple of times and losing her dagger, but she wouldn't let anyone know just how much she hurt. There was much more at stake here than the small amount of pain she felt.

She gave Gabriel a nod and watched as Elle took her bow and arrows, and Mina took her sword. Nicole and Shannon each got a dagger much like hers that they hid, as well.

"We're ready," Mina said as they came forward.

Gabriel motioned to Roderick. "It's going to take both of us to get Hugh outside."

"The hell it is," Hugh said as he gained his feet. "I'll suffer what little pain this will give me. You two are needed elsewhere."

Jayna could see that neither Gabriel nor Roderick liked the idea of Hugh going alone.

Thankfully, Mina solved the problem by wrapping her arm around Hugh.

"I'll make sure he gets there," she said stoically.

Roderick pulled Elle behind him. "I'll take the lead. Nicole, get behind Elle. Mina and Hugh need to be in the middle."

Shannon quickly moved behind Mina and Hugh without being told, which left Jayna and Gabriel.

"I suppose I go next," Jayna said as she moved behind Shannon.

Gabriel nodded. "You'll be safe."

She wasn't worried about herself, she was worried about Gabriel, but she didn't tell him that.

"Roderick will set the pace," Hugh said quietly. "Don't stop until we reach the stables."

Roderick gave everyone a nod before he trotted from the solar. Jayna and the other women lifted their skirts and quickly followed. She glanced over her shoulder to find Gabriel behind her.

"Don't worry. I'll be here. Keep your gaze ahead," he warned her.

But it was too late. She had already caught a glimpse of what was coming after them. It was the servants of Stone Crest, and they all held weapons as they raced toward the group. The intent to kill obvious.

"Run!" Gabriel shouted.

Roderick looked over his shoulder before he sprinted for the door. He jerked it open and pushed the others through. Jayna didn't know how they were going to make it to the stables. The servants looked ready to kill, and she knew they would given the chance.

She stumbled and felt a hand on her arm. "Keep moving, sweetheart," Gabriel whispered as he pulled her to her feet.

Tears blinded her eyes. The endearment had been something he'd always called her. He'd said it was her sweet heart that had calmed a warrior and turned him into a man of love.

They raced down the steps of the castle and into the bailey. Roderick ran past them to the front again, pointing to his right as he did.

Jayna followed his finger and found the guards slumped over dead. With her heart beating like a drum, Jayna saw the stables before them. Thankfully, Cole and Val stood at the entry waiting for them.

"We've got company," Roderick shouted as they raced inside.

Cole groaned. "I see that. We'll have to go out the back way."

Ten horses stood waiting for them, but only five were saddled. Before Jayna could even reach for the reins, Gabriel lifted her onto the horse. He placed the reins in her hands and gave them a squeeze.

"Ride like the devil is after you."

She tried to smile. "I will."

He swung up onto his mount and moved beside her. "No matter what, don't stop. Follow the others to the ruins. And, Jayna, whatever you do, don't look behind you."

She swallowed past the lump in her throat and leaned over to place a kiss on his lips. "I wish you would have let me tell you what I need to."

"Nay," he stopped her and leaned his forehead against hers. "Stay alive. That is all you need to be concerned with."

"Everyone ready?" Cole called.

She nodded when Gabriel raised a questioning brow. Just as she threaded the reins through her fingers, the rear doors of the stable were thrown open and they raced out.

Only then did she think about the gate. The gate was shut and the guards dead. They were trapped.

Yet as they neared, she saw the door within the massive gate opened a fraction. Val's mount kicked it open as he barreled through it.

Jayna leaned low over her horse and gave her a little pat on the neck. "Race like the wind," she whispered.

The horse's ear flickered and then her strides lengthened as she raced through the door and away from the castle. Jayna knew better than to shout with joy. They had a perilous road ahead of them yet to travel.

With the ground flying beneath them as the horses braved the cold wind and deep snow, Jayna made sure that Gabriel was near her at all times. She could face anything as long as he was beside her. She never realized it was he who gave her strength until now. It had always been him.

It would always be him.

When it seemed like they would make the Druid ruins without any problems, the screech of the harpy resonated around them. It was just a heartbeat later that they heard the unmistakable sound of her metal wings.

Jayna didn't know what to do next, but she should have known the Shields would have a plan. They always had a plan. With Mina in the lead, Shannon, Elle, Nicole, and

Jayna suddenly found themselves surrounded by the men.

She looked over at Gabriel who gave her an encouraging nod. Then, suddenly before them was Aimery on a magnificent white stallion, his flaxen hair flying out behind him as his horse sped across the ground.

Seeing the Fae commander seemed to give all of them the extra bit of hope they needed. As the harpy swooped over them, her scream of anger nearly froze Jayna's blood in her veins. It would attack soon if they didn't hurry and reach the ruins.

"Up ahead," Gabriel called over the pounding of the horses hooves.

Jayna trembled, as the cold seemed to seep into her very bones. She looked ahead and saw the ancient Druid ruins. Pillars had been knocked to the ground, some still intact, others broken into bits. A large flat stone lay atop two thick rocks in the middle.

So this was where the battle for Earth and the Fae realm would take place.

Val raced ahead and leapt from his horse. He took the reins of those who dismounted and hurried inside the ruins. Jayna slid to the ground and turned to find Gabriel beside her.

"Get inside with the others," he said.

"What of you?"

He didn't answer her, but pushed her toward Elle and Shannon, who pulled her into the ruins. Jayna tried to jerk out of their grasp when she saw Gabriel reach for his bow and arrow. The harpy was bearing down on them, ready to rip someone to shreds, and aiming straight for Gabriel.

CHAPTER THIRTY-FIVE

Gabriel drew back his bow and aimed for the harpy's eyes. Without her precious eyesight, they might be a little harder to hunt.

He saw her spread her wings as her talons opened wide. She was coming for him. He released the arrow and watched as it imbedded in her eye. Instantly the harpy vanished.

"It was as I thought," Aimery said. "The harpy and gargoyle were nothing more than the shapeshifter."

Cole nodded. "It explains why neither creature acted as it did before."

"Or attacked," Mina added.

"It was toying with us," Gabriel said as he glanced around the area. "The Great Evil is coming."

Hugh leaned against a fallen stone and held his crossbow up. "We'll be ready for him."

But Gabriel knew differently. The Great Evil wanted him, needed him. How Gabriel didn't realize this sooner he didn't know. But it made perfect sense. It was why the Evil didn't kill him in the forest. He had only spoken to him.

Gabriel shook his head and placed a hand on his temple.

"Something wrong?" Jayna's sweet voice reached him as her soft hand touched his.

"I thought all of my memories had returned, but I was wrong. There are some still hidden."

Her face blanched and her mouth parted in surprise. "You remember?"

"I've wanted to tell you."

Her hand dropped limply to her side. "For how long?"

"Since we made love that first time."

"You know why I've come then." She sounded defeated, the light gone from her eyes.

He took her face in his hands and made her look at him. "I know you didn't kill me when you had the chance. That's all that matters."

"There's so much more, Gabriel," she said as tears fell onto her cheeks.

Roderick cursed in his native tongue of Thales, drawing everyone's gaze to the mist rolling toward them.

"It's him," Gabriel said as he released Jayna and readied his weapons.

The mist was dense and thick as it quickly surrounded them. "Do you think you could hide from me here?" the ominous voice asked.

"We came out here to fight you," Hugh bellowed.

A chuckle sounded around them as mist encircled Hugh. "Ah, the leader of the Shields. Wounded and barely able to stand. What good are you to them, then?"

"Don't listen to him," Roderick said. "He's preying on our weakness."

"Weakness?" the ominous voice repeated. "Weakness is your fear that you won't be able to stop me from taking over Thales. I hate to disappoint you, prince, but your realm no longer exists."

"Nay," Cole bellowed and hacked at the fog with his massive double-headed war axe.

The Great Evil only laughed at Cole's weak attempts. "You cannot kill me. Not even these so called Chosen will be able to carry out your wishes...Aimery."

They all turned to the Fae commander who looked bored as he leaned against one of the stones with his arms folded over his chest and his feet crossed at the ankles.

"What are you doing here?" the Great Evil demanded.

Aimery shrugged. "The same as you."

"You cannot interfere."

"Hmmm. It does say that, doesn't it?"

The Great Evil gave a vicious growl before the mist moved to Gabriel. "I've longed to speak to you, Gabriel. To refresh the memories that are lost to you. I wonder if the Shields would be most interested in the man you were before you came to them."

"The past is the past. It doesn't matter what I was before," Gabriel said. He refused to look at the others for fear that he would see the distrust in their gazes.

"Ah, but it does." Suddenly, the mist turned from him to Jayna.

Gabriel felt real alarm then. Jayna had said there was more, and he feared his suspicions that she was somehow connected to the Great Evil had been right.

She stood her ground as the mist enveloped her. "My Jayna. You aligned your soul with mine just so you could mete out your retribution. How is it that you didn't know I was the one that ended your realm? Your stupid little mind thought Gabriel had done it, but Gabriel was just my pawn."

"Stop it," she said through clenched teeth.

The evil laughed. "Nay. I think it's time the truth be revealed. Have you told your new friends that you came to kill Gabriel? That you hunted him through time and space just to plunge your dagger in his heart?"

Gabriel's heart twisted as he saw Jayna's eyes close and defeat surround her.

"I shifted you through time, kept you alive, and gave you the means with which to kill Gabriel." The Great Evil's voice had turned hard, cold. "Yet you betrayed your vow to me."

The mist suddenly pulled away. Gabriel started toward Jayna when she gave a startled gasp, and her eyes widened. He stood in shock as the tip of a sword pushed through her chest.

He didn't know whether to go after the shapeshifter that had snuck up on them or to Jayna. The look of terror on Jayna's face propelled him toward her as the sword pulled from her and she crumpled to the ground.

"Nay," Gabriel said as he ran to her. "Nay. Look at me, Jayna. Focus those beautiful hazel eyes on me." He pulled out his black bag and reached for the delicate white flower that would save her life.

Only to find nothing.

It was then he remembered using it on Hugh and never replacing it. He gritted his teeth as a wail of anger built inside him. This couldn't be happening. Not now. Not to Jayna.

"Shhhhh," Jayna whispered as her cold hand rose up to touch his cheek. "It was not meant for you to save me, my love. I'm so sorry. For everything. I was such a fool."

"Nay," he said again, his throat closing with agony. Tears burned his eyes as he struggled to think of other herbs that could save her. "You won't die. I am a great healer, you know. I will save you."

Tears poured from her eyes to fall down into her hair. "You cannot."

"I lost you once, I won't do so again," Gabriel vowed as he looked through his black bag, seeing herbs, but nothing that could bring her back from the death that was coming to claim her.

He turned back to her then and placed his hands on either side of her head. "Jayna."

"I love you. I've always loved you."

"Forgive me for betraying you."

She smiled. "I already have."

Gabriel raised his gaze to Aimery. "Save her. Please. My life for hers. Take my life and give it to her."

"I wish I could do as you ask." Aimery lowered his gaze.

With a curse, Gabriel returned his gaze to Jayna. "Don't leave me," he begged as her eyes began to close. "Jayna. Please."

"I never have," she whispered.

Gabriel took her hand. Her grip was light, barely there. "Dammit, Jayna, fight. Fight death as you fought me," he bellowed.

Her eyes slowly opened. "Let me go, Gabriel. Let me find the peace I seek."

Gabriel could only watch as her life slowly ebbed from her to paint the snow red.

Her hand fell from his, signaling the end. He had never felt so useless, never felt so...empty as he did now.

His entire body shook as he kissed her forehead before placing her hands together. After a deep breath, he stood and faced Aimery and the Shields. He looked at each of them, hoping they would say something. Yet no one moved. The loss of Jayna touched him to his very soul, and the need to hunt the Great Evil was all that kept him from lying down beside Jayna and wishing for death.

"You know the truth now," he said slowly. "The

memories I feared were much worse than you could imagine. I am from an ancient race of this realm – Babylonians. I was gifted with healing abilities, and so was sent from realm to realm learning all that I could.

"Eventually, I knew how much power I wielded in these hands," he said as he gazed upon his hands. "With my healing powers, vast knowledge of herbs and then the magic I learned, I could bring people back from the brink of death. The offers I received were numerous, the sums...enormous. But I wanted more."

"That's how the Great Evil found you," Aimery said.

Gabriel nodded slowly. "I was an easy target. I was power hungry, and he gave me that power. He shifted me through time and made me near invincible. All that he asked was that I help him in one small task."

He hesitated as unwanted memories flooded him. "He sent me to Jayna's realm. A realm rich in minerals, life and...magic. What I didn't know was that the evil had been steadily going from realm to realm, destroying them. I helped him get into the realm, and once in, it didn't take him long to annihilate it."

"I don't understand," Mina said. "How did this realm manage to keep him out?"

Aimery sighed loudly. "This realm was small, but their magic was strong and true. The Fae had helped to combine our magic with theirs to keep any unwanted evil out of the realm. There has to be a balance of good and evil, so they couldn't extinguish the evil that already resided on the realm."

"How exactly did Gabriel get in then?" Hugh asked.

Gabriel inwardly cringed at Hugh's words. He didn't blame Hugh though for he knew if he was in Hugh's place, he'd think him evil, as well.

Aimery glanced at Gabriel. "Because for all of Gabriel's

faults, the evil knew Gabriel wasn't evil. Gabriel's thirst for power is what allowed him to be seduced by the dark side, much like Nicole's brother."

"My brother was trapped for centuries," Nicole whispered as her gaze rose to Gabriel. "How did you manage to get out from the Evil's grasp?"

Gabriel turned and looked at Jayna. "My orders were to make sure I was in the fray, I didn't realize what that meant until the attack started. I refused, and the Evil threatened Jayna's life, which left me no choice. I kept my sword in my hand and stood to the side sickened at the destruction."

He licked his lips and turned back to the group. "When I saw one of the many creatures enter the palace, I charged in after it since I knew Jayna was there with her family. I battled the creature and wounded it, but it was already too late for most of Jayna's family. Her father was the first killed. I found her at the back of the castle hunched over her two small sisters that had been slain.

"She knew I was part of it, knew I had brought the evil to her realm. She attacked me, and I let her. I deserved death and she deserved her retribution."

Silence filled the air then. Gabriel looked around to find the mist completely gone.

"The Great Evil has left," Shannon said.

Aimery shook his head. "Nay, he's gathering his forces. To leave these ruins would be folly. We wait here for the attack, for he will attack us first. He wants Gabriel."

"Why?" Val asked as he moved toward Gabriel. "You betrayed him."

Gabriel shrugged. "I wish I knew."

"Tell us what happened next," Cole prompted.

Gabriel wasn't deceived by their even tone. He knew they felt betrayed themselves, and he couldn't blame them. "As much as Jayna hated me, she couldn't kill me. She had wounded me gravely in her grief, though I'm not sure she realized what she had done. I knew it was just a matter of time before I died, but before I did I wanted to end the evil."

Roderick snorted. "Fool. You are only human."

"True. Yet, I knew I could. I made it back into the castle and stood guard as a group of people stood together fighting the evil. I don't know what they chanted for I couldn't understand the words, but they were defeating the Great Evil."

Elle's mouth parted as hope filled her eyes. "You mean, like we are supposed to do?"

Gabriel nodded but couldn't meet her eyes. "That's when the evil sent in another creature, a hydra, a nine-headed beast. There was nothing between the creature and these people but me. I fought him as best I could, but I was no match for him since I was already wounded. He got past me and killed most of the small group. That's when the evil came for me."

CHAPTER THIRTY-SIX

"Yet he forgot the gift he had given you," Aimery interrupted.

"Aye," Gabriel said as he met Aimery's gaze. The Fae commander's gaze was steady, no hatred or disgust showed in his fine features. It gave Gabriel a small measure of hope. "My immortality. I tried to find Jayna to take her with me, but she was gone. The realm was about to implode, so I opened a doorway."

Aimery gave a quick nod. "And was found by us. The Great Evil cannot venture into our realm, which shielded Gabriel from him."

"And his memories?" Hugh asked. "Did he lie to us all this time?"

"Nay," Gabriel nearly shouted. "I would never deceive you like that."

"He's speaking true," Aimery said calmly. "Theron, Rufina, and I were able to discern some of his memories but not all before they were closed off to us all together. At the time, we thought Gabriel had closed himself off to us, but I realize now that wasn't the case. The Great Evil might not have been able to reach Gabriel, but he still had enough power over him to keep his memories locked."

Gabriel ran a hand down his face. "Why? Why does the bastard want me so badly? I'm of no use to him now."

"Really?" Aimery cocked his head to the side as he regarded him. "You said that some of your memories were still hidden. Think, Gabriel. What could you have seen that the Great Evil went to such lengths to keep from you?"

Gabriel turned to the women. "I'm sorry. What Jayna knew and never said was that her realm...Elrain...is the very realm you four come from."

There was a pause as each considered Gabriel's words. The silence was deafening. Gabriel glanced at Jayna. She looked as though she slept, but he knew differently. It was the only time he had failed to save someone, the only someone he had never wanted to fail.

Suddenly Val pointed to the sky. "It's about to start."

They all looked skyward to see the sun being blocked by a wave of blackness.

Elle moved toward Gabriel and took his hands. "Do as Aimery said. Think back to when you saw the group chanting. Can you remember anything? You must have seen something that could aid us."

Gabriel shook his head sadly. "Elle, I wish to God that I could. All I remember is the small group standing over...." He blinked as a smile pulled at his lips. "Water.

It was a small basin of water."

"We don't have any water," Cole said. His voice was soft, but held a note of disappointment.

Mina stepped forward then. "There is some. To the back and surrounded by stones."

"What else?" Elle urged him.

Gabriel took a deep breath and closed his eyes as he gathered his memories around him.

He saw the group, felt the fire of the palace as it burned. He was weak due to his wounds and knew the evil was coming for him, could feel the hatred nearly devouring him.

The group standing around the pool of water began to chant some incoherent language he didn't understand, and the water glowed a bright purple before fading to a milky white. Mist began to float above the water as if soaking in the magic of the group.

And that's when he saw it. The rock in the middle of the shallow water.

Gabriel's eyes flew open to look at Elle as he smiled down at her. "I know what you need."

"Hurry," Aimery urged. "The Evil is nearly here."

Gabriel rushed to his black bag beside Jayna and ripped open the lining where a small rock no bigger than a child's palm was nestled safely.

He picked the rock up and rushed to Mina where she led him to the small pool of water surrounding by tall stones that hadn't been touched by erosion or time. He looked down at the stone where the same symbol that marked the Chosen was branded on the stone.

"Place it in the center of the water," he said as he handed it to Mina. He turned to move away only to find that Aimery carried Jayna toward him. "What are you doing?" he demanded.

"Trust me," Aimery said softly.

Gabriel clenched his jaw and swallowed past the urge to seize Jayna's body from him. He stepped aside and let Aimery move toward the women. Jayna was placed near them as they circled the water.

"Get ready," Aimery yelled as he raised his hand over his head and a line of white magic shot from his hand that then fell over the women to surround them in a type of bubble.

Hugh moved toward his wife, but Aimery held him

back as a line of Fae suddenly appeared and surrounded the Chosen.

"Fight the Great Evil," Aimery said. "The Fae will keep the women safe."

Gabriel didn't wait for Hugh's answer as he turned on his heel to retrieve his bow. He might have lost Jayna, but he wouldn't let the men he considered brothers lose their mates. The black cloud was almost upon them, the stench of evil nearly suffocating.

That's when he felt the shapeshifter near. Gabriel notched an arrow and let it fly. He heard a sharp hiss of pain as the arrow embedded itself in the shifter. The smile of triumph pulling at Gabriel's lips didn't last long as the shapeshifter shifted into the harpy.

Gabriel barely had time to duck and roll away before the harpy's talons reached him. He jumped to his feet and ran away from the ruins and the Shields. The Great Evil wanted him after all.

"Gabriel!" Hugh bellowed.

But he wasn't listening. He didn't need to look over his shoulder to see if the harpy followed, he knew it was right behind him by the clang of its wings.

"Damn shapeshifter," he cursed as he stumbled to his knees. He reached for an arrow as he rolled to his back. The harpy flew over him and he released the arrow to watch it root itself in the metal feathers.

Gabriel chuckled, thankful he always kept a few of the arrows full of Fae magic with him.

The harpy shrieked as it tried to pull out the arrow. Gabriel waited for the harpy to realize this arrow was different than the others. The Fae arrow held a dose of magic.

Gabriel rolled to his feet and watched as the harpy's eyes widened as the magic took effect, robbing the creature of its ability to move. The creature plummeted to the ground, its screams of terror and pain echoing around them.

He moved toward the creature and notched another arrow as he did. Before his eyes, the creature changed from the harpy to Aimery to Hugh then to Gabriel.

He stared down at himself wondering what trick the shapeshifter was trying. Gabriel backed away from the creature slowly. He was about to release his arrow in the creature's other eye when he gagged on the stench of evil.

"Hello, Gabriel," the Great Evil said in his ear.

Gabriel sighed and lowered his bow. He turned to find the mist now surrounded him and blocked the ruins from his view.

"Oh, they cannot help you now," the voice said with a chuckle. "I've waited a long time to once again have you in my clutches. I'm not about to let you go now."

Gabriel threw down his bow and arrow. With Jayna gone he no longer cared about living. "What do you want from me?"

"Did I block your memories too well?" The voice spoke softly as it drifted around him, but Gabriel wasn't fooled. The Great Evil had a vicious temper and it was just a matter of time before it was released.

"It appears so," Gabriel answered. "You did hide Jayna's mark well, just not well enough, as we discovered it."

An eerie chuckle filled the air. "As if I care that you discovered Jayna was a Chosen now that she's dead. I allowed her to think she was tracking you all these years, when in fact I kept her from you."

Gabriel felt his heart clutch painfully. "Why?"

"Because it wasn't time for her to find you. The timing had to be perfect for her death."

Gabriel clenched his hands in an attempt to gain control of his growing anger. The need to kill the Great Evil was strong, so strong that it overruled everything else.

"That's it, Gabriel," the voice whispered. "Give in to the anger, the hate. Let loose the rage that consumes you."

"Gabriel!"

He turned to find Aimery standing beside him. "Don't listen to the Evil."

Gabriel shook his head. "I have no more hope. It died with Jayna."

"Yes," the Great Evil hissed.

Aimery grabbed ahold of Gabriel's arm. "Nay. You must trust me."

Gabriel pulled out of Aimery's hold. Only once had he ever asked the Fae commander for anything, and Aimery didn't respond. Jayna lay dead now because Aimery refused to help him. Gabriel took a step back and tried to swallow past the guilt and anger inside himself.

The Great Evil laughed as the mist swirled toward the sky. Gabriel slashed his hands through the mist as he growled in frustration.

"Don't laugh yet, you bastard," Gabriel yelled. "I told the Chosen what they needed to do to defeat you. Its just a matter of time before they succeed."

In an instant, Gabriel was hurled through the air to slam into one of the Druid stones. For a moment, the world went black just before he slid to the ground. The impact of the landing jarred him awake.

"You better pray they don't succeed," the Great Evil shouted. "I will have my true form again. I will rule the Realm of Nations as only I can."

Gabriel threw back his head and laughed while he staggered to his feet. Out of the corner of his eye he saw Aimery walking slowly toward him and the Shields on the other side of the ancient stones.

He gripped the stone as he swayed. "If you are so powerful then show yourself now," he demanded of the Evil. "Show us just who we're up against."

Silence greeted his words. The only movement was that of the mist that continued to mill around him. Gabriel suddenly found himself very tired. All he wanted to do was find Jayna and lay down beside her.

With a heavy heart, Gabriel turned to enter the stones when he was thrown backwards. He hit the snow packed earth heavily. With a groan, he turned onto his side and rose up on his hands and knees.

"What do you hate more," he asked the Great Evil. "The fact that you won't succeed, or that I remembered the one thing you tried to keep from me?"

The mist rushed to his face, nearly suffocating him before falling back. He took a deep breath and let his head drop.

"I thought you wanted power, Gabriel."

He was really becoming to hate that bodiless voice. With a sigh, Gabriel rose to his feet. "Things change."

"I don't."

"And that will be your downfall."

CHAPTER THIRTY-SEVEN

"Hurry," Aimery whispered as he joined the Chosen.

Mina turned to him. "We aren't sure what to do."

Aimery cursed and glanced at Gabriel. He didn't want to leave him alone any longer than he had to. The Great Evil was up to something, but what, Aimery didn't know. Yet.

"Concentrate," he told the Chosen. "Your parents gave you the information you needed. You just need to find it. Stand around the water and close your eyes. Let the magic of these stones release what is keeping your mind locked."

He stepped back and watched as the women did as he commanded. If they didn't succeed soon, the Great Evil would win, and Aimery refused to let that happen. He opened his arms and closed his eyes as he focused all his energy on Jayna. Hidden deep in her subconscious were the answers they desperately needed. He just needed to find them.

He had no idea how long he searched her mind, and he was just about to give up when he found what he looked for. With only a thought, he gave the other Chosen Jayna's memories.

"Bold move, my friend," Theron said as he moved beside him.

Aimery clenched his jaw for he knew he had broken several rules. "Punish me after we defeat the evil."

He glanced at the Chosen to see their hands spread over the water, their eyes closed and their mouths moving in a chant.

He smiled and turned to Gabriel.

"I need out of these stones, Aimery," Val growled. "Gabriel needs us."

"Aye," Roderick, Cole, and Hugh agreed in unison.

Aimery sighed. "I know you want to help him, but Gabriel must fight this battle alone."

Val stepped forward. "I'll not let him suffer against that Diabolus."

Before Aimery could respond Val and the others walked out of the safety of the stones to join Gabriel.

"Let them go," Theron said. "They fight as one."

Aimery glanced at his king. "Can we win this?"

"I plan to make sure we do."

A slow smile spread over Aimery's face as the chanting of the Chosen rose in crescendo.

They had found the key to kill the Great Evil.

~ ~ ~

Gabriel knew the Great Evil was purposefully pushing him to become angry, and he knew he should turn away. But he couldn't. The urge, the need, to retaliate on the evil grew with his every breath.

"You've hunted me for years, toyed with me for too long," Gabriel called as he spread his arms wide. "You want me? Come and claim me!"

The malicious laughter that sounded around him brought chills of foreboding to his skin. He tried to see through the dense mist. The shapeshifter was out there somewhere, waiting.

"The real demonstration is about to begin," the voice whispered in his ear.

Just then the mist cleared enough for Gabriel to see the rest of the Shields leaving the sacred stones. He opened his mouth to shout a warning when he was robbed of his speech and jerked back against two trees.

He could only watch in despair as the Great Evil held him immobile and the shapeshifter walked towards the Shields...as him.

Gabriel jerked against his invisible bonds, but the more he struggled against the Great Evil, the less he was able to breath.

"Just watch, Gabriel," the Evil said near him. "This could prove interesting."

Gabriel tried to turn away, but he couldn't. He had to know what was going on in case he was able to break free of the Evil. If the Chosen had discovered what they were supposed to do there was a chance the Great Evil would weaken enough for Gabriel to break free.

His jaw clenched as he watched the shapeshifter approach his brethren. Gabriel himself had been tricked by the shapeshifter so he knew just how difficult it was to discern between the creature and the actual person.

Suddenly, Gabriel had a thought. He called to Aimery hoping the Fae could aid the Shields before the shapeshifter killed them.

A tsking noise sounded around him. "Come, come, Gabriel. You didn't really believe I would hold you here and not block your thoughts from those meddlesome Fae, did you?"

"You will be defeated," Gabriel choked out.

The Great Evil laughed. "I think not. You see, I've made sure that I survive. Though the Shields might have found the remaining Chosen, not a single one of them remember what to do."

Frustration and anger rolled through Gabriel. "I had the stone they needed. The stone of Elrain."

"Aye. I certainly didn't expect that of you, however, that still doesn't help. The women will fail. Even now they stand over the water wondering what to do, and with Jayna dead, there is no one to help them."

"Nay," Gabriel said, defeat ringing in his ears. He closed his eyes and hung his head.

"Oh, aye," the voice murmured. "I warned the Fae long ago that I would not be stopped. They thought to end me the first time, but they only succeeded in killing my body, not my soul."

But Gabriel didn't care. He had failed everyone. Jayna was gone, the Shields were soon to be dead, and the Great Evil would defeat both his realm and the Fae realm simultaneously.

Don't give up.

His head jerked up at the voice in his mind. It had sounded so very much like Jayna, but he knew it couldn't be her. She was gone from him forever now.

Unable to stop himself, he turned his gaze to his brethren. They stood facing the shapeshifter now, speaking to it as if it were Gabriel himself.

"Nay," Gabriel ground out as he pulled against the evil. "Nay. Nay. Nay."

He had betrayed too many people, failed too many times for him not to warn the Shields what they faced. Even if it meant a slow agonizing death he would strain against the evil.

With each pump of his heart, he felt power flow into him. His muscles strained, his blood pulsed, and his heart pounded like thunder. His only thought to warn the Shields, to give them the time they needed to see that it wasn't him they spoke with.

"Give up," the Great Evil taunted. "You will only succeed in bringing about your own death."

But Gabriel refused to listen.

Every breath became more difficult to take, yet Gabriel didn't stop. He could feel his skin stretching against the Evil's hold, feel the burn as the Great Evil fought to keep him against the tree.

Just as he was about to give up, Gabriel found his feet touching the ground. He blinked and glanced at the Shields. Based on the way Val glared at the shapeshifter, something was about to happen. And Gabriel needed to be there.

Deep, ragged breathing reached his ears, and a smile pulled at his lips. The Chosen had succeeded. They had recalled the chant that would weaken and ultimately destroy the evil.

Gabriel didn't stop to gloat or even taunt the Great Evil. He continued to push against the evil, and little by little he felt the iron control of the Great Evil slipping. Gabriel fell face first into the snow.

He spit the snow from his mouth as he grabbed his weapons and raced toward the shapeshifter. As he ran in the thick snow, he notched an arrow and knelt to aim. He didn't hesitate in releasing the arrow, and just when he thought it would puncture the creature's neck, the shapeshifter ducked. And Gabriel's arrow soared harmlessly past.

"Damn," Gabriel muttered as he rose to his feet.

The shapeshifter turned towards him a sardonic smile. "It's the shapeshifter," the creature said over his shoulder to the Shields.

"The hell I am," Gabriel growled as he stalked toward the creature.

"Which one is Gabriel?" Cole asked as he held up his war axe.

Hugh held up his hand. "Hold," he ordered the Shields. "We don't do anything until we know for sure which is the real Gabriel."

"I'm the real Gabriel," the shapeshifter stated.

Gabriel growled as he circled the creature. "Your race was hunted to extinction for a reason. I'm going to end your kind forever now."

He didn't give the creature time to react as he charged and pushed his shoulder into the shapeshifter's stomach. He heard a grunt and then a curse as the creature fell to the ground. Gabriel gained his feet first and kicked the shifter in the face twice. The sound of bone crunching brought a smile to Gabriel's face.

Blood gushed from the creature's broken nose. He wiped away the blood as he sat up, his eyes blazing with anger.

Gabriel motioned for the creature to attack. "What are you waiting for?"

The creature circled Gabriel slowly. "If you are the real Gabriel, where have you been?"

Gabriel chuckled. The creature was manipulative, and he needed to remember that. "I was being held, watching as you changed from the harpy into me."

The creature raised his dark brows. "Truly? If the Great Evil did have you, he certainly wouldn't have let you free."

"He didn't have much of a choice since the Chosen discovered what needed to be done to destroy him."

The creature glanced to the forest behind him, giving Gabriel the time he needed to unsheathe his sword. Before he could sink the blade into the creature's chest, he rolled out of the way and unsheathed his own sword.

Gabriel lunged at him, his sword slicing open the shapeshifter's chest. He laughed at the look of outrage on the creature's face.

"You don't seriously think I would allow you to harm my friends, did you?" Gabriel asked the creature.

The shapeshifter shrugged. "You don't really have a say in anything."

In a blink, the shapeshifter attacked. His sword met Gabriel's time and again, and each time Gabriel felt more and more of his strength leave him.

He hissed and leapt back as the creature's sword left a deep cut in his left shoulder. He glanced down to see how severe the wound was and realized he would have to kill the creature before he himself died.

Gabriel adjusted his grip on his sword and pivoted swiftly as he brought his sword down and around. As his blade sunk into the shifter's body he felt a sharp pain in his side. He looked down to see the creature's blade was embedded in his body.

With a jerk, Gabriel pulled his sword away from the creature and bit the inside of his mouth from crying out as the sword pulled from his skin.

Every breath was agonizing torture. Gabriel raised his eyes and watched as the shifter waned in and out of focus. He blinked several times and felt the world tilt around him.

He heard a laugh just before he opened his eyes and saw the shifter attack. Gabriel didn't know how many times he felt the blade cut into him before he fell to a knee.

It took every ounce of strength he had to keep the sword in his hand when all he wanted to do was lay down and ease some of his pain.

He heard voices behind him and made out Val and

Cole's voice though he couldn't discern what they shouted. He licked his dry lips as he heard the shifter walk up behind him.

Gabriel had this one chance to kill the creature, this one chance to end it all. And it was going to take every bit of his strength to do it.

"Such a pity," the shapeshifter whispered. "I had hoped for a better fight from you after listening to the Great Evil talk of how fine a warrior you were."

Gabriel pulled his sword next to him, as his eyes grew heavier. He could barely move his left arm and his back screamed in pain, but he blocked it all out as he concentrated on the creature behind him.

As soon as he felt the shifter raise his sword, Gabriel took a deep breath and jerked his sword backwards. A loud moan resonated around him as his blade sank into the creature's stomach.

Gabriel rose to his feet and turned to look at the shapeshifter. The creature's eyes grew round as he realized he was finished.

Without wasting any time, Gabriel pulled his sword from the creature and with one movement of his arm, beheaded him. He watched as the creature's head fell to the ground with a thud as his body languished upright for a moment before it toppled over and black liquid stained the snow.

Gabriel turned to his brethren as the shifter changed from his look-alike to Aimery and then to the harpy before disappearing. The Shields smiled and took a step toward Gabriel, but the sudden concern in their eyes told Gabriel that all was not over yet.

"I may not win, but you won't live to enjoy it," the Great Evil shouted.

Gabriel, with no more strength, fell to his knees. There

was an odd pain in his chest, which made it difficult to breathe. He raised his gaze to Hugh to see his leader's face crumple. Gabriel looked down and saw a sword sticking out of him.

There was a loud bang and a horrible scream behind him, but he couldn't turn to see if it was the evil. He felt himself falling and winced as the side of his face hit the snow.

There was so much he wanted to tell the Shields and Aimery, so much they needed to understand. He couldn't let them think he was evil.

"Gabriel," Val shouted as he ran to him. "By the gods, someone do something!"

Gabriel tried to laugh but only managed to choke on the blood that now filled his mouth. "Nothing to be done."

"Shhhh," Mina said as she bent down to take his hand. "You need your strength."

"Sorry," he said as he looked to each of the Shields. "Made. Mistake."

Hugh nodded. "We know, Gabriel. But you saved us, and the Fae. That's all that matters now."

Gabriel nodded and began to close his eyes as the world grew dark. "So cold."

A memory of him and Jayna by the sea flashed in his mind. Her golden hair blew in the wind as her beautiful hazel eyes sparkled with love and laughter. He could join her now and find the peace she spoke of.

Aimery raced up to see the Shields and their wives huddled around Gabriel. "Nay," he whispered as he knelt beside Gabriel. He felt along Gabriel's neck and found a heartbeat that grew steadily weaker. "Gabriel, nay. Listen to me. Follow my voice."

"Jayna."

Aimery raised his head and let out a bellow of rage. He

took Gabriel's hand and felt the life draining from his friend. He should have been there to stop the shapeshifter instead of watching the Great Evil. He should have been there to save Gabriel.

"Do not blame yourself."

Aimery sighed and raised his face to his king and queen. In Theron's blue eyes, Aimery saw the truth of it, but he had given the Shields his vow of protection, and he hadn't honored it.

Gabriel had been the best at healing, never giving up until the person was long past dead. Suddenly Aimery had an idea. He pulled the sword from Gabriel and lifted his body into his arms.

"Aimery," Rufina cautioned.

But he was no longer listening to his lieges. He had a friend to save. He looked Theron in the eye before disappearing.

"What the hell!" Hugh shouted. "Where has he gone with Gabriel?"

Theron sighed and turned to the Shields. "Aimery is hoping to save him."

Val stepped forward, his face hard and unyielding. "Where did he take him?"

"To Stone Crest."

No sooner were the words out of his mouth than the group rushed to their horses and galloped toward the castle.

"Aimery is going to need help," Rufina said as she took Theron's hand.

"Aye." He glanced into the stones and nodded to the Fae soldiers to gather Jayna's body and follow.

CHAPTER THIRTY-EIGHT

Aimery stared down at Gabriel's body as he focused all his magic. He felt something beside him, and glanced over to see Rufina. She gave a soft smile and moved her eyes across the bed. Aimery followed and found Theron waiting patiently.

"You used most of your magic on Jayna. You're going to need us," Theron said softly.

Aimery nodded and focused on Gabriel as he felt Rufina and Theron's magic join his. He had to save Gabriel at all costs.

~ ~ ~

Gabriel turned his face away from the bright light and sought the darkness that claimed him. Something soft touched his cheek, and for a moment he allowed himself to believe it was Jayna.

His sweet Jayna.

Gone from him forever.

"Gabriel?"

His heart plummeted to his feet as he heard Jayna's voice.

"Gabriel, please come back to me," she whispered.

For a moment, Gabriel was afraid to move, afraid to even think that he could open his eyes and find his beloved beside him. But the need to see Jayna outweighed his fear.

Slowly he opened his eyes and found himself staring at the bed hangings of his chamber. He moved his gaze to the left and found bright light streaming through his window.

Then, he turned his gaze to the right and saw...Jayna. Tears fell down her cheeks as she gave him a heart-stopping smile.

"You came back to me," she cried as she leaned over to place her lips atop his.

Gabriel didn't care how either of them was alive as he raised his arms and brought her atop him. He placed his hands on either side of her head and gazed into her hazel eyes.

"I love you. I've always loved you, and nothing will ever change that. I cannot take back the betrayal of your family and realm, but I will do whatever you ask in the hope that one day you will trust me again."

A soft sob was her only response, and Gabriel panicked, thinking that she could never forgive him.

"You silly fool," Jayna said through her tears. "I forgave you the moment I saw you in the bailey. I know what you did was a mistake and not something you knew would happen to my realm."

Gabriel let out a pent up breath and crushed her to his chest, and he rained kisses over her face. "Don't ever leave me again. I cannot survive without you."

She pushed up and wiped the tears from her face. "Thanks to Aimery, I'll be with you for some time."

Gabriel felt peace surround him for the first time as he

held Jayna in his arms. Finally, he was whole again, and a bright future awaited them.

"As much as I'd love to stay in your chamber, the others are waiting for you," Jayna said as she slowly climbed off the bed.

Gabriel sat up and took a deep breath. The skin was still pink from his many wounds, but nearly all the pain was gone. "How long have I been asleep?"

"Days," she said and clasped her hands in front of her.

There was relief in her eyes, proof that she had sat by his side worrying for some time.

He pulled on the tunic she handed him, then pushed the covers away from his legs and rose from the bed. He tugged on his trousers and then his boots before he faced her again.

"I thought you had died."

"She nearly did."

Gabriel spun around to find Aimery leaning against the stones of the hearth. He smiled at the Fae and gave a nod of thanks. "Why didn't you tell me you helped her?"

Aimery pushed away from the stones. "The Great Evil needed to believe she was dead. I didn't have time to tell you otherwise."

"You did what you had to do. Thank you. For Jayna and myself."

Aimery bowed his head and smiled. "It was the least we could do after all the Shields had done. There was a huge celebration on my realm."

Gabriel laughed then stopped to listen. "Why is there not one here?"

"Because Hugh wanted to make sure you were with them," Jayna answered.

"Go," Aimery said. "Celebrate with the Shields."

Gabriel held out his arm and waited for Aimery to grip

his forearm. "I don't have the words," Gabriel began.

Aimery smiled and held up a hand. "There's no need. Go. Celebrate and rejoice, my friend. You deserve it."

Gabriel turned to Jayna and took her hand in his. "Ready?"

"As long as I'm with you I'm ready for anything."

Gabriel didn't look back as they strode from the chamber. He didn't need to. He knew that it wasn't the last time he would see Aimery.

When he and Jayna reached the great hall, a massive cheer rose. Gabriel looked around the room at the people of Stone Crest once again smiling and laughing as the Great Evil's hold was gone. When his gaze moved to the dais, it was to find his four friends and their wives standing as they waited for him.

With a little squeeze of Jayna's hand to let him know she was ready, they walked to the dais and stood before Hugh and Mina.

"I'm glad to have you back," Hugh said. "You had us all worried."

Gabriel sighed. "I'm glad to be back. I owe each of you an explanation."

"Nay," Val said. "Aimery told us everything."

Gabriel blinked. "What? How?"

"It seems once the Great Evil was defeated, the block on your memories was gone," Cole said.

Roderick nodded. "Which allowed Aimery, Theron, and Rufina into your mind to see what actually happened."

"They then told us everything," Hugh said softly. "It takes a man of great character and strength to do what you did for us."

"I was merely trying to make up for a mistake," Gabriel said. "There is no apology good enough or deep enough to make up for my betrayal."

Jayna turned to him. "Don't. You didn't destroy my realm, Gabriel. The Great Evil did. He used you just as he used me. The lies he told me..." She trailed off unable to finish.

Gabriel took her face in his hands and kissed her tenderly. "I don't care what he did or said. You're with me now. That's all that matters."

"Which is how we all feel," Val said which brought a chuckle from everyone.

Hugh raised his goblet. "A toast. To a Shield. A warrior. A friend."

Gabriel choked on the emotion filling him. He accepted the goblet handed to him and raised it up with the others as a loud "here, here" filled the great hall.

Once the cheers had settled down, the group moved to the solar for a move private place to speak.

"What happens now?" Cole asked.

Hugh shrugged. "I'm not sure, though I think we'll find out soon."

No sooner had the words left his mouth than Aimery appeared. He gave them a bright smile. "Each of you have put your life on the line numerous times. You fought not only for this realm and the Fae realm, but also for all realms. You fought against an evil of just power that there seemed no hope of a victory. Yet triumph you did."

His gaze moved from one Shield to the next. "The evil is gone and the realms once again safe. In return for your dedication and loyalty, King Theron, Queen Rufina, and I would like to grant each of you a gift of your choice."

Hugh took Mina's hand and smiled. "I only want to stay here, Aimery. I've found a home at last, and I cannot imagine living anywhere else."

"That gift was already granted to you, Hugh. However, the Fae will bless this land, you, and your descendants."

Aimery then turned to Roderick.

For a moment, Roderick sat there and returned Aimery's stare. "You've already given me my gift by saving my father."

Aimery smiled. "Many Fae have gone to Thales to help rebuild your realm. As soon as you are ready, I'll escort you and Elle home."

"Thank you," Roderick said softly. "I speak for all of Thales when I say how grateful we are for the aid."

"And you, Cole?" Aimery asked. "What would you ask?"

Cole turned to Shannon. "What do you want?" he asked her. "Do you want to return to your time and live there?"

Shannon shook her head. "I just want to be with you."

"Anywhere?"

"Anywhere," she responded.

Cole turned to Aimery.

"We would like to return to the Realm of the Fae."

"So be it," Aimery said before he turned to Val. "And you? Would you like to return to Rome?"

Val shook his head. "Nay. Nicole and I would like to return to Scotland."

Aimery nodded and smiled. "You will find a home for you and Nicole that I think will be most agreeable to both of you." Aimery then turned to Gabriel.

Gabriel shook his head. "I've already been given more gifts than I deserve. I was given Jayna, my memories, life, and then forgiveness. That is all I need."

"Maybe so," Aimery said. "However, you and Jayna deserve a new start."

Gabriel looked down at the woman that held his heart. "I asked you once already, but I need to ask it again. Will you be my wife?"

Her lips pulled back in a smile. "The answer hasn't changed. Aye, I'll gladly be your wife."

"Where would you like to live?"

Jayna shrugged. "Surprise me."

Gabriel laughed and looked at Aimery. "You heard her. Surprise us."

EPILOGUE

Gabriel couldn't believe Jayna was actually his wife. It seemed he had waited for an eternity to call her his, and now that they were joined he couldn't wait to start their life together.

He was both joyous and sad, for while he wanted to begin a life with Jayna, it meant he and the Shields would be parted. Possibly forever.

Already Aimery had taken Roderick and Elle to Thales, and Val and Nicole had left just moments ago for Scotland. Theron and Rufina had escorted Cole and Shannon to the Realm of the Fae, which left only him and Jayna.

"Are you sure you want to let Aimery surprise you?" Hugh asked as he walked towards them.

Gabriel and Jayna shared a laugh. "Aye," he answered. "I've no wish to return to my people, and we cannot return to Jayna's realm."

"I'm going to miss you."

Silence filled the air after Hugh's admission.

"It's been an honor," Gabriel said. "You're the finest leader I've ever known."

Hugh took a deep breath before he gave a quick nod. "Thank you. For everything, Gabriel."

Gabriel looked down at his wife to find her and Mina crying as they embraced. If he thought leaving the Shields was difficult, he could only imagine how the Chosen felt. It almost didn't seem right that the Shields would no longer exist.

"That's not exactly correct," Aimery said from beside him. "Once you're a Shield, you're always a Shield."

Gabriel felt his lips lift in a slow smile. "Is that so?"

"Aye. Now, are you and Jayna ready?"

Gabriel took Jayna's hand and waited for her nod before he turned to Aimery. "Show us our new life."

~ ~ ~

As one last gift, Aimery gave each of the Shields the ability to shift through time and space to visit each other.

He smiled as he looked over *Caer Rhoemyr*. All had worked out as it should.

"You seem mighty pleased with yourself," Theron said as he joined him on the balcony of the palace.

Aimery chuckled. "You're the one that should be pleased. How exactly did you explain my execution, then explain my return?"

Theron shrugged. "Once our people realized a shapeshifter was involved, they knew it wasn't you. Besides, I never made the announcement that you were executed. I just didn't tell them you weren't."

Aimery sighed. "Peace. Finally."

"Don't get too comfortable, my friend. You know as well as I when one evil is defeated another rises to take its place. 'Tis the way it has always been."

Aimery shrugged. "Maybe. But for now, there is peace,

and I'm going to enjoy it."

~ ~ ~

There wasn't a week that went by that Aimery didn't visit his Shields.

Hugh and Mina lived a long, happy life together with their five children. Stone Crest prospered for centuries, and it was a place known for its great lord and gentle lady.

Roderick and Elle returned to Thales and rebuilt the realm to its former glory. Roderick took his father's place as king soon after his return, ruling Thales with wisdom and justice. The love between him and Elle helped set a steady foundation in Thales, and they were blessed with two children.

It didn't take Cole and Shannon long to find that the Realm of the Fae was the perfect home for them. Because of his service and his battle abilities, Cole found himself in the service of Aimery and his legendary Fae army. Their love was blessed by four children, and as a gift, Queen Rufina gave Shannon immortality so she and Cole could spend eternity together.

Val and Nicole returned to Scotland. The home Aimery had given them wasn't the small cottage they expected, but a sizable castle situated on a beautiful loch. Val soon came to embrace his role as lord of the castle, and he was known as a fair and just lord, much loved by his people. He and Nicole spent many hours in the loch they loved so dearly. Their blessings were frequent and numerous in their eight children.

As for Gabriel and Jayna, Aimery surprised them well when he sent them to Elrain's sister realm, Newvale, where Jayna's mother had fled after Jayna left in search of Gabriel. As another surprise, Gabriel's beloved wolfhound, Laird, was waiting for him. The couple lived a long and happy life together, content in their love and their three children.

Thank you for reading **A Warrior's Heart**. I hope you enjoyed it! If you liked this book – or any of my other releases – please consider rating the book at the online retailer of your choice. Your ratings and reviews help other readers find new favorites, and of course there is no better or more appreciated support for an author than word of mouth recommendations from happy readers. Thanks again for your interest in my books!

Donna Grant

www.DonnaGrant.com

**Never miss a new book
From Donna Grant!**

Sign up for Donna's email newsletter at
www.DonnaGrant.com

**Be the first to get notified of new releases and be
eligible for special subscribers-only exclusive content
and giveaways. Sign up today!**

ABOUT THE AUTHOR

New York Times and *USA Today* bestselling author Donna Grant has been praised for her "totally addictive" and "unique and sensual" stories. She's written more than thirty novels spanning multiple genres of romance including the bestselling Dark King stories, *Dark Craving, Night's Awakening,* and *Dawn's Desire* featuring immortal Highlanders who are dark, dangerous, and irresistible. She lives with her husband, two children, a dog, and four cats in Texas.

Connect online at:

www.DonnaGrant.com

www.facebook.com/AuthorDonnaGrant

www.twitter.com/donna_grant

www.goodreads.com/donna_grant/